FOREVER SHELTERED

DEANNA ROY

Forever Sheltered

Casey Shay Press
PO Box 160116
Austin, TX 78716
www.caseyshaypress.com

Paperback: ISBN: 9781938150265

Hardcover: ISBN: 9781938150289
Ebook-ISBN: 9781938150272

Library of Congress Control Number: 2014911601

Other books by Deanna Roy

Forever Innocent
Part 1 of the Forever Series

Forever Loved
The shattering sequel to Forever Innocent

Stella & Dane
A new adult contemporary romance

Baby Dust: A Novel about Miscarriage
Women's fiction on baby loss

Jinnie Wishmaker
Marcus Mender
an adventure series for 9-12 year olds under the name DD Roy

Dust Bunnies: Secret Agents
an iPad story book app for children ages 3-9

Learn more about the author at

www.deannaroy.com

For Janice Roy
My mom
Over ten years cancer free

Jan Korfmacher
My mother-in-law
Decades cancer free

Stan Korfmacher
My father-in-law
Lost to prostate cancer in 2010

Mary Ballard Roy Wright
My grandmother
Survived breast cancer and lived another 20 years

And for all those lost to cancer
and those who have survived it,
including the hundreds listed
in the final pages of this book
by fans and readers

•*¨`*•♥•*¨`*•

1

TINA

Oh, that idiot jerk doctor just walked in here and demanded a favor.

A favor.

Demanded.

He strode into my art therapy room like he owned the place, with his high-dollar shoes and custom-tailored khakis, and said, “You have to do something for me.”

Right. I *have* to.

I whirled away from him to pick up a box of tempera paints and clutched it tightly with both hands.

It was either that or punch him in the face.

This was *my* room at the hospital. Where doctors weren’t the big shots. Where patients came to *escape.*

My cheeks were hot. “I didn’t expect to see you again,” I said, pointedly refusing to ask what the *something* he wanted me to do entailed. “You didn’t show up the last time you asked to meet with me.”

This same doctor blew me off two weeks ago. Set up a meeting and didn't show.

Like his time was valuable, and mine was not.

I kept my back to him. A long moment passed. He stayed quiet, so I began to wonder if he'd snuck out.

Not a bad idea. Nobody likes me when I'm pissed off.

I checked the paints, chucking any colors that had dried out. I had less than ten minutes until my next therapy group arrived, a set of children from the cancer ward. It often took all my emotional strength to get through that hour. I wouldn't give the doctor another thought.

Those kids had it so hard. They lost their hair. Threw up spontaneously. Dealt daily with the idea of death. Many were far from home, sent here to the specialty wing for cancer patients after their own hospitals had exhausted all options.

My days felt like battles, miniature war zones.

And yet here was this Dr. Darion Marks, asking me to do something for *him.*

I was so sure he was gone that I jumped when he spoke again.

"I'm sorry I didn't let you know I couldn't make our meeting two weeks ago," he said.

Still no explanation. I turned a little so I could see the doctor, tall and stalwart in his white coat. He reminded me of a statue, perfect, chiseled, and cold as granite. I dropped the box of paints on the low table with a satisfying clunk.

"Hey." His voice carried an impatient tone that sparked my anger into rage.

I glared at him. I was ready to give him a real piece of my mind when he switched tactics.

"Maybe we can start over," he said with a smile I'm sure he thought was charming. "Hello, Ms. Schwartz. Could I ask you to help me with one of my patients?"

I hated him with a fury I usually reserved for people who kicked dogs. And my parents.

I grasped the back of a chair and leaned over it. Menacingly, I hoped.

"Dr. —" I pretended I couldn't remember his name and peered at his badge, even though this doctor was pretty unforgettable. A classic face complete with dimples and a jaw of steel. Broad shoulders and a lean body. Well dressed. Most of the doctors here wore scrubs and took a laid-back approach. This Darion dude was clearly on the path to administration, even though he barely looked over thirty.

"Dr. Marks," I said, "I treat all the patients who come into my room the same. Each one gets equal attention."

"But this one lost her mother," he said. He adjusted his tie, as if suddenly it was too tight. "Let me show her to you."

I tried to avoid noticing how his pale blue dress shirt stretched over his chest as he reached around for his back pocket. He must use the workout room available to staff.

Use it a lot, actually.

I felt that familiar pounding that connected my heart to other interested body parts, but that was fine. I could ignore it. Or I could do a one-and-done with the doctor. That was no skin off my back, unless carpet burns were involved. I'd taken in men more powerful than this guy and showed them the door right after.

That sort of challenge was what made life interesting.

The doctor opened a hand-tooled brown leather wallet. One

glance told me it cost as much as my entire outfit. Probably more, actually, since I got everything at resale shops.

Dr. Marks flipped the wallet open to a picture of a girl. Even with the mop of blond curls in this image, I recognized Cynthia. Her little head was smooth and bald from chemotherapy now. She used to come to art every day. Sometimes twice, if she could sneak in. I always let her.

Cynthia had been missing from my class for a couple weeks. She was the first of my patients to leave without warning, and I had been afraid to ask anyone why.

"I know her," I said. "She's very sweet." I stuck my hands on my hips, purposely showing him some attitude. "Why do you have a picture of your patient in your wallet?"

This got him. He snapped it shut. "She gave it to me. Couldn't exactly throw it away."

I watched him with suspicion. Keeping it and putting it in his wallet were two very different things. Now that I looked closer, I could see something haunted in those gray eyes. Something that told me he had a past. Maybe not as bad as mine. I was hard to beat. But something had happened to him. Maybe this girl brought it back.

I felt my disdain soften a little.

A nurse I knew, Marlena, pushed an empty wheelchair through the door. "Just tucking this in here," she said.

I smiled at her, ignoring the doctor. "Who's it for?"

"Jake is going to come in on crutches today," she said, smoothing back her perfect curtain of black braids. "PT went well. But I suspect he'll be plumb worn out by the end. We'll have this for him just in case."

"I'll keep an eye on him."

"Thanks, love," Marlena said. She cast a furtive glance over at the doctor, raised her eyebrows at me, then left again.

When I turned back, the doctor's face had grown angry. "So, you'll watch Jake but not Cynthia?" he asked.

I heaved a long, annoyed sigh, one designed to make a point. I summoned my best whiny, put-out voice. "I already make sure they seem okay, don't get too upset, that their IVs aren't tangled or their tubes pinched or their color doesn't alter or their breathing isn't labored and a million other things on top of my actual job, which is to help them feel better about being in the hospital."

Dr. Marks shoved his wallet back in his pocket. A muscle twitched in his jaw, and I had the craziest urge to press my hand to it, to calm him. I shook it off. I was supposed to be getting him out of here, not mooning over his dimples. I was hoping the whiny voice would make him leave.

He seemed disgusted by what he had to say next. "Cynthia likes you, Tina. She talks about you all the time." Dr. Marks shoved both his hands in his lab coat pockets. The stethoscope around his neck was cocked sideways, one side longer than the other. If he didn't adjust it, it was going to hit the floor. I resisted the urge to fix it.

I was watching him way too closely.

I relented. "I know," I said in a more normal tone. "She wraps her arms around my leg and begs the nurse not to make her leave." The image of the little girl, Cynthia, doing this softened my feelings yet another notch. Maybe this doctor had a similar experience with the child. The nurses doted on her.

"You're important to her. Just — just don't forget that. That's all I ask." Dr. Marks wouldn't meet my eye now and stared down at his polished black shoes. "Your approval or disapproval of her drastically affects her day. How she does with her treatment. How much she eats. You're important."

I had no idea.

"I understand," I said. "I'll be careful."

"That's all I ask," he said.

We both sounded different now. Like real people.

I plucked at my sleeves. "She's been missing art class. Is she all right?"

Technically, I wasn't allowed to be informed about a patient's medical condition. I wasn't a nurse, and I had zero medical credentials. I was just an artist with a college degree who had been hired as an emergency measure to fill a vacant slot no one else would take. The pay was crap. My job was temporary and had no benefits. But it was mine. I liked it. I helped patients color, paint, and sculpt to escape the awfulness of their treatments.

What I did here mattered. Maybe for the first time in my life.

The doctor cleared his throat. "She went to Houston seeking eligibility for a clinical trial of a new chemotherapy drug. She's back. We're hoping her leukemia will go into remission." His jaw twitched again, and I could tell this time it was from upset, not anger. "It's basically our only hope."

I gave up on my bad attitude altogether. I didn't know much about leukemia, but I did know Cynthia was fighting very hard. For some reason, this doctor had taken her case to his heart. He couldn't be all bad.

I shifted a stack of paper to avoid having to look at him. "I'll keep an eye on her," I said.

He got quiet, so I glanced back up. His eyebrows drew together. This was hard for him. I hadn't seen him around much, although I knew he was an oncologist, one of the hotshots working on a new specialty. I was never sure I could handle such constant contact with so much loss, in children so young. Although, who knows, maybe I was perfect for it. Anything longer than the three short hours my own baby had lived felt like forever.

"Thank you," he said.

Time to just play it straight. "You're welcome, Dr. Marks."

"Darion, please." He flashed a small smile, this one without the forced charm. I remembered our last meeting, when he asked me out for coffee. My friend Corabelle had encouraged it. But Corabelle didn't know I had a rule I never violated. One date. One night. And that's it.

But to do any of that — either the night OR the brush-off — with a coworker seemed like a bad idea. Especially with a devastatingly handsome doctor who was pretending to be a jerk but was really utterly vulnerable.

"Darion, then," I said.

Damn, I might as well climb into his bed. I was done for. The gears of my interest had already gotten engaged. No telling what direction they would grind.

But there would definitely be grinding.

One of the volunteers led in two children by the hand. My next group was about to start.

"Looks like it's time for me to go," Darion said. He passed the two kids, patting one on the shoulder, and left the room.

Marlena returned, this time with Jake. He seemed pleased to be on the crutches, hobbling along. Half of his head was still shaved from his surgery, the suture angry and red but no longer hidden under bandages. He was recovering. It was such a relief when some of them did.

When the three kids were settled, Marlena said over their heads, "What was Marks doing here?"

I shrugged. "Just asking about a patient of his."

"That boy is as cold as ice," she said. "He's been here a couple of months and hasn't made a peep to anyone other than 'Where are so-and-so's test results?'" Marlena shook her head, sending her braids bouncing. "Nobody knows a thing about him."

I set a piece of construction paper in front of each of the children. I could see how people would find him cold. He had walked in that way. But later, not so much. He'd been sort of emotional, actually. And he had that picture in his wallet.

The man was definitely a mystery.

A very intriguing mystery.

2

DR. DARION

The art teacher was definitely on my mind as I made my rounds through the oncology ward. Such a funny girl, with her striped stockings and bohemian style. I'd never known anyone with a college degree who wore their hair in pigtails.

Still, something about her was refreshing and easy. Not her attitude, certainly. Borderline insolent. But she let you know where you stood, good or bad. I could talk to her.

Showing her the picture in my wallet was probably a mistake. And I couldn't afford many.

But it had worked. Cynthia would be looked after. For some reason, the two of them had a bond. I couldn't question anything that helped her with this struggle. Cynthia needed as many people as possible in her corner.

I made sure I nodded cordially at the nurses who passed. Despite my best efforts since arriving two months ago, I had already gained a reputation for being a stoic.

I wasn't sure how anyone could be emotionally involved in this specialty. More and more, it seemed the cases that were assigned to this floor were palliative and not curative. I spent more time establishing a comfortable, lingering decline than trying to make anyone healthy and well.

But St. Anthony's was a subspecialty clinic within the bigger hospital. The people who came here were at the end of their cancer battle, seeking experimental treatments and any last shred of hope.

I recognized Harriet Parker trundling down the hall. Her husband rolled an IV alongside her. She must be coming from the chemo room. She'd asked to be able to take it with the outpatients. Anything to be among other people. I understood that.

I carefully memorized each patient's name using alliteration, a trick I learned from a middle school teacher I dated briefly in med school. Harriet was always in a hurry, so I nicknamed her Harried Harriet.

"Hello, Harriet," I said. "You haven't slowed down a bit."

She straightened her orange flowered head cap. "Oh, I'm not as spry as I was when I went through this as a kid." She banged the metal stand of her IV. "Sloppy seconds are no fun."

I tried to laugh, but I knew it wasn't convincing. Harriet had beat childhood leukemia only to get secondary cancer as an adult. Nothing about any of this was really funny, although I could appreciate Harriet's willingness to find humor in her situation.

"I'll be down to see you in a bit," I said.

She waved her hand. "No rush, Dr. Marks. I got nowhere else to be."

I turned the corner of the hallway, this one bustling with nurses and aides. All the outpatient chemotherapy rooms were stationed along this corridor. Bedraggled family members sprawled on chairs in the waiting lounge, knitting or reading or staring up at television screens. Treatments could take hours, depending on the drug and the protocol. And the aftermath was often worse.

I knew this all too well, when my own mother went through it. Multiple cancers erupted at once, as though her body just gave up on fighting. I was midway through my residency. My involvement with her illness led to switching to oncology. While we struggled to manage her condition, I learned how important holistic care could be.

We added at least a year — a good productive year — to her life because I was there to help the doctors talk to each other. We coordinated everything from surgery to chemotherapy to nutrition to mental health as a team, even though I was not allowed to oversee her care myself due to the family connection.

But I ruffled a lot of feathers. Several doctors felt I should have stayed out of it and resented non-medical caregivers recommending changes to her protocol.

I vowed that from then on I would work only someplace that incorporated holistic care. St. Anthony's wasn't quite it, but life had led me here after Mayo turned me down. I'd make the best of it.

I paused at the desk in the hub of the ward to log in and check which patients I needed to visit, but more importantly, to see if I had a moment to drop by and visit Cynthia before going on the longer rounds.

Something about talking to Tina made me want to see Cynthia sooner rather than later. I knew she was exhausted from the trip to Houston.

But we'd been treating her for two years. Inductive therapy. Radiation. Stem cell transplant. She couldn't go on forever. Damage to her remaining kidney was becoming serious. She'd go into failure soon and end up on dialysis and a donor list. Then everything would change. The minute I stepped up to donate, whether a kidney or another round of stem cells, everyone would know our relationship.

Screw it. I would see her now. I whirled around and headed quickly back through the ward. Now I knew my reputation was preceding me, as my pace and determination made everyone move out of my way without greeting.

I couldn't help that.

When I got to Cynthia's door, I paused. Drawings in paint and marker and crosshatched pencil covered all the available space. The art teacher did not seem to realize that the person Cynthia drew holding her hand in so many of the images was her. She probably assumed it was a member of the family.

I focused on one of the drawings. In it, Cynthia had drawn all three of us — me, Tina, and herself. She positioned herself between us, all holding hands. My throat tightened a little. She deserved so much more than what life had handed her.

I knocked on the door in case a hospital nurse was with her, but when I stepped in, only Cynthia and the private nurse I had hired were inside.

"Dary!" Cynthia cried. She disentangled her legs from the sheets and gingerly stepped to the floor to come over to me.

My heart hurt, as it always did, when her small bare head buried into my belly. She was eight, but her thinness and slow growth made her seem younger. The only thing that kept me going as she fought this battle was that I could be here to manage her care, like I had our mother's. Rules be damned. I had seen too many doctors with too big a caseload miss important things.

Nurse Angela adjusted a pair of lime green glasses to peer at her notes. "She's eaten a little today. Urine a bit concerning."

I held the back of Cynthia's head. "I'll order a blood test."

Cynthia's face popped up. "Not another one!"

"You have a new port," I said, pointing to the neck of her gown. "No more sticks now that it's working again." Her central line had stopped functioning while we were in Houston, but I had a new one put in the minute we got back. It was a risk, a surgery when her immune system was down, but we needed to be able to put meds in her, and so many of her veins were already blown.

Cynthia touched her shoulder. "That's right," she said. "My space port is operational." She laid her cheek against me again, clinging like it was hard to stay standing.

"She still seems a bit tired, so I canceled her extra activities today," the nurse said.

Cynthia popped her head up again. "But I get to go to art, right?"

"She should go to art," I told the nurse.

Angela lowered her glasses and glanced at the clock. "She's already missed it."

"Dary! You promised!" Cynthia's hands scrunched the fabric of my lab coat.

"You'll get to go tomorrow," I told her. "I'll make sure."

I scooped her up and carried her back to the bed. "I heard about a special kind of marker today," I said. "One that if you cross one line over the other, it makes a new color."

"Ooooh," Cynthia said. "Can we get some?"

"We can," I said. "If you eat your dinner."

Cynthia frowned. "But it makes me sick."

I squeezed her hand. "Just do the best you can." I glanced up at Angela. "All okay with the staff?"

When we were readmitted after the trip, one of the nurses seemed to suspect Angela wasn't family after all. We created an elaborate ruse that Angela was Cynthia's aunt. No one could know that Cynthia was my sister, or I'd be taken off her case.

"It seems all right. I made up a big ol' story about all the crawfish boils I took Miss Cynthia to when she was a baby."

"I even drew a picture," Cynthia said. She sorted through a pile at the foot of her bed, producing an image of a blood-red crab diving into a pot.

I hated that she had to be involved in the lie, but she couldn't tell anyone I was her brother. "That's real good, Cyn," I said.

I had to get back on rounds. Sometimes it felt like an illicit affair, the time I would steal to sneak in and check on Cynthia. I knew of no other way to work these long hours and still stay close to her. "I'll see you before you go to sleep."

"Okay." Cynthia leaned back against her pillows, pale and fragile with shadows under her eyes. I cursed the genetic marker I'd discovered in both my mother and my sister, one that bypassed me. The tumor suppressing gene T53 was mutated in them both. Mom made it to her fifties before it caught up with her. But Cynthia hadn't been so lucky. She was only six, just two years after Mom died, when she started showing symptoms of leukemia — deep bruising, weight loss, and fevers.

This would be a battle all her life. And I would be there to help her fight it.

3

TINA

I had little time to think of Dr. Darion Marks or his peculiar attachment to his patient as my day spiraled out of control.

My attempt to teach a set of young teens to paint away their pain had gone completely south when the girls got the bright idea to color themselves instead. Soon I had four giggling rainbow heads and a set of nurses grumbling about the mess.

I wiped down the tables, still speckled with paint. I couldn't admit it to anyone at the hospital, but I applauded their misbehavior. They had it tough, running around in hospital garb, no makeup, no dating or school angst or socializing. In their shoes, I would be doing much worse than a bit of temporary color.

My own teen years were complex and strange. I had gone "goth" and continually covered my pale hair with black dye. I ran with a crowd just like me, full of attitude and railing against authority. Everything had to be about me — my wants, my refusal to assimilate.

I didn't get the big picture until life smacked me hard.

My hand automatically moved to my throat to finger the charm on my necklace, a photo pendant.

The image was of Peanut, the baby I had when I was seventeen. He was born terribly premature and lived only three hours. Three long, sweet hours.

His father never acknowledged him or saw him. He ditched me in the hospital during my premature labor. By the time I tracked him down again, he was already poking some other hole.

I frowned at the dirty cuffs of my sweater, smeared with paint and magic marker. I would love to be able to wear short sleeves to make my job easier, but it seemed unwise. People would notice the scars. I slid the sleeve up my arm. Even five years later, the raised white lines on my wrists were obvious at a glance.

I'd been so stupid. So young. So unable to think about anything beyond the pain I was in at that moment and how to make it go away.

A tiny bare head peeped around the edge of the doorframe. "Miss Tina?" a little voice asked.

Cynthia. Dr. Darion's favored patient. She wore a pale blue gown and the nubby-bottomed socks the nurses preferred. She wasn't hooked up to anything today. No drip or oxygen tube. With her quirky smile and cheerful demeanor, she could be any small girl.

But a closer look revealed the shadows under her eyes. And of course the lack of lashes as well as hair. Her hands were marred with nicks and scars from IVs. If the neckline of her gown shifted just right, you could see the port they had installed for her chemotherapy.

I pulled my sleeve down over my own scars.

"Hello, Cynthia," I said. "You missed class today."

"I wanted to come."

"Does anybody know you are here?" I remembered Dr. Darion saying she had lost her mother. He hadn't mentioned a father.

"I told Aunt Angela."

"Is she in your room?"

"She said I could come." She slid into a chair. Her body was tiny, smaller than a typical eight-year-old. More like a kindergartner. She propped her chin on her hands. "She went with me on the trip to Houston."

My boss had told me not to ask medical questions of the young patients, but to redirect if they said anything their parents might not like non-staffers to know.

This policy insulted me on several levels. One, it's pretty damn hard to do art therapy if you're not supposed to know how or why they are sick. Two, I signed enough paperwork on privacy to fill a file cabinet. And third — why wasn't I considered staff?

But I said nothing. If it wasn't for this job, I'd be serving coffee with Corabelle and Jenny at Cool Beans. At least they had the excuse of not having their degree yet.

My other option was worse. Going home and living with my parents.

I'd rather live in a gutter.

"Would you like to color?" I asked.

"Yes, please."

I slid a piece of paper toward her and retrieved the bin of crayons. I cleaned each one with an antibacterial wipe before handing it to her. That was another difference between this job and other art positions. The absolute necessity of sterility.

I sat opposite her. "What do you want to draw?"

"Something pretty," she said.

"A beach?" I suggested. "Or maybe a place you remember from a happy memory?"

She nodded. Her chin was tiny and pointed. "Can I have two kinds of pink?"

I sifted through the box. By the time I set the new crayons by her paper, she had already drawn a stage with fancy red curtains. "Did you go to a play?" I asked.

"My mama was a singer."

"Really?" I sat opposite her to watch the scene unfold.

Maybe I didn't have formal training in this. But I had done a lot of speaking tours about suicide during the past four years, and I had talked to hundreds of people about their best and worst times. I knew that when you sat down and purposefully brought a memory forward, it was usually one that mattered.

On center stage a woman began to emerge from the squiggles and lines. Cynthia was fairly typical for her age and skill level. Mostly stick figures with two-dimensional details, like the flare of a pink dress, the kick of the elbows. She did understand feet, though, and instead of making the toes go out like a ballerina's, her mother's shoes were at a natural angle.

"What is she singing?" I asked.

I didn't expect what happened next.

Cynthia stood up from the table and held an invisible microphone in front of her chest. Her arms were all bones and elbows, thin, fragile, like a marionette. She drew in a deep breath, and what came out next blew me away.

She sang her heart out. "I spent my life in old Kentucky. Moved to Cali when I got real lucky in love."

Cynthia nodded and winked at me, and I knew she was playing

the role of her mother onstage. She sang with sass and self-confidence. Her voice took on a hint of a twang. "He took me home and showed me lovin'. We had a lotta love but a whole lotta nothin' but love."

Cynthia turned in a slow circle, holding the microphone out, arms outstretched. I could almost hear the interlude of a piano, or a guitar, as she made her way around. "Then you found a whole new love to make you happy. T'weren't another woman but a job overseas. You traded workin' for my love."

Cynthia took on a sober expression, and the next verse slowed down. "I held our baby tight on the night that you left me. My little golden boy with the eyes of gray. My only love. My own sweet love."

I clapped as she bowed. "Wow, Cynthia! I've never heard that song before."

"My mama wrote it."

I stopped clapping. "Really?"

Her face got all serious. "Her husband left her to get a fancy job in England."

"Was he your daddy?" Illegal question, but I asked it anyway.

She shook her head. "I don't have a daddy."

An elderly nurse stepped into the room. "Cynthia? What in the world are you doing in here?"

Cynthia turned around. "Where's Aunt Angela?"

"Out looking for you," the nurse said. She placed her hands on Cynthia's shoulders. "Come on now."

The woman narrowed her eyes at me. "She's neutropenic and high risk," she said. I had no idea what that meant.

"I'm sorry," I said.

"You should have reported her to the nurses' desk immediately. I'll be speaking to your supervisor."

I stood up from the chair. She was right. I should have buzzed them as soon as I saw her. Pediatric patients were not allowed to wander. Damn.

"I don't want to go!" Cynthia cried. "I want to be here with Tina!"

The nurse firmly turned her toward the door. "You can come back when it's time for your class," she said.

Cynthia looked back with a mournful gaze, staring at me until she was out the door. My heart clenched for her. I hated rules too. There were always so many things standing in the way of what you wanted.

I picked up the image of her mother singing. So, if the song was true, then Cynthia's mother had another child, a son. Probably not much older than Cynthia, I'd guess. Ten, maybe twelve. I wondered where he was. With his father, maybe. Must be quite a story there.

I set the image high on a cabinet. I would take it to Cynthia's room later and apologize to the undoubtedly worried aunt. See if I could salvage the situation. My position at the hospital was perilous at best. I had to do better if I wanted to keep it. Even if only to keep my promise to Dr. Darion.

I leaned against the cabinet, picturing the doctor standing in the middle of my room. That familiar ache pulsed in me again. It had been a while since I'd gotten tangled up with a man. My sociology professor, actually.

He had so not been worth it. Clammy hands, and gave me a damn B in the class. After that, there had been the rush of moving out of the dorms, scraping up enough cash to sublease the equivalent of a closet in a house owned by a cat lady. It was dumb luck that Corabelle took me to the airport a month ago, then wound up in the hospital around the same time the social services director was giving up on filling this slot with someone who had real credentials.

I was lucky. I knew it. I could use this experience for something better, as long as I could keep the job long enough for a recommendation. I'd been given a chance to do something real. I couldn't waste it on attitude or screwups.

Or blow it with a passionate one-and-done with a handsome doctor.

4

TINA

I saw Corabelle's car in front of her apartment, so I wasn't surprised when she turned up in the kitchen.

"I'm sorry to be here so late," Corabelle said. "I just needed to grab a few things."

"It's your place," I said. Corabelle had moved in with her boyfriend, Gavin. Their wedding was just a month away. I was living in her apartment until her lease was up or I got fired, whichever came first.

I was starting to lean toward getting fired.

"You look sort of strung out," Corabelle said. Her black hair was tied up on top of her head, so thick and tall even in a bundle that she reminded me of a geisha. She plunked herself down on the sofa.

I sat on the floor and leaned against the wall. It was a small room without a lot of furniture. None of us had much money, although our friend Jenny had found some rich movie director guy who kept buying her pink furniture and jewelry.

I kicked off my shoes and set them next to the wall so I

wouldn't trip over them later. "Every day I leave that hospital, I'm shocked I haven't been fired yet," I said.

"It's because you're good," Corabelle said. "Anybody with half a brain would see that you really help those people."

I shrugged. "Hospitals are all about pieces of paper. Credentials. Diplomas. And nepotism. Always the nepotism." I had nobody watching my back whatsoever. It couldn't possibly last.

"So, get the paper," Corabelle said.

"Paper's expensive. And time consuming." I tugged the ponytails from my hair and ran my fingers through the strands. It was getting long. I should cut it all off again. Maybe dye it black again.

Except, expensive. Blond I would have to stay, unless I found my own sugar daddy.

"Any sign of that hot doctor?" Corabelle asked.

She questioned me about this at least once a week. She had been in the room when Dr. Darion first showed up and asked me out for coffee. She thought he would be good for me. Right. Like a needle full of rat poison.

But I wouldn't lie. "He showed back up today."

She sat up instantly. "What? Really?"

"Yep. Right back with the old favor he wanted the first time. Help with a kid patient."

"You said you'd do it, right?" Corabelle's eyes were lighting up like a neon sign.

"Well, not right away…"

"What?" Corabelle scooted forward on the sofa, her hands clasped together. "Why not?"

"The doctor is a jerk!" I said, although admittedly only when he first came in. Still, I didn't want to encourage her.

"Oh." She sat back again. "Then screw him."

Now I felt like defending him. "It wasn't that bad. He just has this gruff exterior. It's probably hard, all these dying patients."

Corabelle watched me carefully, as if trying to figure out which parts were true, my disdain or my understanding. "So, there was something good about the doctor," she said.

I wasn't up for being questioned. I didn't know how I felt myself.

5

TINA

"Tina! You're here!" Cynthia's eyes lit up from her position on the bed when I walked into her room the next morning.

I had an hour at the start of each day when I was expected to write reports on patients who might need additional mental health referrals. That took no time at all, so I usually wandered the hospital a bit.

"I brought you your picture," I said, holding out the image she had drawn of her mother singing.

"Thank you!" Cynthia struggled to push herself to sitting. She seemed weaker than yesterday, even though her smile was huge.

A woman seated near the bed peered at me over green glasses. "So, you're the famous Tina?"

"Are you Aunt Angela?" I asked. "I am so sorry I didn't let the nurses know Cynthia had escaped to my room. She was singing the cutest song."

The woman waved my words away. "I knew where she went. It would have been fine if that bossy nurse hadn't wanted a urine sample just then."

I relaxed a little. If the family didn't make a fuss, then it would probably be okay. When no one came for me yesterday after the incident, I wondered if I had managed to escape trouble.

"Are you Cynthia's mom's sister?" I asked.

Angela's expression froze for a second, and I worried I had been too nosy.

"I'm more of a distant aunt," Angela said.

I didn't know what to make of that. "I loved that song her mother wrote. Such a sad tale of love!" I hoped this might prompt some details about how the lyrics related to the family.

Angela looked behind me, her hands so tight on the arms of the chair that her knuckles were turning white.

The voice that came from the door was like an icy blast. "Do you have any more personal questions that are completely out of line for your relationship with my patient?"

I whipped around. Dr. Darion stood in the door, glowering like a gargoyle.

"I—I was just asking about a song Cynthia performed for me yesterday."

His eyes narrowed. I wondered what I possibly saw in him before, because now he was clearly the biggest jerk in the universe.

He snatched my arm and dragged me from the room.

I tried to wrench free as he moved us down the hall. "What is going ON with you?" I asked.

"Hush," he said.

We turned down a narrow corridor, and he buzzed us through a door with his ID. I had never been in this part of the hospital and tried to figure out where we were. The back side of ICU, maybe.

He shouldered open a door marked Surgical Suite B. The room

was dim and empty. Boxes were stacked along one wall, and it had an unused smell to it, stuffy and antiseptic. A pair of gurneys were pushed together next to a line of cabinets.

"What is this about?" I asked, jerking my arm out of his grasp.

"Why were you in Cynthia's room asking questions?"

"Why are you dragging me through the hospital like a lunatic?"

We were only inches apart, me defiantly on my toes to try to eliminate the advantage of his height.

"You have no business questioning my patients or their family."

"She's my patient too."

"You don't have patients. You are not practicing anything but how to draw a goddamn picture."

Oh, I wanted to punch him. My hand curled into a fist. My voice came out bitter and hard. "It was just a friendly conversation," I said. "Cynthia snuck away to the art room and got in trouble."

I was so close I could feel his breath on my face.

When he didn't comment on that, I said, "I wanted to make sure she was okay." I poked his shirt front with each word. "Like. You. Asked."

Darion exhaled like a tire leaking air. "When did that happen?"

"About an hour after you came to see me yesterday."

He ran his hands through his hair. His anger seemed to be evaporating. "The nurse kept her from going to art class."

I plopped back down on my heels. "Really? A nurse? Which one was authorized to cancel her therapy?" I had been told that only doctors could override the schedule except in an emergency.

This got him. His mouth opened. Then closed. "Actually it was her aunt Angela."

I crossed my arms. "Really?"

Something was wrong here. The woman in her room seemed fine with the girl sneaking off to see me. But not go to class?

His Adam's apple bobbed up, then down, like he had swallowed something nasty. "I'm sorry I dragged you down here," he said.

I shoved at his chest. "Sorry? You just embarrassed the hell out of me! No telling who saw that. And I'm already in trouble for not reporting your precious patient after she came to see me!"

I pushed him again. I was really in a fury. "Are you TRYING to get me fired?"

He backed up against the wall. "I'll talk to the head nurse. Take responsibility." He seemed a little panicked. I had no idea why.

"You better!"

His hands went back to my arms, gentler this time. "I'm sorry. I'll make sure nothing happens to you."

The contact between us sparked, like a match being lit. I forgot why I was mad. He was so freaking close. He wore cologne, just a hint of it. He smelled like heaven. My heart sped up. Crap.

I tried to think how to get out of this. I needed to just walk away. We were alone in a dark room.

Shoot. I could already tell my body was getting ahead of my head. It was calculating distance. Seeing how far I could push this man. How close I could get.

Remembering how long it had been since my last tryst with anybody.

I would have to do the one-and-done with Dr. Darion after all.

I leaned in, just to see what he would do.

6

DR. DARION

Bloody hell, this girl was trouble.

Tina's eyes flashed at me like cannon fire just seconds ago, but now everything had changed. She was breathing differently, little huffs like her respiration was speeding up. Maybe she thought I was a threat.

Or not.

I knew all the reasons for accelerated respiration.

Her arms were slender but strong. The pale blue sweater cushioned my grip. I should let her go, and I knew it. But I couldn't make my hands move. They wanted to stay where they were.

I didn't have time for any kind of affair. And if it blew up, Cynthia would suffer. Obviously this art teacher was nosy, and her curiosity had been engaged. She didn't have any of the training she ought to have about professional distance, how to manage your feelings about patients and keep them separate from your life.

But I'd involved her. I'd asked her to care. Stupid. I should have known better. Tina wasn't equipped for this. She was going to start watching. And she might figure things out. And then everything I had built to create a safe place for Cynthia would be for nothing.

And yet, here she was. I'd dragged her into this space with my own hands.

Hands that refused to let her go.

I recognized exactly when she made some new decision, one that I knew better than to allow. She leaned in, up on her toes again. She didn't come quite all the way. I was, after all, the one holding on to her.

I could smell her. Shampoo. Lotion. Just a hint of flowers, jasmine maybe.

Before I realized what I was doing, I had closed the gap.

Her lips were like a soft landing. As soon as I felt it, I wanted more. I wanted it all. My arms went around her and dragged her lithe body flush against mine.

I kissed her harder, probing, insisting she open for me. Her passion flared, and our mouths moved with a mission of their own.

I felt out of control in an instant. I craved everything about her. I wanted it all at once.

My hands cupped her head, loosening the pigtails. Her hair was sleek and fine, cool beneath my fingers. Her head was delicate, and her neck long and slender. Every part of her ignited another fire in me, until I had no choice but to draw her even closer.

I reached down for her thighs and lifted her to straddle my waist. If she missed my desire for her before, she definitely felt it now.

She was so tiny, so light, it was easy to keep her in place. I ground against her. I chided myself even as I did it. But still it wasn't enough.

The gurney was only two steps away, so I crossed the distance and sat her on it. Now I could use my hands on the rest of her.

I encircled her waist, our mouths still working over each other. I lifted the bottom edge of her sweater, and my fingers brushed her hot skin. God, I couldn't take it anymore. I wanted her here, in the damn hospital, where anybody could find us.

She lurched against me, and I felt completely out of control. She wanted this too. But hell, I didn't know anything about her. She could have a boyfriend. A big nasty boyfriend.

My hand slid up her ribs, and I realized she was a hippie to the core when my thumb brushed a naked nipple. How did I not notice that? Her little gasp against my mouth sent me into a frenzy of why and how. Condom? Not on me. Was she on the Pill? Hell, she could have any number of —

Both her breasts were in my palms now, and any other thought got lost. Her fingers were in my hair, and every stroke of my hands on her body made her jolt against me.

I lowered my arm and started feeling around for the bottom of her skirt. Hell, if she wasn't wearing a bra, maybe there would be no barriers below either. My pulse hammered in my throat. This was the craziest damn thing I'd done in my life.

I found her knee.

Then the surgery room door swung wide, blasting the room with light.

Damn.

7

TINA

What the hell was I about to do with this doctor?

The light blinding my eyes told me in no uncertain terms — get out of there.

I pushed at Darion and jumped from the gurney. My first class was probably about to start, and here we'd been discovered by a custodian.

Hopefully he had some discretion.

I whipped past the tiny man in blue coveralls and a ball cap, praying he didn't know me.

The halls were a blur as I dashed back to my own wing. Only when I got into my empty room did my breathing slow down.

What just happened?

I had no time to think about it as an orderly wheeled in one of my adult patients. I smoothed down my hair, tightened my ponytails, then realized they were a mess, so I pulled them out and tucked the elastic bands into my skirt pocket.

The man in the wheelchair was Albert. He had declined quickly in the weeks he had been coming to art therapy, but this was the first time he wasn't walking. Still, I was happy to see him. He would take my mind off the doctor and our torrid moment in the unused surgical suite.

Albert's gnarled hands grasped at the arms of the chair. I knew he did this to hide the shaking. He had Parkinson's, although that wasn't why he was hospitalized. He and I had something in common, long scars on our wrists. His were still fairly fresh, red and raw, although no longer bandaged.

Mine might have been old, but when I first saw Albert's a couple weeks ago, they throbbed in recognition like the wounds had opened up yesterday.

"Hello, Albert," I said. "I see you've got your own set of wheels now."

The bright yellow FALL RISK bracelet stood out from the cuff of Albert's faded flannel shirt. I glanced up at the orderly and nodded as an acknowledgement that I had seen it. Calling attention to it would make Albert feel worse. The whole reason for his attempted suicide a couple months ago was his inability to paint anymore. The lack of mobility had to be another blow.

Albert grunted. His pale eyes went immediately to one of his paintings on the wall, a castle in blues and grays that I had framed. It was his first breakthrough work since his arrival at the hospital. He made it during my first week on the job.

The image was bleak, blustery from a storm on one side of the castle and roiling with black spirits on the other. But on the day he painted it, I spotted an unlit hurricane lamp in one of the windows.

And I asked him to light it.

So now the image had one bright spot of color, the warm red glow of a single window. Albert looked for it each time he came.

Probably to remind himself that even where he was, and the dark, dark places he'd been to get here, he still had something to look forward to, something to do.

I sat opposite him at the table. "What are you up for today, Albert? Watercolors? Crosshatch? Markers?" I liked to get an idea of how much he was shaking that day before I chose something. But his grip on the armrests was unrelenting.

"I might just pound some clay today, milady," he said, and managed a small smile.

His face was kind and gentle, surrounded by a thick mop of gray curls. He always reminded me of that painter Bob Ross on the PBS show, the one who showed you how to make "happy trees" on canvas. He had the same calm demeanor, and on a good day the joy about his art was palpable.

Albert really must have fallen hard to attempt suicide when his talent was so visceral. Even with the struggle to control his movements, he was easily the best artist I'd ever met or studied under, even in college.

I pulled the container of clay from the shelves. If I were unable to do the one thing I loved, if some disease took that away, I'm not sure I would do any better. One thing I told the students who attended my suicide talks is that once you choose death as your destination, it never goes away. Every upset, every disappointment, every setback has the same way out. You don't even have to search for it to know it's still out there, waiting for you to stumble one more time.

In that, suicide wasn't that much different from alcoholism or drug addiction. You could go to rehab or therapy. You could get it out of your mind for a while. And life could go well for months or years or decades.

But the moment it didn't, in that instant when your depression or your struggle or your exhaustion hit that critical point, it all rushed back. And your mind went straight to the place you thought you'd twelve-stepped or group-sessioned out of existence. The needle. The bottle. The knife.

"Where's Clementine?" I asked. Normally Albert arrived with a sullen woman who complained the entire hour about having to be there.

Albert lifted his arms, wiggling his fingers through the air. "She flew the cuckoo's nest."

"Really? She went home?"

He nodded. "But the beds never stay empty in the loony bin."

I set a lump of clay in front of him. "I'm always surprised more people on your wing don't end up here."

He swung his narrow arm and brought his fist down on the clay with a hearty thwack. "It's a pretty wild bunch." He waggled his eyebrows at me. "We're crazy, you know."

"We're all crazy," I said.

Albert continued to mash at the clay, making it more malleable.

I wasn't allowed on the psychiatric ward. I had six patients from there, or I used to. I guess I was down to five.

Two were Albert and Clementine. The other four were girls closer to my age, also there in the aftermath of suicide attempts.

The majority of people who came through my door were cancer patients from the specialized clinic housed inside the hospital. Thinking of this, though, turned my mind back to Dr. Darion, so I took out a ball of clay of my own and began to shape it alongside Albert.

We had not gotten a chance to talk alone since my arrival at St. Anthony's. He'd always come with Clementine, whose cantankerousness required my full attention.

Albert pinched off a section of clay and rolled it into a fat tube.

"So, what did you do on the outside?" I asked him.

"A little of this, a little of that," he said. Despite the shake in his hands, he skillfully molded the clay into the rough shape of a fish. "I don't guess you have a modeling stick?"

"There is a set here somewhere." I dropped my lump of clay and headed back to the cabinets. I spotted the shaping tools a week ago. I didn't think I would have cause to use them. They were sharp and fine, expert tools rather than something I would hand a child or a psychiatric patient. I wasn't sure why they were even here.

Albert clearly had experience in several areas of art. I would wheedle information out of him. Anything to avoid thinking about the doctor.

I dug around until I found the tray of chisels and taper tools.

Albert poked through them and extracted a long-handled hook. For a moment, I worried I'd done the wrong thing, imagining him dragging the sharp point into his wrist again. But maybe I was the only one who thought of those things. He laid the handle expertly between his fingers and began picking at the body of the fish, giving it texture and shape.

I gave up on my own lump of clay and watched him work. The curve of the clay became clear as a woman's shape appeared in the upper half. When Albert's fingers fused the fins to the body, I saw it. A mermaid.

"You are amazing," I said to him. Once again, he'd found a way to work so fast that the shake in his hands was minimized. It's something we had been practicing. If he could move quickly enough, he could stay ahead of the trembling, incorporate it even. If he slowed down, then the tremors took over, ruining the work.

The wheelchair worried me. I knew Parkinson's was debilitating. I just didn't think I'd see him change so fast.

Albert's pale lips were drawn tight in concentration. He picked up a different tool, rapidly cutting into the clay to create scales along the fins.

I could only watch in awe. The minutes ticked by. We didn't need to talk or go through the list of recommended questions and answers left by my supervisor to encourage therapeutic discussion. Albert was an artist in the truest sense. The work was his therapy. Just doing it. Being able to do it.

He moved to the female figure, pressing in her belly, separating her arms from her torso with neat, lean lines. The smooth swell of her skin gradually transitioned into the rippled scales.

The castle he had painted was also by the sea. The ocean must have been an influence. There was so much I wanted to know about him. The sense that time was passing, not just for class, but to have the opportunity to learn about him, made me want to interrupt him, to insist on answers. But I let him work.

The hour was almost up by the time he set down the last tool and held out the mermaid. She was beautiful, graceful, and well detailed. Only after I held her in my nervous hands, anxious that I would smudge or damage his work, did I realize that instead of long flowing hair, Albert's mermaid had pigtails.

He had sculpted me. My eyes pricked with emotion. Of all the people I'd run with in art school, graffiti artists, painters, illustrators, none of them had done something like this of me. Not one.

My voice didn't quite hold steady. "Where did you train?" I asked. I hadn't learned to do this at my liberal arts college. Maybe it couldn't be taught in a class, only in an apprenticeship, or in long hours of trial and error.

Albert sat back in the wheelchair. His hands gripped the armrests again. "I was lucky. I lived only a mile from a great sculptor by the name of Jean Luc Mireau. He left Europe during the war and settled not too far from my father's fishing enterprise."

"And he trained you?"

Albert laughed. "He let me clean up his messes. But I learned."

"And the painting?"

"I picked up a few things here and there in school."

"You're wonderful." I hoped he didn't think I was gushing. I still cradled the mermaid in my hands.

"Just an old man with a few skills."

I didn't believe him, but nothing I'd found on him proved any different. I had his name on my patient roster, and a Google search turned up only a few courses he had taught at a small liberal arts college in the 1970s.

I set the mermaid high on a cabinet so none of the kids who came through could reach it. "I wish I could set it in a firing oven. This is that silly sort of nondrying clay for kids."

Albert brushed some errant gray curls out of his eye, and I could see how pronounced the trembling was again. "It's just a quick-and-dirty job," he said. "Nothing worth saving."

The orderly from Albert's ward entered the room to take him back. I squeezed his shoulder. "If only all of us could do such amazing work in an hour," I said.

He laid his hand on mine. His skin was chilly, the bones

pronounced. "I'm glad I could get in a few last works."

His tone made my throat feel tight. "I'll see you tomorrow," I said.

"Tomorrow."

The orderly began rolling him toward the door.

I perched on the edge of the table and picked up the lump of leftover clay. I couldn't do anything with it. But Albert was the real article. I headed back over to the mermaid to examine it more closely. The pigtails gave it a youthful look at first glance. But the seriousness in the girl's face belied the innocence of the hair. Her mouth was pulled down, as though she were thinking of something troubling. One of her hands was tightly clenched, holding her worries.

Is this how Albert saw me? Is this how I looked to the world? I glanced down at the knee socks below my skirt, blue and red argyle diamonds. Now that I looked closely at the mermaid's scales, I could see the same pattern repeated on her fins.

Albert didn't just notice my appearance, the way I presented myself. He also seemed to understand why I still wore my hair that way, what made me put on these stockings, a relic from my teens.

Maybe he even somehow knew my one fervent wish. That I could be back in that time, as hard as it was, those three special hours with my baby, Peanut. It was the only short period of my life that had ever really mattered.

Me and my baby, the only family that belonged just to me. I couldn't get past it. Didn't really try to.

Albert saw me for who I was.

8

DR. DARION

Charles leaned on the handle of his mop. "Didn't fancy meeting you here, doc," he said.

I straightened the stethoscope around my neck before it fell. "Just having a chat with a staff member."

Charles coughed into his hand with an audible chortle and adjusted the blue ball cap that topped his uniform. I had no idea how much he'd seen.

But things could be much worse. Charles was one of the few people at the hospital I had spoken with more than in passing. He was the reason I knew about this unused surgical suite. He sometimes snuck a smoke in here, then sprayed everything down with cleaner to cover the smell.

I wouldn't talk if he didn't.

"She's a cute girl," Charles said, tapping a cigarette from the pack he kept hidden in his cart. "Not like you're the only doc around here sneaking a quickie with someone."

I would have corrected him about the situation with Tina, but he'd seen enough. Five more minutes, and he would have been right. I ran my hands through my hair, trying to bring myself down from the encounter. I was not impulsive like that. I had to get it together.

Charles motioned over his shoulder at the door. "It's got a lock on it, you know. You might want to use it."

"I just brought her in here to talk."

Another chortle. He lit a match, illuminating his face with the flare. Charles was easily sixty, Hispanic, fuzzy facial hair covering his jaw, gray intermingling with black. I met him a month ago after he spotted me in Cynthia's room at three a.m. She was sleeping on my lap, her head on my shoulder.

I knew when he came in and saw us that he had discovered my secret, that I was family to Cynthia. I chased him down later and asked for his discretion. We talked here in Surgical Suite B.

I hadn't hired Angela at that point. That incident is what prompted me to do it. Cynthia needed someone with her, and we had no one to step in. Our mother was an only child. Her mother had died young as well. Probably the same damn T53 gene.

Our grandfather lived in a nursing home in Houston, an impossible drive or flight in his condition. We had visited him on our trip to M. D. Anderson last week. He was recuperating from stomach surgery, but was alert and in decent spirits. Seeing Cynthia without hair was hard on him. I imagined how impossible it was to lose a wife, daughter, and granddaughter. No, I caught myself. Cynthia would be fine. We would get her in remission.

The whiff of smoke reached my nose. I would reek of it myself if I didn't go. "See you around, Charles," I said. "Don't set off the fire alarms." I glanced at the ceiling.

He lowered the cigarette. "Disabled them in '09," he said. "Tell the pretty art lady I said hello." He guffawed again. "Your secret's safe with me. I got a ton of them. I could be a rich man if I were the blackmailing kind."

"I bet." I strode out and walked briskly, deciding to cut through an exterior courtyard to hopefully remove any lingering smell on me. Smoke or Tina.

Just saying her name in my head made my crotch tighten again. I had to get it together on this. I didn't have time for a love affair, and the last thing I needed was another random person knowing about Cynthia.

But she wasn't random. She was like a child herself in her pigtails and colored stockings, petite and full of energy. But her attitude was all woman.

And so was the response of her body.

New subject.

A couple of families lingered in the courtyard by the fountain. The air was chilly, but the sun pleasant. I recognized one of my patients. Melancholy Melanie. I waved hello and called out a greeting. Melanie waved from where she perched on a concrete bench, gazing down at a few winter flowers. Another leukemia case. Her visit was routine, unlike Cynthia's. Her remission had lasted four years. Still, she was sad, always, as though the cancer cells might be subdued but she would not forget the years they stole from her.

Back inside the corridor, the smells and sounds of a busy hospital helped drive the past half-hour from my head. By the time I made it back to the nurses' desk to check on my rounds and what patients were lined up to fill my morning, my distraction with the art therapist had been shoved into the deepest recesses of my mind.

9

TINA

My biggest art therapy group was eight adults from the traumatic brain injury ward. This class was always challenging. I had two aides who assisted, since four of the patients were just regaining use of their arms and hands and two of them often erupted into unexpected shouting matches.

I quickly learned what types of activities would frustrate them the least. I wanted my time with them to be relaxing and productive, not upsetting.

But still, this hour was the one with the most flung paint, torn paper, and angry outbursts. I felt acutely undertrained for this group, although I wasn't sure anyone could be prepared when a hulking three-hundred-pound man hurled a pair of scissors at your head.

I ducked. The plastic safety scissors meant for young children crashed against the wall and broke in two.

"Maybe we should skip cutting today," a heavyset nurse said, rolling the patient away from the table before he could get his hands on any more missiles.

You think? I thought, but I just smiled. "I'll get some clay." Sculpting was always a foolproof art activity. Pretty much anyone could roll a ball around, and punching at it was as good a therapy as anything.

I glanced up at the mermaid on the tallest cabinet. Thinking of Albert and our quiet time always gave me something to look forward to. Just meeting him made all the other groups worth it. Maybe I could ask someone in administration if we could showcase his work somewhere in the hospital.

When I turned back around, Sabrina, my supervisor, was standing unsmiling in the doorway. I waved and pried open the plastic bin.

"Class is ending a little early today," Sabrina announced. She seemed anxious, clutching a folder full of papers to her chest. She'd decided to dye her hair red a week ago, and the color made her wild hair appear to be flames shooting around her face. With black cat's-eye glasses and a zebra-print dress, she looked like she stepped from a 1960s magazine.

I set the bin on the desk. The aides helped their patients make the tight turn to head toward the door. One man hunched over his drawing of an angry rooster as though he would refuse to leave. And actually, without someone coming to escort him back, I wasn't sure how to get him out.

"What's going on?" I asked Sabrina.

She flashed an artificial smile, one that seemed more menacing with her dark red-black lips. Corabelle had been totally creeped out by Sabrina when she was in the hospital. The clothes, the glasses, the busybody attitude. But I'd hung out with stranger people than this. Sabrina was all right by me. Maybe a little excitable. I hoped this emptying of my class was just another dramatic act, and not an indication of something more serious.

I thought back to my moment in the surgical suite with the doctor and yesterday's upset nurse when Cynthia snuck to my room. Plenty of errors to be held accountable for.

Only the rooster picture patient remained, filling in the blue sky on his page. I knew he couldn't get back to his room on his own. Since his car accident, he had struggled with basic tasks. He talked only in quotes from cartoons he had watched as a child, and preferred to spend class drawing the characters.

"Toby?" I said, kneeling next to him. "I'm going to call a nurse from your ward to come get you."

He turned away from me, and I saw a tear drip from his eye onto the table, as though he were a child losing something he cherished. This was so hard, as otherwise he was a full-grown man with a beard and big beefy arms. No one knew how or when he would recover. The brain was so mysterious.

I glanced over at Sabrina, still hugging the file and standing to one side of the door, as I reviewed the list of patients and called the nurses' desk for Toby's ward. No one answered at first, but finally a clipped voice said she'd send someone after him.

A puddle of tears had formed on the table when I went back to him. I was irritated at Sabrina now. For many patients, this was their refuge, a place that wasn't like the rest of the hospital. She was taking this away from them. Why couldn't she have come between groups? She had my schedule. She was in charge of it.

"Tell me about this picture," I said gently. Sabrina could just stand and rot over there for all I cared.

"Who's responsible, I say, who's responsible for this ruckus?"

he asked.

"It's Foghorn Leghorn!" I said. "You did a great job on him." The rooster in his drawing had his arms folded across his chest. Toby had done a remarkable job capturing the details of the character. "What is he saying?"

"Son, you're dimmer than a ten-year-old lightbulb," Toby said.

My throat tightened at that. It could have been a random quote. Or Toby could be projecting the way he felt about himself. If he was, it would indicate higher-level thinking skills, an awareness of his condition. I'd have to write that up in his report.

If I got a chance to make a report.

"Can you write that sentence at the bottom?" I asked. Toby had been relearning to read and write. The skills came back in spurts, as though he wasn't actually learning, but remembering.

He shook his head. At the rooster's feet, he began to sketch out the baby bird from the cartoon, one with giant round glasses. I waited and watched, not just to avoid Sabrina, but also to give Toby some attention since I had him one-on-one.

The minutes ticked by. There must not have been anyone available to come get Toby, which didn't surprise me. Hospitals were nothing if not highly scheduled.

Sabrina wandered the room, looking at the pictures and paintings I had taped to the walls. She paused when she got to the clay mermaid.

My indignation welled up. I didn't want her looking at it. It felt intimate, as though she were spying on some private communication between me and Albert.

The group had only five minutes left when an aide arrived to escort Toby back to his room. Toby picked up his picture and held it tight to his chest as he stood up to leave.

I was doubly irritated now, as group could have gone on as usual. This couldn't be good for the patients. They needed structure, to know what to expect from one hour to the next.

I snatched an antibacterial wipe from the container clipped to the end of the table and began cleaning all the colored pencils.

When the aide and Toby were gone, Sabrina turned around. "I need you to pack any personal things right now," she said.

My face popped up in shock. "What?"

"I have to escort you out of the building."

I jumped from the chair. "What for?"

God, was it that bad with the doctor? Or Cynthia? I couldn't imagine that either transgression would warrant this sort of treatment.

"It's not you. I made a grave error in protocol. You aren't cleared for this job. Not trained. I should have known better. I have to let you go." Sabrina glanced around the room. "At the time I had to hire someone quickly or lose the endowment."

"We should go talk to someone. I think there's been a misunderstanding." I circled the table to confront her. "You don't just escort someone out like this."

"No choice. You're not a licensed therapist."

"I thought you said you couldn't find one."

"The hospital director is quite certain I could have." She pinched her dark lips in a tight line. "Don't worry, you're not alone here. I've been given my notice too."

"What?"

"Yep. After dealing with paint splatters and irate patients myself before you came, PLUS my regular flow of referrals and paperwork." She leaned against the counter, and I could tell she wanted to cry. "He's a difficult man. He knows social workers like me are a dime a dozen, and he'll have a hundred applicants."

"This is ridiculous. What are you going to do?" And what was I going to do? It hadn't really sunk in. I'd moved across the country for this job, and now I had nothing.

"I don't know yet. I'll figure something out." She huffed out a rueful little laugh. "Maybe I'll marry a doctor and give up on the whole career thing. Pop out babies and complain about my house cleaner."

"Can I meet with this guy? Talk some sense into him?" I thought about Albert, and Toby, and the teen girls with cancer. And Cynthia. "He has to know the trauma some of my patients are going to feel if I just disappear."

"You couldn't get to him if you tried," Sabrina said. "He doesn't exactly make himself available to the little people."

"Watch me."

Sabrina held out her arm. "Tina, don't. It's not worth it. He could really make a mess for you. Technically, your working here broke a lot of rules. There's no telling what he might do."

I plunked back down in a chair. "You must have really been desperate to bring me on, then."

"I didn't think it would be as big a deal as it was." She set the folder on the table, and I saw it was my personnel file. "I thought we could get you certified once you were established."

"I don't even get to say good-bye to anyone?"

"He wants you out and the records gone," she said.

I reached for them. "I'm not above blackmail," I said.

Sabrina shoved them away. "You don't even want to go there," she said. "He's gotten doctors stripped of their credentials. Nurses blacklisted."

"Why is he even here, then? It's a hospital!"

"It's nice to think that everybody has the patients' interests at heart," she said. "But really, it's all about careers and power." She sighed. "At least once you're above the peons like us."

I glanced at the clock. I should be having another class, Cynthia's little group, in fifteen minutes. "Have my other classes been canceled?" I asked.

Sabrina nodded, her flaming hair dancing around her face. "All the nurses have been notified not to bring patients down."

I wondered how long until Dr. Darion would check on Cynthia and find out I was gone. If he would step in.

For a moment I let myself focus in on him, his smell, his hands on my skin. That encounter felt like a lifetime ago already. I wondered if he could do anything to stop this.

But Marlena said he'd only been here a couple months. He probably didn't have any pull. And if this director was as horrible as Sabrina said, it wouldn't matter anyway.

"Do you need a box or anything?" she asked.

"I have one," I said. "Let me just gather a few things."

"I have to get you to sign this," she said. Reluctantly, she pulled a sheet of paper from inside the folder. "It's a nondisclosure and an agreement to stay off the premises."

"Why the hell would I sign that if I'm already fired?"

"Withholding of your last paycheck," she said meekly.

God, what a lunatic. If I signed it, I couldn't come back and say good-bye to Albert or Cynthia. If I didn't, I wouldn't be able to pay Corabelle's rent on the apartment I was subleasing from her.

But you know, the thing about agreeing to stay away is that it relied on something important — getting caught.

"Give me that," I said. I scrawled my name across the bottom.

They'd have to arrest me.

10

DR. DARION

I was back at the nurses' desk checking the paper records against the glitchy iPad software when I saw Tina out of the corner of my eye.

She looked even angrier than usual, and she'd taken her ponytails out. Maybe someone had suggested she not wear them anymore. I could imagine that would rile her. Now that I knew about her lack of a bra, it was hard to keep my eyes from drifting to the sweater. But the corded weave was thick enough to hide it. She was pretty slight.

The memory of her skin beneath my hands made my blood pressure rise.

When she got closer, I saw she was carrying a box with a potted plant sticking out the top, some books, and various odds and ends. Another woman, one of the social workers, if memory served, walked alongside her. She didn't seem too happy either.

I knew I shouldn't speak to Tina, but I couldn't help it. "Leaving early today?" I asked. It dawned on me as I said it that she hadn't had her art class with Cynthia yet.

"Leaving for good is more like it." She turned away from me and punched a button on the elevator.

When her words actually sank in, I strode over and grabbed her arm.

She looked down at it and raised an eyebrow as if to say, "Again?"

I let go. "What do you mean 'for good'?"

"I got fired," she said.

Now my blood boiled. "Who found out?" Charles wouldn't dare tell anyone about our encounter in the surgical suite.

She rolled her eyes. "Not that."

This made the other woman snap her head around and look at us. God, I could already see the rumors trailing through the halls, as visible as kite strings.

The elevator dinged. "I'm apparently not qualified," Tina said. "That time you called me the art teacher? I'm not even certified for that."

The doors opened, and she stepped through.

Damn it.

I looked left and right, not sure what to do. Impulsively, I dashed into the elevator as the doors were closing.

She and the retro social worker were the only ones inside. "What about Cynthia?" I asked.

Tina shrugged. "I'm out. And I'm not allowed back on the premises."

"That seems a little extreme."

"They don't want me to make a ruckus."

"You struck me as the kind of person who likes a good ruckus."

Tina stared at the list of floors and wards printed on the wall.

The flame-haired social worker peered at my badge. I resisted the urge to turn away.

"Dr. Marks," she said, "I would advise you to stay out of this. It's a personnel matter."

"But I have a patient who will be dramatically affected by Tina's unexpected departure," I said, knowing the words sounded false.

"We have already identified a qualified candidate for the position," the woman said. "There will be minimal disruption to the schedule."

The elevator stopped. We were at the bottom floor. Panic started to rise in me. Cynthia would be devastated. She wouldn't eat. She would go into a vicious cycle of nausea and lack of appetite. Mental health affected physical health. I knew this to be a fact.

The two women stepped out. I was about to lose her. God, I couldn't let that happen. I followed them. "I would like for us to go to HR right now," I said. "I want an explanation."

The social worker stared at me from behind black cat's-eye glasses. "I assure you that you do not want to do that. This goes all the way up."

"Then I'll take it all the way up." Hell, what was I saying? I was in hot water with HR myself after taking a two-week leave of absence only two months into my tenure at the hospital. But Cynthia had to go to Houston. I had to see what our options were beyond St. Anthony's.

Tina spoke up, her voice unexpectedly soft. "Darion, I'll find a way to see Cynthia, okay? I'll figure it out."

The way the social worker shot daggers at her told me that her job was probably tied to Tina's obedience on this matter.

"I don't have any way to contact you," I said.

She smiled, which couldn't have been easy under the circumstances. "But I know how to contact you."

The two women crossed the broad atrium toward the exit. For all I knew, Tina didn't even care. She could breeze out of here and never look back. And I would have to deal with the fallout for my sister.

I had no choice but to trust her. I had to hope she'd do the right thing.

11

TINA

I collapsed on the sofa in Corabelle's apartment. I officially could not afford it anymore, although I guess I had a month until I wasn't able to pay. Sabrina assured me once we made it to the parking lot without further incident that I would receive my last paycheck in the mail within a week as long as I stayed away.

I reached into the box on the floor and lifted out Albert's mermaid. I handled it carefully to avoid disturbing the soft clay. The girl who was me looked serious and sad. I wasn't sure how I would find him to say good-bye. I couldn't get on his ward even as staff.

"Maybe Albert can predict the future," I said aloud, setting the mermaid on the coffee table. "Sad was just around the corner."

And in the past. Loads of it. I was nowhere near the emotional upheaval that led to my scars, but every upset always brought my mind back to it, as though it were the measuring stick to gauge my current level of unhappiness.

I let myself drift to my happy spot, that bittersweet memory I called up whenever life got hard. Me and Peanut, curled up together on a hospital bed.

We had been alone, just me and the baby. Somewhere in this quiet space, after the doctor took off his monitor and said it was time, and when I noticed that he no longer moved anymore, we became a family.

I wasn't close to my parents. I was a late-in-life baby, a surprise that came fifteen years after my older brother. He was out of the house, graduated and gone, before I was old enough to really know him.

What my parents called the generation gap, I called the Grand Canyon. I had nothing in common with the people who raised me. Once I had my own opinions about things, I was nothing but a confusing, ill-mannered hellion. I didn't belong to them, and they didn't belong to me.

But not Peanut. He had been mine. From that moment I found out I was pregnant until the nurses took him away to be cremated, he was mine.

I flopped back on the cushions to stare at the water-stained ceiling.

At this point, I couldn't imagine having a life stable enough for a kid. But I lived vicariously through Corabelle and three-year-old Manuelito. I liked watching the boy if I got the chance. I could probably do it more now. He and I could be wacked-out maniacs together.

Eventually I would have to find another job.

I got up and started pacing Corabelle's apartment.

Most of my stuff was still in storage. I hadn't been able to afford to ship it here. I brought as many suitcases as I could get away with on the bus to San Diego when I moved here for the hospital job. I figured once I got a few paychecks under my belt, I could have the rest trucked over.

But not now. I couldn't live much more cheaply than I was. Corabelle's apartment was about as low as it got without living someplace seriously sketchy. And I'd avoided deposits or transfer fees by subleasing from her.

She lived here on a coffee-shop wage, so I probably could too. I kept things simple. Fancy didn't suit me. It would be all right.

I dug my phone out of the box and sent Corabelle and Jenny a text. *So, is Cool Beans hiring?*

Corabelle was probably in class. No telling with Jenny. She was skipping half her courses these days to hang out with her eccentric sugar daddy.

But the phone buzzed within seconds.

From Corabelle: *What happened?*

From Jenny: *Glad you're home. I'm coming right now.*

I tapped off a quick note saying I'd been escorted from the hospital like a common criminal.

Within fifteen minutes, Jenny was barging through the door, her pink hair streaming behind her like cotton candy unraveling from a cone.

She yanked a giant pair of designer sunglasses from her face. "What the hell is wrong with those hospital people?" she asked. "I thought they signed some hypocritical oath to take care of people!"

I could only stare at her. Jenny had always been a little larger than life. Crazy colored clothes. Wild hair. An attitude to match. But today. Wow. Shiny black knee boots stood high on five-inch platforms. A teeny black vinyl skirt flared out below a matching jacket. A black and white striped sweater pulled it together. With all that lack of color, her hair stood out like neon paint on newspaper.

"Never mind," Jenny said. "We'll catch up after the delivery guys are gone." She stood in the open doorway. "In here, boys!"

I came up behind her. "What is going on?"

"Frankie bought me another sofa. Like my apartment had one more foot of space!" She waved at two men standing by a truck.

Frankie was the movie director Jenny had hooked up with a few weeks ago. She dumped her poor teaching-assistant boyfriend in an instant and jumped straight into endless nights of B-list parties. Her picture had been in a tabloid last week, and she was still gushing about it.

"You're having the sofa brought here?" I asked.

Jenny whirled around. "Corabelle has room. Besides, she'll take her stuff, and then this place will be empty. And this beauty will be all yours!"

She stepped aside as the two men brought in a sofa that I instantly nicknamed "The Pink Monster."

It had a rounded back that curved into the arms. Two fat cushions looked bouncy enough to launch you to the ceiling.

And it was fluffy.

Like a stuffed animal.

Or a bathroom rug.

Or a shag carpet from the 1970s.

Only now it was in my living room.

"Jenny, what the hell is this?"

She pointed for the men to set it down at an angle from Corabelle's sofa and jumped onto it, striking a pose as though a magazine photographer would be snapping her for the cover of *Where Trash Meets Money* magazine.

The two guys headed out. I ran my hand along the fuzzy

surface. "You're really leaving it here?"

"It's all yours, baby," Jenny said.

I moved past it to sit on a sofa that *didn't* look like a set piece for Strawberry Shortcake. "Why don't you just tell him to stop buying you this stuff?"

Jenny flipped over on her stomach. "Have you lost your mind? These have been the best weeks of my LIFE!"

"Is he at least handsome and sexy?" I asked. Jenny hadn't brought Frankie around to meet her friends.

"Oh, no. He's short and balding and really into licking," Jenny said. "Not that I mind that." She rolled onto her back again, like she couldn't get enough of the fur. "And temporary. I get that. I'm not looking to be Mrs. Short and Balding."

"You sure you know what you're getting into?"

Jenny sat up and began unzipping the boots. "I'm a plaything. I might as well have fun with it. I know where I stand." She dropped the first boot with a sigh of relief. "Besides, you know how I feel about sex with strangers."

"It's good for your complexion," I said. "Or is it your metabolism?"

Jenny chucked the second boot to the floor. "It's good for what ails ya," she said. "Unless you catch something that isn't cured with a round of antibiotics."

I shook my head. I wasn't any better. One-and-done. This was something Jenny and I could agree on.

She propped her feet in little green socks on the coffee table. "So, what happened in the Land of Hot Docs? You got canned before I got a chance to be examined by any of your coworkers."

I pulled my elastic bands from my skirt pocket and twisted my hair back into pigtails. "Turns out the paperwork mattered a lot. They want someone with an art degree AND a therapist license."

"Gawd. They should have known that before they brought you here." Jenny smoothed down the vinyl skirt. "What are you going to do now?"

"Find some other work. No reason to go back to that college town. And definitely not going home." I shuddered. "I'll manage."

"I've been skipping shifts at Cool Beans, or I'd recommend you. But Corabelle can. That girl doesn't make a mistake."

The walls seemed to echo her words as we both realized that Corabelle had probably had the biggest life screw ups of us all. Punched a professor and got arrested. Then kicked out of her last college. Stripped of her scholarships.

Jenny seemed to know the direction both of our thoughts had gone. "Well, NOW she doesn't," she corrected. "Straight arrow, that girl."

"I'll take a look around," I said. "There's bound to be something."

"Christmas is coming," Jenny said. "Everybody starts hiring."

"Some of the people at the hospital are going to be very upset that I left so suddenly," I said.

Jenny leaned forward. "Would any of them be that doctor who asked you out for coffee?"

"He never showed up, remember?"

"Corabelle said he talked to you yesterday."

I pulled the plant from the box and set it on the coffee table. "He and I sort of had…a moment."

Jenny scooted to the end of the pink sofa, closer to me. "What kind of moment?"

"He got upset that I was talking to one of his patients in her room." I could still see Darion's angry scowl as he dragged me through the halls. "And we ended up in this empty surgery room."

"Oh my God. Did you bone him?"

I had to laugh. "No, I didn't bone him." I plucked a dead leaf from the ivy.

"But something happened, or you wouldn't be bringing it up."

I shrugged. "Maybe we got a little…involved."

Jenny transferred from the fuzzy sofa to the old one to sit next to me. "You can't leave out the details!"

"None of our clothes came off." I crossed my arms over my belly. I could still feel the doctor's hands on me.

"Not like that's necessary," Jenny said. She picked up the mermaid and turned it over. "Where did this come from?"

"One of my patients made it." I resisted the urge to ask her to set it back down. The clay was so soft.

But she handled it carefully. "It's beautiful."

"I know. I wish I could get back in there and say good-bye to some of them. I can't believe they just escorted me out."

Jenny placed the mermaid back on the coffee table. "That's not right. What's the hot doctor going to say?"

"He saw me leaving. There's nothing we can do. I'm just not qualified."

Jenny flopped back on the sofa. "Uggh. That just sucks." She lifted her wrist to examine a diamond-encrusted watch, probably another gift from her director. "It's five o'clock somewhere. Let's find something to drink."

12

DR. DARION

I tried not to be distracted as I went on patient rounds. Everyone deserved my full attention. But I kept pausing between the rooms, picturing Tina with her box of belongings. I couldn't believe I didn't have something to do with this, despite what they said.

About an hour after my run-in with Tina, I spotted the custodian, Charles, mopping an empty room. I stepped inside and closed the door.

"Did you mention me and Tina to anyone?" I asked, trying to keep my voice casual. "Because she just got fired."

Charles leaned on his mop. "Not to nobody," he said. "But her boss lady got the axe too."

"That's ridiculous. Why would they be firing people randomly?"

"Just sayin' what I heard."

I could believe that Charles, virtually invisible to people as he cleaned floors in his blue uniform, might hear things others didn't. He'd probably seen hundreds of doctors and nurses come and go.

Administrators too.

Charles straightened his ball cap. "Your Miss Tina has a lot of champions. I think she'll be back."

"What do you mean?"

Charles resumed his mopping. "Just saying that money talks around here. And there's some money going to be flappin' like a squawking bird when the word gets out that she's gone."

I had to get back to my rounds. If Charles was right, then something would happen. But that man was as vague as a fortune cookie. I couldn't risk it. I knew who I had to talk to.

***

My father's office was a twenty-minute drive from St. Anthony's Hospital, and he wasn't expecting me.

I did take the precaution of calling his secretary to make sure he was in, but otherwise I felt it better to not announce my intent to see him in advance.

As I pulled into the parking garage, I girded myself for the visit. We did not have a good relationship. I rarely saw him, even on holidays, as he refused to allow me to bring Cynthia around him.

My main goal today, the same as any time we met, was to avoid an argument. He had made some terrible choices, and they had cost my mother and my sister dearly. But he wielded a lot of power, and sometimes I needed him for that.

He wasn't someone to make your enemy, although I had tried my darnedest in the years after he left my mother and refused to acknowledge Cynthia as his.

The California Board of Medicine was housed eight hours away in Sacramento, but being on the board didn't require being there. My father, and his father before him, had a lot of political influence that got them appointed to the right places.

My face reflected in the mirrored walls of the elevator looked stressed and haggard. It was hard to imagine that earlier that day I had been in the surgical suite with Tina. The last day as emotional as this had been the one when my sister was born and my father had refused to come, insisting the child wasn't his.

He hadn't attended my mother's funeral either.

I had to strike these things from my mind, or the resentment would cause an emotional backlash that might hurt me while dealing with the issue at hand. Someone needed to exert some pressure on the hospital director regarding Tina's job, and my father was the man to do it.

I had two ways to play it. I could start with self-righteous indignation over my patients' suffering, but he'd see through that quickly. Still, applying a gloss of professional interest would grease the later conversation, which would be a lie built on truth.

My father's weakness was his intense desire to continue a long family tradition of physicians. I was his only son. He wanted to see me comfortably set up with family and kids, whom he could also bully into becoming doctors.

So, to save Tina's job, she would have to be exalted to the position of future mother of his grandchildren. She would never even know this behind-the-scenes action was taken on her behalf.

My father's secretary, Martha, had been with him since I was a boy, first answering phones at the clinic where he practiced. Even when he left us for Oxford, the move that split our family apart, she had remained with him.

"Darion, so good to see you," she said. "Let me buzz your father."

"Thank you."

I didn't sit down, but stood by the windows overlooking San Diego. Winter had settled in, gray and dull. But California had its fans for a reason. Temperate weather. Beaches. I pictured Tina in other places in the city, sitting beneath the trees in Balboa Park, walking along the path by the lighthouse on Point Loma.

Good grief. I barely knew her. I remembered her angry tirade when I spoke to her yesterday. She'd probably just as soon whack me with a roll of art paper as go out on a date.

But then there was the way she'd stood on tiptoe, leaning toward me like it was a dare. And how she responded, as though we were two swimmers caught in a current.

"You can go see him now," Martha said. "He cut his conference call short."

I nodded curtly at her. She beamed like I was still the tyke who dug through her bottom drawer for the butterscotch candies she kept for me. She was a lovely woman who had aged well, spinsterly in a handsome way. I often wondered if there was something going on between her and my father, but even after his divorce from my mother, she never seemed to be anything more than an employee.

I turned the gold knob to my father's office. He stood up from behind the polished mahogany desk and held out his hand for a solid shake. "To what do I owe this unexpected surprise?"

"Just wanted your opinion on an issue at St. Anthony's."

He settled back into his oversized leather chair and gestured for me to sit as well. "How is the new position suiting you?"

"Good. I see pediatric patients as well as the second-onset

adults who were treated as children."

"That's a very good subspecialty. Not a lot of literature exists on the long-term genotoxic effects of chemotherapeutic intervention in children. You could really make your mark there."

His smile was genuine, a rare thing. I could see something of Cynthia in it, which is what always riled me when he insisted she was not his. It was obvious to anyone who looked, despite the paternity test.

"It's a growing population." I decided to indulge him in his fantasy that I would achieve some medical breakthrough that would give the family name a place in history.

"Has there been some resistance to your handling both adult and pediatric cases?"

"Some. But I've been approved for the alternate track to pediatrics."

Another proud smile. I wanted to wipe it off his face. I hadn't repeated all that work just to show off. He wasn't aware that Cynthia was so ill, and that I needed the credentials to remain involved in her care. I wasn't certified in pediatrics, but my oncology work had gotten me into St. Anthony's specialized wing to manage both, even if Mayo had turned me down.

With Cynthia at the hospital, I was fine doing extra rounds, extra work, extra everything. My supervising doctor in pediatrics felt I would easily complete my pediatric hours inside a year if I chose to go that direction.

I could only hope Cynthia would be in remission well before then.

"I think it's a good course. It will lend credibility to your papers on the adult second-onset work. Maybe you'll find the treatments that prevent it."

It was a good goal for someone else. Right now I felt in the thick of battle, and thinking about my own future was for later.

"But that's not what you're here for, is it?" he said. "Do you need someone to supervise this alternate track? I could contact Dr. Libson. He's done work in that field."

"No. It's not that." Here was the moment. After all that overblown talk about changing medical history, I couldn't figure out a way to bring up saving the job of the girl I'd felt up in a dark surgical suite.

But this wasn't about her. It was about Cynthia.

"St. Anthony's has taken some bizarre stance on social workers and has fired several. One of them was making a huge difference with my patients."

My father's face was impassive and blank, a forced expression I knew well. He braced his elbows on his desk, his hands folded in front of a face that looked remarkably like mine, albeit with a hairline I was sure I could expect in twenty years.

His voice barely held back his disdain. "And you're bringing this little staffing matter to me."

"The director has a stick up his ass."

"John Duffrey is a highly respected hospital director. I expect to see him on this board inside of five years."

"He's being shortsighted."

"On social workers?" My father leaned back in his chair. "Leave that to HR."

"The directive comes from him. He should be corrected."

His eyebrows shot up. "Why are you taking on Duffrey over this?"

Time to break out the second salvo. "A woman."

This brought out a smile. "Ah. Is the mighty bachelor finally settling down?"

"Not if she moves six states away." *Nice touch.*

"Is she just a social worker?" He tried and failed to remove the disapproval from his voice.

Hell, I didn't know what she was. "A therapist, actually."

He touched his telephone, then pulled back. "She should be protected, then."

Crap. I was talking out my ass. "Well, she's more of a layman. The art therapy program."

I realized my mistake immediately when his face darkened with disgust.

"I see you're still hung up on your little drawings."

We were back to that. He had swooped back into my life when I applied to art schools instead of going premed after high school.

"I went to medical school. I have two subspecialties. Let it rest."

He held up his hands. "I'll let it rest."

But he wouldn't. He knew my love of art came from my mother, and that the years he was gone meant that his family legacy of physicians was salvaged only by his monetary bullying.

"This art therapist got let go?"

I tried to salvage my argument. "Yes. Since it's systemic and not just her, I thought it might need looking into."

Now came the expression I knew well. Condemnation. "You realize you're getting involved in something very serious over something very small."

"Not small to me." I managed to keep my voice straight and

even, something he'd taught me well, but inside I knew I had lost.

"You're not going to get very far in your career if you take every woman problem straight to the top. If you want this therapist to stay around, then get her to stand by your side."

"Right, just like you did for Mom."

My words rang off the walls as he stared at me. "I'm not getting into this old argument."

"Right, because you know damn well you did the wrong thing. I'm trying to do the right one here."

He picked up a pen and began flipping through a calendar, signaling that the conversation was over.

I wanted to smash my hands on his desk. Make him listen. One phone call from him to Duffrey would get Tina back. We both knew this.

I hadn't played it right.

"It would mean a lot to me personally if Tina Schwartz were reinstated to her position. I'll go to Duffrey myself if I have to."

My father stared at me, impassive, but his eyes flashed in warning. "You'd jeopardize your relationship with a very powerful player at your hospital over this girl?"

"I would."

"Then I haven't taught you a goddamned thing." He picked up his phone and began dialing.

Obviously we were done here. I stood up. "Nice seeing you, Father," I said.

He waved me away, looking out the window as he pressed the phone against his ear.

Disappointment in me was nothing new to him.

The feeling was definitely mutual.

13

TINA

By the time Corabelle made it over, Jenny and I were halfway through my box of wine and not making much sense.

"Drunk by midafternoon?" she said, dropping her backpack by the door. She looked at Jenny. "Don't you have class?"

Then she noticed the big pink sofa. "What in the world is this?"

"My newest acquisition," Jenny said. Her voice might have been slurred. I wasn't sure if I was an accurate judge at this point.

"Frankie buying you things again?" Corabelle asked. She sat delicately on the furry cushions, as if the sofa might drag her into its pink clutches.

"He won't stop," Jenny said. She was sitting on the floor now, her glass of wine sloshing precariously.

Corabelle leaned down and took the glass. "And it's in Tina's apartment because…"

"I ran out of room!" Jenny slapped the floor. She'd ditched her shiny black jacket and tied the flowing pink mane into a ponytail.

I wasn't nearly as drunk as her. Probably. I couldn't tell for sure. I sat at the kitchen table a few feet away.

Corabelle got up and came over. "So, they fired you?"

"Not qualified," I said. "No certification." I might have added an extra syllable in there.

She picked up my wine glass as well and placed them both in the sink. "Are you going to go back to Massachusetts?"

I laid my head on my forearms. Damn, I was tired suddenly. "I'll probably marry the doctor instead."

Corabelle whipped around. "What?"

Jenny's voice had a singsong quality. "Tina and the doctor sitting in a tree…" she trailed off.

Corabelle sat opposite me. "I'm guessing things progressed."

"Yep. Right there on the gurney in Surgical Suite B." Even though I was talking flip about it, I couldn't get the feel of his hands on me out of my head. One-and-done. I needed the one-and-done.

Why had I said something about marrying him?

No more wine.

"You had sex with him at the hospital?"

I lifted my head. Corabelle's face was bright red.

"No, no," I said. "Just, oh, I don't know. Stuff."

Jenny stumbled to her feet. "No orifices were penetrated. I already checked." She went into the kitchen and retrieved her wine glass. "I mean, I didn't CHECK check. But I asked."

Jenny paused in front of the Pink Monster. "I promise not to puke on the new sofa. You should take it since Tina doesn't want it," she said.

Corabelle shook her head. "I don't think it's Gavin's style."

"Little Manny will love it," Jenny said. "He'll think it's a giant stuffed animal." She paused. "What's big and pink and furry?"

"Your brain with Frankie," I said, and we both laughed so hard I almost fell out of the chair.

My cell phone buzzed, but I had no idea where it was.

"I don't think you should get that," Corabelle said.

I struggled to my feet. "But it could be the good doctor," I said, although there was no way that was true. I'd refused to give him my number. Said I'd contact him. Silly me.

The phone was out on the coffee table. "It says St. Anthony's Hospital," I told them. "Maybe they're hiring me back." I fumbled and hit the talk button.

"Give me that!" Corabelle hissed and took the phone. "This is Corabelle, assistant to Tina Schwartz." She flashed me a horrible look, but this just made me giggle. I plunked down on the sofa.

"No, she isn't here at the moment," Corabelle said. "Can I take a message for her?" She looked around for a piece of paper, saw none, and snatched up a pen to write on her palm. "Okay, got it. Yes. That's great. I'll let her know."

"Well, good news." She set the phone back down. "The director of the hospital wants to see you first thing in the morning about enrolling in some program. Sounds like you may have your job back."

No way. Things never went right for me. Somebody had pulled a string. A big one.

I had underestimated the doctor.

14

DR. DARION

Cynthia wasn't in her hospital bed when I checked on her that afternoon. A quick glance at the empty bathroom told me no one was there. Panic threatened to consume me as I jerked my phone from my pocket to call Nurse Angela. Cynthia's ANC was under one hundred. She had no immune system to help her fight off contagion right now. None. Anything could happen.

Staph infection.

Fungus.

Bacteria.

God, even the common cold could kill her right now.

I paced the small room as I rang Angela. She was a nurse. And smart. She would make sure Cynthia was double masked. They were probably outside in the courtyard getting some air. That was safe enough as long as they watched what they touched, who they talked to.

Angela answered within two rings. "I'm going to have to call the alert code," she said without any greeting. "I assume you're in her room?"

"Yes." I strode straight out the door. "How long has she been missing?"

"Ten minutes. Should I call the code?"

A missing child was a Code Amber to alert the staff. Cynthia was willful and prone to wandering since she knew I was near, so I asked Angela to hold the code unless we had to call it.

"You checked the art room?" I asked.

"First thing. It was empty."

Nurses looked at me curiously as I passed. I was probably radiating fear. "Where are you now?" I asked.

"Heading to the cafeteria. She talked about ice cream earlier. Maybe she thought she could sweet-talk someone into some."

I didn't bother to ask how Cynthia got away. The girl was sly. If Angela went to the bathroom, or even nodded off for a few minutes, my sister would find a way to escape her room.

Particularly to find Tina.

I snapped the phone shut. I had to bring myself down. I couldn't seem overly alarmed for a doctor asking after a patient. But my heart was practically beating outside my chest. Why did Cynthia do this? Maybe we would need to put an IV back in her just to keep her tied down.

I blew past the art room, then slowed down and turned around. How carefully had Angela looked in there?

I headed for the door. Tina was gone, so it was surely unused. My stomach turned over again just thinking about her holding that box of possessions.

It opened easily. Like Angela said, the room was silent and forlorn. The walls were blank, and the string to hold drying artwork cut across the room with nothing but clips on it.

I stepped inside. I could picture Tina standing by the cabinet, clutching a box of paints, so mad at me she could almost spit fire. The grief of the loss of her added to my upset. These past few days simply could not have gone any worse.

I turned around to head out when I heard the smallest noise, like a sniffle. I paused, listening. Yes, someone was in here.

I couldn't see where. The room was open, with shelving on the walls and a table in the center.

But then a little curtain rippled. The bottom section of one of the shelves was covered with fabric to hide the contents.

And I could see a small nubby sock sticking out.

Everything began to settle as I moved slowly toward the shelf. I didn't want to startle her. "Cynthia, I can see your foot."

The fuzzy toes shifted back under the curtain.

I sat on the floor next to the shelf. "Will you come out?"

Her voice was small and tearful. "Not until Tina comes back."

I exhaled slowly. "What makes you think she's gone?"

"The nurse said no class. And when I came here, her Happy Face Man was gone." Another sniffle.

"Her what?"

"Happy Face Man. The one she looks at when she's sad. She let me hold him whenever I wanted to. He's soft and fluffy and yellow, like sunshine."

I tugged the curtain back. Cynthia sat curled up in a ball, bending down to fit beneath the shelf, her back against a tall stack of construction paper.

"Will you come out?" I asked.

She shook her head. "Not without Tina."

"I don't know that I can get her back. But she did tell me she would try to visit you."

Cynthia looked up. "Really? When?"

"As soon as she could."

"Why did she leave?" Her cheeks were streaked with tears.

"She didn't want to."

Cynthia dropped her face against her bony knees. She was so thin. My heart hurt. This was more than anyone should have to bear.

"I'll find her," I said. "Maybe she can work with you by herself. You'd like that, wouldn't you?"

She nodded against her legs.

"Will you come out now?"

Her back made a long, hard shudder. "Why does everybody always go away?"

"I'm here, Cyn-Cyn."

"But what if you die like Mommy?"

God, I hated this world. I hated T53 genes. I hated cancer.

"I am not going to die," I said.

"Everybody dies. I am going to die."

I slid my arm beneath her knees and the other at her back. "Not for a very long time. Not until all *my* hair falls out." I slid her out from under the shelf to pull her onto my lap.

"When you have chemo?" she asked. Her brown eyes looked up into mine, lashless and dark like an infant's.

"Nope, when it all falls out because I'm very very old."

"You're already very very old," she said, and cracked her first smile.

"I am indeed."

I couldn't carry her through the halls. That would look

inappropriate for a doctor and patient. So, I sent Angela a text to come fetch her, and we sat there for a while, on the floor of Tina's room, both of us wishing for the same thing.

That she was back.

15

TINA

Dang it, I was early.

I had never met the director of the hospital, John Duffrey. Rumors about him weren't good, and Sabrina had confirmed that when she escorted me out. He was old, mean, and determined to power-play his way to the top, wherever that was. I didn't keep track of this stuff. I didn't even know what power a doctor or administrator could wield.

But my nerves meant I got up at the crack of dawn. Dressed conservatively, a bra this time, and a jacket. And no pigtails. I hesitated with the striped stockings. I rarely went without, especially in winter. They were my connection to Peanut, my good luck.

In the end I wore them, but put on the longest skirt I owned so only the ankles showed above a pair of black flats.

I wandered through the gift shop, killing time. I was tempted to go see what was happening in my room, if anything had been moved or changed. But it had only been one day. I'm sure it was all the same.

The doctor worked fast. He was bound to be the reason I got

my job back.

I glanced over the shelves of Bibles and rosary beads and little plaques with expressions about faith, hope, and healing. My mother would eat this stuff up.

Then I saw him. Dr. Darion. He was speed-walking down the hall. He'd pass right by the windowed wall of the gift shop in a second. I hid behind the shelves of stuffed animals and toys.

Maybe he had a sixth sense about me, though, because when he got close enough, he spotted me through the glass.

And halted.

I gave a little wave. He looked to the right and left, as if considering whether he should be seen with me. Then he turned and came into the shop.

"You're here?" He seemed shocked.

"I assumed you would know."

He glanced over at the volunteer behind the counter. "Why are you in here?"

"I meet with the director in half an hour."

The shop lady looked up at us. Darion pinched his lips together. "Come with me."

At least he wasn't dragging me this time. I followed him past the main elevators down a long corridor to a set of stairs. We went up a floor, then onto the hall I recognized from yesterday. The surgical suites.

Back there again.

He buzzed us through. My heart was pounding before we even got into the room. Something about getting fired yesterday, his desperation over it, and I'm guessing knowing he had done something to get me back lit a flame that licked through me.

But I was a one-and-done. I couldn't do this with him. Couldn't do anything.

In fact, why were we here? Was he expecting it? Did he really think I'd bang him for getting me my job back?

Now indignation drowned out my interest. What an asshole twit!

He locked the door this time, but before he could even turn around, I was on him like a wasp. "You looking for payment for services rendered?" I spat out.

"What? No. What?"

I poked his shirt front. "We should at least wait and see if I actually GET the job back before you crawl between my legs."

He took a couple steps away. "I just wanted to get away from anyone who might gossip. We're not here to —"

"Really? You didn't come here to finish what we started?" Everything in me was at war, reality not quite meshing with the accusations in my head. He was acting so confused. I would have expected something more cocky.

"Why are you meeting with Duffrey?" he asked.

"You tell me. They said they needed me to enroll in some program." The woman had told Corabelle they wanted me to get certified, paid for by the hospital. I wasn't sure what all it entailed.

Darion straightened his stethoscope. "So, you're not gone?"

"Shouldn't you be telling me that?" I was so confused. Was he part of this or not?

When he came at me this time, I was sure it was going to be one of those kisses you see on movies, the slanting-mouths crush-you kind.

But when he got to me, he just pulled me into him, my head on his chest. "Jesus Christ," he said. "I didn't even know how to find you."

His heart was hammering ninety to nothing. I had no idea why. We had a moment in the surgical suite. That was it.

Or maybe it was the girl.

I pulled away. "Is Cynthia okay?"

His eyes wouldn't leave mine. "She ran away. Hid in your art room until I promised I would find you." He grabbed my hand like he would drag me out. "Let's go see her now."

I resisted. "Hey, wait. Let's be sure what's happening first."

He ran his hand through his hair in agitation. "I don't care about that. I'll hire you myself. I just need you near her."

"Near Cynthia?" I might have hated him two minutes ago, but the idea that he only wanted me for his patient was a bit of a blow.

He watched me for a really long moment. There wasn't a lot of light in here, just a bit coming in from the high transom windows near the ceiling. But I could see him, his hair all askew, his eyes on me like I was something he'd found after a desperate search.

I didn't think anyone had ever looked at me quite like that before.

His voice shook a little when he said, "Maybe I should tell you something."

16

DR. DARION

I had to tell her, didn't I? That Cynthia was my sister. That the mother in the song Cynthia sang belonged to both of us. That her father — my father — wouldn't claim her. That she was the only thing in this godforsaken world that I cared about.

Tina's hair was bright yellow in that darkened room, like a goddess, like an angel. She was a mess, no doubt, quick to anger, sparking like a fuse. But beautiful. Mesmerizing.

I hadn't entirely lied to my father yesterday. I really could see her inside all my possibilities. I wanted to take her places, be with her.

Maybe it was too soon to trust her. I had to know her more.

But I wouldn't let her get away again.

Instead of talking to her and revealing my secret, I gave in to my second most pressing urge, and kissed her again.

This collision was more intense than the first. I needed her, had to keep her close. For Cynthia, I told myself, refusing to admit anything else.

She seemed reserved this time. I didn't care. I had her back, and I wasn't going to let her go without knowing I had definitely started something. I wanted her to think about it. To consider me. To feel enough that she would at least let me know who she was, how to get in touch with her.

My hands didn't appreciate the rough sturdy jacket she wore and slid beneath it. The silky camisole I found there was much better, cool and slippery, hugging her ribs.

A bra today, disappointing, but still, I didn't want to stop. Her mouth softened as I caressed her. She began to relent. My fingers pulled the shirt from the waist of her skirt. Then I was back to skin, warm and smooth, her belly, the definition of the base of her rib cage. Then up to the band of her bra.

My thumb crossed the thin satin cup and was rewarded with the tautness of a nipple. I became obsessed with the idea of it in my mouth. I unfastened the button holding her suit jacket closed and pushed it off her shoulders.

Just a thin spaghetti strap held the camisole in place. My lips left hers to trail across her jaw, down her neck, and to her shoulder.

She smelled like a dream, gently floral. I let go of thoughts of my schedule, the bustle outside the doors, and the patients in their rooms as I pushed aside the two straps to expose her skin.

Her breathing came fast, and her hands on my shoulders gripped me tightly as I made my way along her collarbone. I was determined to get to my destination. The door was locked.

The slippery top slid down her front like a waterfall once the strap was down. Her bra needed a gentle tug. But then I had it, my mouth closing over the tender breast. She arched against me, clutching me now, a small mewling sound escaping her throat.

I didn't want to be anywhere but there, her body curved into mine, intimate parts of her exposed to me. The need grew fierce, expanding from desire to a gnawing ache.

Tina's hands moved, pushing at my lab coat, running up over my chest. I had her now. She'd engaged.

I wanted to see her and pulled back. Her shoulder glowed pale in the light from the transoms overhead. The small pert breast glistened, the nipple puckered tight. I leaned into it again, savoring the texture and taste, letting my tongue encircle the areola. I'd let this part of my life languish too long, deep in the fight for Cynthia's health, transferring hospitals, getting us moved and settled in a new city. I had no time for it.

Tina stilled, her head falling to my neck. She breathed against me, her torso shifting beneath my hands and mouth. The intensity dropped a notch. I lifted my head.

"The meeting," she said softly. "I have that meeting."

I straightened. Of course. God, I hadn't meant for this. Or maybe I had. I tugged her bra and camisole back into place.

She sighed as she stepped back and pulled the jacket onto her shoulders, looking anywhere but at me.

"Will you come see Cynthia after?" I asked.

This was the wrong thing, I knew it as soon as I said it. Her face got a pinched expression. "Is that what this is about? You sure are willing to go to extremes for a patient."

"No, no, I mean...Shit." I straightened my lab coat. "I'm sorry. I meant to say me. Can I see you after? Can we meet somewhere? Lunch? Dinner?"

She turned her eyes to me. I couldn't see their color in the low light, but I knew they were gray, like mine, like my mother's. "I don't know. This seems like a bad idea."

I took her hands. "It's not. No. Just let me have a little time."

"I can take care of my own problems. I can get my own jobs."

I wasn't sure why she said that. I wasn't solving anything. But I said, "Everybody needs somebody."

Saying it made me feel like a hypocrite. I refused to rely on anybody myself. I wouldn't even let anyone else take care of my sister. Nobody cared more about what happened to her than me.

Her voice was quiet when she spoke again. "People will let you down." She glanced up at me, and her expression was so haunted that my chest tightened. "Definitely lovers."

"I won't," I answered quickly. Too quickly. What did I know?

Tina took a step back. "I don't need anyone. I don't want to need anybody. So, I won't."

She seemed so lost. Like she had nowhere to be. No one to protect her, take her side.

But maybe that's not what she wanted. Some people liked to be lost. Tina was extraordinary. Probably I seemed like too straight an arrow. Too dull.

"Just one dinner," I said. "I'll try not to be boring. I won't talk about blood toxicity OR bone density."

This got her to crack a small smile. "But I might like talking about blood and bone."

I pulled her to me again, not to kiss, just to hold. "I want to know how it goes with Duffrey. Will you talk to me later?"

She wouldn't answer. God, she wouldn't relent even that much. She let me hold on to her a moment more, then stepped away again.

I released her and tugged out my phone. "Let me send you a text so you know how to reach me. I promise to let you make the next move. If it's just for Cynthia, I will live with that."

Tina told me her number, her voice heavy with reluctance, then headed for the door. She fussed a moment with the lock and was gone.

My phone screen gradually grew dim as I stared at it.

I tried to think of what to say to Tina in that first important message. She was so upset. I had to convey what I felt. I wanted her to know where I was coming from.

I respected that she was tough. But I didn't agree with her. People need other people. You can't go through life alone.

I tapped the phone awake and typed one simple sentence, with almost no hope that it would work, that she would allow it:

Let me shelter you.

17

TINA

I forced the doctor from my mind as I hurried through the hospital to meet with the director.

The admin offices were housed in a maze of halls and connecting rooms tucked away behind the information desk at the main entrance of the hospital.

I felt my anxiety rising and convinced myself that this was nothing. So what if my temporary art job landed me a meeting with the top dog at St. Anthony's?

So what if my old boss, Sabrina, had been too frightened to even say his name, like he was Voldemort?

He was just a man. And this was just a job.

My hands shook anyway.

Duffrey's secretary looked harried and distracted. "Who are you?" she asked, scrolling her mouse to search through his appointments.

"Tina Schwartz. The art therapist."

"We have an art therapist?" She stuck a pencil behind her ear. She was in her late sixties, with a puffed-up hairdo of brushed-out curls that looked like a Halloween wig. She probably bought the same bottles of Aqua Net that had sustained her in the 1970s.

I was always snarky when I was nervous.

"Sit over there," she said. "He'll be with you in a moment."

I perched on a narrow hard-backed chair you might have expected in a boarding school for criminal boys. It was punishment just to sit on it. I sat and stewed, adjusting every few seconds as the wooden seat crunched my butt bone.

My phone buzzed with a message, but I refused to look at it. I didn't need the distraction of Dr. Darion right now. Or whoever it might be. Corabelle or Jenny. I wanted to focus. And Duffrey probably wouldn't be too pleased if his first impression was me staring at my cell phone like a social-media addict.

I tried to picture this guy everyone seemed so afraid of. Even Dr. Darion had been incredulous that I was meeting him. I imagined him as a cross between Mr. Burns on *The Simpsons* and some dictator. Stalin, maybe.

Half an hour passed, and my back started killing me. There was no way to get comfortable on this chair. This had to be some sort of intimidation tactic. Now when I visualized Duffrey, I saw Satan.

By the time Ms. Aqua Net told me, "The director will see you now," I was ready to rumble.

She didn't bother to get up, so I painfully stood and headed to what I assumed was his door, since it was the only one. I guessed Duffrey couldn't be bothered to escort me inside either.

Inside was an opulent room lined with bookshelves neatly filled with medical tomes. An enormous gleaming desk sat in front of a window that let in filtered light through parchment blinds.

Near the entrance were a sofa, coffee table, and two chairs.

Nobody was in the room.

Another door led off to one side. I assumed this must be a private bathroom, the sort you see in movies showing executive offices. They always had little bathrooms. And the men would come out and seem surprised that you were there.

Viewing the situation cinematically helped calm my nerves. I was the upstart young employee, making waves. Duffrey was the pompous jerk boss who would get what was coming to him before the credits rolled.

I heard water running, and my bravado evaporated. This wasn't a movie. And I had been fired. Whatever force had brought me back here might be pushing this man to do something he didn't want. He could be ready to take it out on me.

By the time the door swung open, I was prepared for something awful. But the man who strode out wasn't nearly as old as I expected. Barely fifty. Aged well. His face lit up with welcome and charm when he saw me.

"You must be Tina. Come sit." He gestured to the sofa and chairs. "I'm John Duffrey. I run this little funhouse."

I was probably supposed to laugh, but I was sort of freaked out. This was the horrible and imposing head administrator? Instead of some evil dictator, this guy was more like a talk-show host.

I lowered myself to the edge of a sofa cushion. Duffrey dropped into one of the wing chairs.

"This is a beautiful office," I said.

Duffrey glanced around. "It's part of the original hospital core. Took a little sprucing up when I got it."

"How long have you been the director?" I smoothed my skirt

over my knees so that it would fall evenly, trying not to show too much striped stocking.

"Two years now." Duffrey leaned back in his chair, hands behind his head, elbows out, like he was about to watch football at home. Boyish black curls topped his head, out of sync with his age. But something in his eyes was sly, like he was putting on a show.

I tensed up, my senses going on alert.

"You're probably wondering what the heck happened yesterday," he said, crossing one perfectly pressed trouser leg over the other.

"It was a strange day," I said. "Getting escorted out like I'd robbed the place. Then getting called back a few hours later."

"Here's the score. Sabrina Longly hired you because she had not done her homework on the position, and she had gotten in a bind. That was a mistake. And hospitals can't afford mistakes."

"I understand you wanted a certified therapist."

Duffrey nodded. "It requires a master's degree in psychology or social work. For a job like yours, not much more. It's not up there on the pay scale."

The way he said it made me feel small and inferior. I burned with a little more anger. *Stay calm, Tina. Don't blow it.*

"The position was funded by a patient. He put some contingencies on a rather extraordinary endowment, one being that the program began, at least rudimentarily, while he was still here."

Duffrey set both feet on the ground and leaned forward. "I'm not one to be pushed around, but a gift of this magnitude doesn't come along very often. Sabrina was asked to get the ball rolling."

"Did the guy take a turn for the worse or something?"

Duffrey chuckled. "Actually, he was doing well."

I felt a trickle of horror. "Did you keep him here just to make the deadline?"

Duffrey held up both his palms. "No, no. That would have been unethical. We just accelerated the plan. Sabrina started the program herself, filling in until we brought someone on."

I remembered how strung out she had been when we first talked. "I think you gave her too much to do."

"Probably. That's often the case in a hospital. Your job is probably one of the easiest there is."

God, this man made assumptions. "Say that when people are chucking scissors at my head."

He smiled briefly, and now I could see the facade slipping. "You see why training is important."

I shrugged. I felt like I had little to lose here. Duffrey's hand was being forced. He didn't want me, and he was having to bring me back. I could probably call him a jerk to his face and suffer nothing but making an enemy.

But I couldn't afford enemies.

I tried to inject a pleasant lilt to my voice. "What am I supposed to do?"

Duffrey jumped up and rummaged around on his desk, producing a file. "We've put together some local programs for you to get your master's degree." He looked up at me. "I assume your bachelor's is in order? Your transcripts will be in good shape?"

I wasn't sure what he was insinuating. That I had lied about my degree? Faked my application? "Yes. I graduated back in May. Won't I have to take the GRE?"

He passed me the folder and sat back down. His voice held a note of bitterness. "Yes, but the score won't matter. With a ringing endorsement from the hospital, you'll get into any of these programs."

"But I can't afford to be in school. I already have loans for undergrad." I tried to picture my life, working all day, night classes, barely paying the bills.

"It will be covered. You can take it slowly. One or two classes a semester." He seemed impatient with my arguments.

"What if I don't want to do my master's? I just finished school. Maybe I don't want to go back."

Duffrey's smile grew pained. "I suppose we could create some administrative position for you within the program. You wouldn't actually be in charge of any patient activities, but you'd be in the room to satisfy the donor."

I was missing something. I flipped through the papers in the folder. "Why are you doing this? I wasn't even here when this money was donated. This can't be about me."

"You've made a very powerful friend since your arrival, Tina." Duffrey leaned forward, and now his dark blue eyes flashed.

I pictured Dr. Darion in here insisting I keep my job. Maybe he involved someone he knew, someone with connections. "Do I get to find out who he is?"

"Anonymity was one of the stipulations." He sat back again. "I hope you'll do the program. I think you'll enjoy it. And I think you'll like Master of Psychology much better than Art Assistant on your resume."

I shrugged. "I'm not in this for titles. But I did like my job."

This did not sway Duffrey at all, and I could see why people thought he was a hard-ass. "Fill out the application so I can get your irate benefactor off my back. If you decide not to do the program, let me know, and we'll go the other route. Either way, I need you back in your room like nothing has happened by midafternoon."

Now it was time for my power play. I had him over a barrel. It was plain as day. "I want a budget for supplies," I said. "And a new table with an adjustable height for the different age groups."

He waved his hand at me. "Those are easy. Just don't go anywhere. We'll be drawing up a contract that will keep you here until the program stipulations are met."

Wow. I was going to be stuck here. "How long?"

"Probably a year at least, possibly for the duration of your master's program."

"If I leave?"

"You forfeit the money for your program and have to pay it back." He frowned. "It's not often you get a free ride for a graduate degree. I'd take it."

"All right."

"Let my secretary know your budget needs. Find this table you want and bring her the ordering information."

"And chairs," I said hastily. "I need both adult and child chairs."

"Just tell her." He walked back to his desk, probably disgusted that I was bringing in petty details. His job was just to make sure the hospital didn't lose the money for this program.

And to appease some powerful person.

I wanted to know who it was.

18

DR. DARION

I had a break in the day around lunch and decided to check on Cynthia. I wanted to make sure her temperature was normal and there were no ill effects of her little expedition yesterday. Her first clinical trial chemotherapy was scheduled for tomorrow. I had hoped her ANC would recover between rounds, but since the clofarabine infusion would destroy her immune system again, it wasn't relevant at the moment. We had to divide and conquer the various complications she was experiencing. At least for now, we were keeping the cancer at bay.

I checked my phone as I crossed through the outdoor courtyard. Tina had not responded to my text. Perhaps I had been too emotional, too emphatic. I regretted the message. I should have been simpler, plainer. *Can we meet for coffee tomorrow?* Or *Let me know how the meeting went.*

But I had been overwrought, affected by her physical proximity. Away from her, I could remain detached, see the situation from the outside.

Maybe.

I still felt an ache, a need for her that I couldn't quite subdue.

Damn nuisance.

I should stay far far away from the spritely art therapist.

But I already knew I wouldn't. I'd gotten my hands on her. There was no direction to go except closer.

The chemotherapy hall was quiet on a Friday afternoon. Few patients were scheduled during this time slot, although a smattering of family members dotted the waiting-room chairs. It always surprised me how many didn't sit directly with their loved ones on the drip. It shamed me that I couldn't sit with Cynthia, not anymore.

At our first hospital, where they knew she was my sister, we would play games. Her favorite was called "Brother Pix." She would start a drawing, then pass it to me, and I would add to it, then return it to her. We'd do this until the page was too full to add anything else to the picture. We had dozens of these now, amassed during the hours we waited on her bag to empty.

But here, after I'd purged her records of my name, I was her doctor. Whenever I felt a twinge of regret that I'd chosen this course, I remembered the mistakes they had made at Children's. Not catching the tumor cells in her kidney until it was too late to save it, misdiagnosing a strep infection that almost killed her. I knew this was what I had to do. I didn't trust anyone else with her care.

In the late evenings, when I was forced to go home to my empty apartment, I studied her charts, placed her stats in spreadsheets, looking for patterns like a fortune-teller might divine the future from tea leaves. If there was a way to save her from this aggressive form of her disease, I would find it.

Here at the hospital, I kept personal interaction with staff to a minimum. I wanted to do my job with competence, to garner respect and not camaraderie, the sort that might get me found out.

The wireless on my iPad usually dropped in certain spots of the courtyard, so I waited until I was back inside to pull up Cynthia's current chart. Her temperature an hour ago was normal. I relaxed a little. She would be able to see Tina, if we got that chance.

If Tina messaged me. It had been two hours since our encounter in Surgical Suite B. Her meeting had to be over.

Before I could make it to Cynthia's room, my hospital phone buzzed with a code. Harriet.

I rushed to her room. The team had already assembled. Abrams was acting as code doctor.

Harriet's husband stood by the window, frozen with fear.

I glanced at the monitor. Ventricular fibrillation. A nurse was sliding a CPR board beneath her while another affixed the pads to her chest.

The respiratory therapist leaned over, pumping air in. "She's fully intubated."

Abrams glanced back and saw me. "You want to handle the code?"

"Yes. Prepare for first shock," I told the cardiac assistant. To the nurse, "Prep one milligram epinephrine."

I turned to the nurse holding an iPad. "She might be septic. When was the last bloodwork?"

The nurse glanced down. "This morning. Bacteria present. Antibiotics started three hours ago."

"Call someone in infectious disease — maybe Dr. Carter — to get on top of this."

The nurse nodded, clicking her stylus on the pad.

"Clear," a man said, and the first electrical pulse went through.

We all stared at the monitor. The pattern settled back to a regular heartbeat.

"Three hundred milligrams of amiodarone, then get her to imaging," I said. "I want to see if there is fluid on her heart."

"We can bring in a portable chest X-ray," the nurse said.

"Perfect."

I kept watch another minute. Harriet's rhythm held. The room visibly relaxed.

"Continuous amiodarone infusion at one milligram a minute," I said. "Get that image, then move her to ICU."

While having a patient code was always an emergency, this particular situation was not unusual during heavy rounds of chemo. I didn't want to cause more damage by overtreating her.

I turned back to the nurse with the iPad and took it from her. They had to be treating the wrong bacteria, or not aggressively enough. We had to get the infection down, or she would have more organ failure.

The code team began to withdraw.

"Is she okay?" her husband asked.

I stepped over to him and placed a hand on his shoulder. He was shaking. "She's stable. This was just a little bump. She has an infection. Her body isn't able to fight it. We started treating it this morning, but it was more aggressive than we expected. We're going to go check her organs now and administer stronger medications to fight the bacteria."

He nodded, although I'm not sure how much he was hearing. Families who witness a code go into a type of shock themselves. I'd repeat all of this to him again later.

"Will she be okay?"

"We'll get that fluid off her, and that will help her heart." I wasn't answering the question, really. Second onset of cancer as an adult after pediatric leukemia was not an easy thing to treat. Harriet had a lot of damage to her body already.

Life was always a risk. Everything about it.

"When will she be back?"

"They will move her to ICU for close monitoring." I glanced up at the waiting aide and squinted at her badge. "Sheila here will show you where the waiting room is for that."

He nodded numbly, his face drawn and tired. They had been here for a week already.

I squeezed his shoulder. "Hang tight. She's a tough woman."

Sheila helped him gather their bags, and I headed out to the hall. I'd go check on Harriet again after imaging. With the amiodarone helping her heart, she would be all right for a while, long enough to treat her.

The code had used up most of my break, but I had about five minutes to eat a sandwich with Cynthia. I turned down the hall toward her room. Angela was by the door, taping another image onto the collage.

"Almost out of room here," she said.

"She's prolific, that's for sure."

The new picture was the one she had drawn with Tina, Mom onstage singing. I could almost hear her voice, clear and pure, belting out one love-gone-wrong ballad or another. My father hadn't seen how much she cared for him. He wasn't wired to recognize it. But I had. I had always known. When he'd accused her of sleeping with other men after her pregnancy became obvious, it had cut her deeply.

I followed Angela inside. Cynthia was sitting on the bed cross-legged. "Dary!" she cried.

"You look good," I said. She was surrounded with a deck of cards all spread out. "What are you doing?"

"I'm learning a card trick!"

Angela rummaged through a soft-sided cooler. "Her little friend Andrew," she said.

"Pick a card!" Cynthia said.

I selected one from the center.

"Not that one!" she said.

I laughed. "Which one, then?"

"Mmmm. This one," she said, pointing to one near the end.

I picked it up.

"Is it the eight of spades?" she asked.

It wasn't. I showed her the card.

"Well, rats." She began stacking the deck back together.

"Just a little more practice."

Angela produced a sandwich and a bottle of water and handed them to me. "Here you go, Dr. Darion," she said.

"How is she today?" I asked as I unwrapped it.

"I was going to suggest some IV fluids, actually, if you want to take a look. She's not getting much output."

Cynthia had tuned us out, her habit lately if we started talking about her illness. She hummed a little tune as she shuffled the cards by pulling a few out and stuffing them back in the stack.

"I'll check her chart," I said, trying not to feel any concern, pushing down emotion so I could retain the same cool detachment in assessing Cynthia as I had done in the room with Harriet.

But her one functioning kidney had to be watched carefully. If the cancer cells liked renal tissue, they could attack the other. I would order a PET scan, just to be sure.

"Dary, will you draw me a picture?"

"Of course. What would you like today? A blue unicorn? A pink bear?"

She giggled as she tugged a drawing pad out from under her pillow. I found it amusing that she slept with it. Mom had pulled my sketchbooks out from under my blankets many nights.

"I want you to draw Miss Tina." She held out the pad and a pencil.

I rewrapped the sandwich and set it down. "But you have so many very good pictures of her."

"But you do it better. Make her a princess!"

My heart hammered a bit as I accepted the sketch pad. "Does she have a castle?"

"Yes! St. Anthony's Castle."

I laughed. "A hospital castle?"

"This is where she will rule!"

"Crown or cone hat?"

"Crown!"

I laid out the lines of the overall image. The flowing gown, the indentation of her waist, the bend of her elbow. "Pigtails?" I asked.

"Of course!" Cyn bounced a little on the bed as I drew in Tina's head and flared out a few arching lines for her hair.

"Ribbons?"

"Big ones!"

I smiled. Tina was not a big-bow kind of girl, so it was fun to sketch in giant ones on either side of her head.

Now that the rough shape was in place, I began filling in features. The detail of the gown. Her eyes and nose and mouth.

I paused, shifting her expression to one I knew, looking up at me with vulnerability. As I formed the dress to her curves, I could feel them again, warm skin under my fingertips.

Behind her I added just a foggy suggestion of a castle with a big red cross on it. Her hands were empty, so I added a paintbrush in one and a palette in the other.

Beneath it, I wrote, "The brush is mightier than the sword."

"What does that mean?" Cynthia asked.

"That art is more powerful than fighting," I said.

"Ooooh," she breathed. "I think so."

Angela peered over my shoulder. "I didn't know you could draw." She picked up the sandwich and passed it to me again, taking the sketch pad.

Right. I had to eat, too. "I did it as a kid."

"You should have kept going," she said, studying the image. "You knocked this out in no time flat. You could be one of those sketch artists in amusement parks."

I smiled as I chewed. She should tell that to my father. Switch a life's ambition of changing medical history for drawing caricatures at Disneyland. Sounded good to me.

Cynthia reached for the pad. "Can I color it in?"

"Absolutely," I said. "Make her face green."

"Noooo!" Cynthia howled. "She's not an ogre!"

"But Fiona is a green princess!"

"Noooo! Tina is a human princess!"

"Did I hear my name?"

We all looked up. I'm not sure whose heart jumped more when we saw Tina's blond head pop around the edge of the door, Cynthia's or mine.

19

TINA

That little girl sure was happy to see me.

Cynthia cried, "It's Tina! It's Tina!" over and over as I walked over to the sink to disinfect my hands.

By the time I turned around, Cynthia had come off the bed and crashed into my leg. "Where did you go?"

I kneeled down. "I had to go buy more art paper!" I bonked her pert little nose. "Somebody I know was using it all up!"

"Come look what Dary did!" she said. Then her eyes got big. "Dr. Darion." Suddenly she hesitated. "Never mind."

I hadn't missed Darion sitting on the edge of Cynthia's bed, eating a sandwich. This was not standard practice anywhere. Clearly he was a family friend. This would explain his closeness to her.

The aunt sat in the corner, watching us. I waved at her.

"What did Dr. Darion do?" I asked.

"Nothing," Cynthia said. She sat back on her bed.

That was odd. I turned back to her quizzically. What was going on?

Darion spoke up. "I was just checking on her. She thought it was funny her doctor was eating lunch." He shoved his sandwich in the pocket of his lab coat.

"You don't have to stop," I said. "And whatever your relationship is with the family, it's no big thing to me." He was covering up something, and this upset me. He can get all up in my shirt in a surgical suite, but he can't tell me he has a personal relationship with a patient? He could have said it on the first day, when he asked me to watch out for her!

Except he didn't trust me.

Or maybe it was something more.

I could see panic in Cynthia's eyes. Were they asking her to lie about it? This little girl? Indignation burned in me. The doctor was going to get a piece of my mind about this later.

But I had come here for a reason. "Cynthia, classes will be back on this afternoon, but just a little off schedule since I missed this morning. Are you going to come?"

"Yes!" she said, her face brightening again.

I passed a half-sheet of paper to her. "Make sure your nurse knows when to bring you. This is the schedule for today and tomorrow."

Cynthia pressed the paper to her chest like it was a treasure. "Okay."

I noticed Angela holding an oversized sketch pad. "Have you been drawing?" I asked Cynthia.

Her eyes got big again. She held up a deck of cards instead. "I've been practicing card tricks."

Weird. Another redirect. I glanced over at Darion, who was studying his iPad as though he needed to memorize something. What was going on here?

"Can I see the picture you made?" I asked.

Nobody answered.

Now the whole room was tense. I decided to back off.

"It's okay," I said. I'd take this up with Darion later. Ask him straight out who this little girl was to him. His niece? The daughter of a colleague?

I hadn't responded to his text. The message had hit me in the gut.

Let me shelter you.

So emotional. So unlike him. Or maybe it was like him, and I was the only one who saw it. I didn't know what to make of it. Instead, I had sat in my room, rearranging the schedule to make sure I saw all the patients today so that whoever had paid for the program would know I was back.

But was it Darion? Could he be the benefactor? Or his family?

I glanced down at his shoes again, expensive and perfectly polished. He had money. Came from money.

Hell, maybe I wouldn't confront him after all. Maybe I should just shut the hell up. He could be my meal ticket. An anonymous one.

What a mess.

"I'll see you in class," I told Cynthia.

"You might not see her tomorrow," Darion said, his voice back in professional mode. "She has a three-hour chemotherapy drip."

I glanced back at Cynthia. She seemed so full of energy today. That would go away after the treatment. "I'll come by your room later." I glanced at Darion. "If that's okay."

Everyone looked at him to see what he would say. "I think that will be fine," he said. "She will be tired but probably not sick for a few days."

"I don't usually start throwing up until the next day," Cynthia said matter-of-factly.

I couldn't even imagine being where she was. "Then I'll come by. See you in class later."

I waved at everyone, Angela still clutching the sketch pad to her chest.

I had no idea what to say to Darion about all of this, IF I talked to him at all.

I barely got back to the art room before the nurse wheeled Albert up to the table. He wore his usual flannel shirt, and his mop of gray curls was as wild as always. I was glad to see him.

"You're back," he said. "I got a message that your class was canceled indefinitely."

"You can't get rid of me that easily," I said. "Just an administrative hiccup."

He nodded thoughtfully. "Glad you got it worked out."

I glanced at his hands. He held them in his lap today instead of gripping the wheelchair. He looked better, just a tremor rather than a hard shake. "How are you doing?"

He held up his hands. "New drugs!" he said. "Started them a ways back, but we tweaked my cocktail. So far, so good."

"That's great. You want to paint, then? Or draw?" I was dying to see what he could do if he had a little more control.

"Everything!" he said. "Let's do everything."

I got out the paints and the pencils, and the highest-quality paper we had in stock. I'd ask for some good stuff when I sent in an order to Duffrey's assistant. I wanted some nice things on hand for Albert, not just kids' paints and crappy construction paper.

I barely got the paper and pencils on the table when he snatched one up and began sketching in long rapid strokes.

Rather than gawk at him, I wandered the room, adjusting small things, thinking about what else I could squeeze Duffrey for. The table was the most important. Then chairs. I wondered if I could get a light board. Tracing might be more fun for the patients with less control, and build motor skills. If only I had a bigger room.

Albert switched colors, and I had to resist walking over to steal a glance. I would get his castle painting back up here tomorrow, although I might keep the mermaid at home. I should probably ask him about it. Technically, it was his art.

Oh, I should have asked Duffrey about a space to showcase the patients' work. Dang it. I wasn't afraid to march up there and request it, but the thought of having to sit on that hard chair again stopped me. I'd send an email.

When Albert picked up a third color, my curiosity couldn't wait another second. I casually moved closer and had to hold back a gasp.

An amazing scene filled the oversized parchment. A circus was poised on the edge of a cliff overlooking the ocean. It had tents and elephants, and clowns stacked ten high teetering on a single unicycle. On the underside of the cliff, the ground and rocks crumbled and fell into the water, while up top, the performers juggled and led lions through hoops with exuberant laughter, unaware of the danger, that the ground beneath their feet was disappearing.

"How did you do so much so fast?" I asked.

"Years of practice," he said, his hand almost a blur over the page, shading in colors, adding depth and texture to the scene.

I gave up on my nonchalance and just sat to watch. As the image filled out, the tone shifted from innocent to a malevolent glee, as if the performers knew exactly where they were and welcomed the impending disaster.

Albert added a boxcar in the distance, then a caged compartment, a train the circus came in on. All the colors so far were subdued, slate blue, sea green, dull yellow, but then he picked up a blood-red pencil to fill in a painted sign on the side of the train. It read "Saints of Circus Anthony."

That reference to the name of the hospital wasn't lost on me. I began to look more closely at the performers. The woman with a chair and whip next to the lion was the nurse who rolled Albert to class.

The tower of clowns seemed familiar too. Really familiar. The one on top had a maniacal look I recognized. From where?

In the center was a man in a top hat and tails, the ringmaster. I bit my lip as I tried to see if he knew what John Duffrey looked like and had drawn him in, but the man's features were obscured by the enormous hat. Perhaps not.

"I love it," I told him. "Did you ever do any cartooning?"

Albert set the pencil down. "No. Some illustration here and there. A few posters."

"So, you DID work as an artist."

He smiled. "Here and there."

I couldn't get anything out of him. "I don't think it takes a psychology degree to figure this one out," I said.

He held his belly as he laughed, and I wondered if he was in any pain. "I don't think so," he said.

"You think they'd let me display this in the entrance?"

"Now that would be something."

I turned the page around. "As your official art therapist, I have to say," I paused as he leaned forward to hear my verdict, "you are quite possibly the only sane person here."

He got serious then and peeled back the cuff of his shirt to reveal the red lines on his wrist.

I grasped his hand and held it for a moment, then shoved up the sleeve to my jacket to show the pale lines of my five-year-old scars.

He swallowed hard and nodded in recognition.

I could feel the tremor in his arm and wondered how he could overcome it. I'd prodded him to try, and he had managed, but now that I could feel it, the tension like a taut wire being plucked, I couldn't see how he even held a pencil, much less drew anything recognizable.

He was amazing.

His free hand touched the pale lines of my wrist and walked tremulously along their paths. Then he gripped me tight, his eyes closed, and we sat there silently wishing that only art bound us, not this terrible shared experience. But even as I knew what he was feeling, that grief about the places life had taken us, I also felt gratitude that we were together now.

We stayed like that, joined hand to wrist to scar, until the evil-eyed nurse returned to roll him back to his ward.

20

DR. DARION

I knew I should let things go. Tina was tipped off about my relationship with Cynthia. And she had her job back and would see to my sister. I should avoid her and not disrupt the arrangement.

But throughout the afternoon, I found myself making excuses to walk by the art room. The door was always closed, but a wide window allowed me to see what was happening. I managed to pass by three times before she looked up and spotted me. Then I had to stop going that direction anymore, or else look like a stalker.

Later that day, when I knew Cynthia had been to art class, I stopped by her hospital room.

Cynthia said, "Did I mess up? Does Tina know?" She covered her face with her hands.

"No, no, don't worry about that. It's okay."

"But I called you Dary!"

"It's all right." I sat on the bed and pulled her hands down. "This is the grown-ups' problem, not yours.

I glanced over at Angela. She raised her eyebrows as if to say, "I told you so."

Angela had agreed to keep the secret, although she didn't

approve of the plan. "You have to learn to trust other people, Dr. Darion," she said.

When I tried to tell her about the missed kidney diagnosis, and the infection, she waved it off. "In my twenty years in a hospital, I saw lots of mistakes. It's part of it. You are not going to be immune to it, and it will hit you so much harder when it happens."

I had to disagree. I went over every number on Cynthia. I ordered every test. Anything that wasn't covered by insurance, I paid out of pocket through my trust. Thankfully, when my father refused to acknowledge Cynthia as his, my mother decided to return to her own family name and give it to my sister as well. The connection between us wasn't nearly as apparent as it might have been.

I scooped Cynthia up for a moment and hugged her. She was so light, so insubstantial. I felt like she could just disappear. If we didn't work very hard, she might.

"What's going to be tomorrow's chemo present?" I asked her. Since we could no longer do our drawings together at this hospital, I always bought her something new.

"Can it be for someone else?" she asked.

I set her back on the bed. "What do you mean?"

"I get lots of chemo presents. But Andrew doesn't have any."

"Who is Andrew?"

"A boy in my art class."

I looked over at Angela. She said, "A.L.L., second relapse, sixty days post."

Almost identical situation as Cynthia. Same leukemia. Failed stem cell transplant. "How old is Andrew?" I asked.

"Nine," Cynthia said. "He doesn't feel very well."

"Is he doing chemo?" I asked.

Cynthia's voice got quiet. "Tomorrow, same as me."

"What would you like for Andrew?"

Her face brightened as she realized I was agreeing. "He loves Pokémon!"

"That's still a thing?"

Cynthia rolled her eyes. "Dary, it will *always* be a thing."

"All righty, then. What do you think? That yellow guy. Peekaboo?"

"Pikachu!" she corrected. "I thought you were so smart."

"Just doctor smart. Not cool-kid smart."

"Well, don't get Pikachu. Everybody has Pikachu. Get Pancham!"

I laughed. "What is that?"

"A panda bear with an attitude!"

"All right, Pancham it is."

She grabbed my arm and hugged it. "Thank you, Dary. He'll really like it."

"He's not going to be your boyfriend, is he?" I teased.

Cynthia thrust my arm away. "No! And don't you say that to him!"

I held up my hands. "Okay, okay. But I'm your big brother. I'm supposed to watch out for boys."

"I'm only eight years old, Dary. I can't get married until I'm at least forty."

I let go with a belly laugh then. "That sounds perfect. Forty." I headed toward the door. I had to get back on rounds. "Don't you forget that."

I was still laughing to myself when I realized I was actually done seeing patients that day. I checked my watch. After six. Tina was probably already gone.

Just in case, I hurried toward her room. I would come up with an excuse about why I was there on the way.

21

TINA

I was never going to get out of here.

Some random lady from HR had come by with a stack of papers a mile high, insisting I fill them out before I left. No way was that going to happen. It was already after six, and probably the whole human resources department was home having dinner. And I was only halfway through the stack.

Statement of intent to do social work.

Consent for psychological evaluation.

Prior coursework.

Grad school application.

I didn't even know what some of this stuff was, and I had no idea if I wanted to go the therapist or social work route. I needed advice. And a better pen.

I shook my hand, trying to work out the cramp. How did Albert draw so intensely for so long without pausing? I knew what he would say. Years of practice.

He was somebody. Had to be. He was too good. And he'd given me some clues. Posters. Illustration work. I had snapped a shot of his work on my phone to study, especially that clown, which was still bugging me. Maybe I could put something together. If not, I would worm it out of him.

The halls were quiet. I left my door open, feeling closed in if I was alone in the room. Sometimes I swore I could sense the patients who once sat around the table but were long gone. I knew someday soon I would lose one I was attached to and the ghosts would feel real.

I lifted my arms high and stretched my back. The HR lady could stuff it. I had to know what I was doing before I could fill out any more forms.

A figure in the doorway caught my eye.

Darion.

I stood up suddenly, and the chair fell backward with a crash.

I whipped around to pick up the chair. I should have known he would show up. Men like him, manipulators, liars, they probably thought they could do anything they wanted.

The chair dropped back into place with another clang.

"You okay?" Darion strode in, concern on his face.

"I'm fine." I crossed my arms. "I thought you were going to let me make the next move."

He glanced back at the door. "I was just walking by."

"Just walking by." I pushed past him to the tiny closet where I kept my bag. "Well, I was just walking out."

"Good," he said. "I'll go with you."

I jerked the closet open, snatched my purse, and closed it again with a slam. "I don't think so."

"What's gotten into you?"

I whipped around. "Well, first of all, there was that promise you made about the first move." I slung the strap over my arm. "And then there was whatever went on with Cynthia. Are you making that little girl lie for you?"

That got him. His jaw went all tight, and his fist locked on the keys in his hand. "You have no idea what she has been through."

"And I sure as hell don't know what's going on now. You should have seen her in class today. Quiet and worried, like the roof was about to fall on her head. What are you doing to her?"

"I am looking out for her like any decent person would. She has no parents."

"Is she in foster care? What is your relationship to her?" I rounded the desk and snatched up a sheet of paper. "You realize I'm about to get clearance for medical records, right? I can look this up myself."

He shrugged. "Go ahead. You'll find a very long list of treatments and setbacks. A family history of a mother who also died of cancer."

"Where is her father?"

Darion's neck went red at that. His jaw ticked.

He didn't have an answer.

And then I got it.

HE was her father.

I took a few steps back. Holy shit. Nobody knew. Nobody was supposed to know.

This explained everything. His secrecy about her. His familiarity. His wanting extra help.

So, the woman who died. The mother Cynthia sang the song

about. Had she been his wife?

I couldn't keep control of my thoughts. I needed to sort all this out.

"Never mind," I said. "Forget I said anything."

"Tina —"

"No. It's none of my business." I set the paper back on my desk. "She's a lovely little girl. And tomorrow will be tough for her." I pictured her hooked up to the bag, the poison that kept her alive flowing into her. "It's fine."

"Can I walk you down?"

His whole demeanor had changed. He wasn't the tall stalwart doctor now. Just a worried father. My heart squeezed a little. His wife had died. Now his daughter might. Damn.

"Okay," I said. "That's fine. Walk me down."

We moved for the door. Darion shrugged off his white coat and laid it over his arm. I kept my distance, since really we were being seen together way too much. I didn't know the hospital policy on dating. I would ask Darion, but then that would be like admitting that we were seeing each other.

And we weren't.

I felt completely tangled up inside. When would he tell me about Cynthia? What was his motive for lying to the whole staff? And who was Angela? His mother? Sister? She had been so taken aback when I asked how she was related to the family.

We passed through the halls, mostly quiet at the dinner hour. Visitors were scarce on these floors. Only maternity and the ER would bustle with people this late.

We took the staff elevator down. No one else rode with us. The silence wasn't awkward, but it had a heaviness to it. He wasn't confessing. I wasn't asking. A thousand unspoken words filled the space.

As the elevator slowed to a stop on the ground floor, Darion asked, "Can I take you to dinner?"

The doors started to open, but Darion pressed the button to make them close. "Please?"

Despite the concern in his eyes, the worry he carried in his heart, he watched me with an earnestness I didn't think I'd ever seen aimed at me by any other man. In my history, I'd seen a lot. Desire, sure. Charisma, sometimes. And definitely cockiness and jackassery.

But earnestness. Honest-to-God need.

I hadn't seen that.

"Okay," I said. I would give a little. Just a little. A moment of comfort for him, nothing more.

I could spend a night. Do the one-and-done. I was good at it. It's not like the past men refused to express emotion. Several had professed undying love. And it wasn't as though they weren't gorgeous or wealthy or powerful or any number of amazing things I should have grasped instead of letting go.

It was me. I could feel all sorts of things leading up to the act, but once it was done, once the man chilled after he got what he wanted, I just didn't want to stick around for the inevitable rejection. It might not happen right away. But it would happen. And I wouldn't let it get that far.

We left the hospital and went into the cool evening air, still not talking.

But my mind raced. The one time I cared about a guy, he left me when I was in premature labor, when I needed him the most.

He missed the three hours our baby lived, Peanut's entire life. And when I went to find him, he had already moved out of our apartment. Gone. Poof. Like none of the previous months mattered.

Not going to happen again. Not with Darion. Not with anybody.

We walked side by side to the physicians' level of the parking garage. People passed, and Darion nodded politely. He steered me gently by the elbow through the rows of cars. He was courteous and kind.

But I would not be moved. Not by the gleaming Mercedes I slid into. Not by any expensive dinner or wine. Not by a mansion or killer condo. Not even by a gold-plated cock.

We'd have our moment. And maybe he'd tell me his secret. Maybe not. We all had them. I'd keep the lights off, my wrists hidden, and tell no tales of my own.

A nice dinner. Friendly conversation. A night of intimacy. Then I would go.

One. And. Done.

22

DR. DARION

Tina was so quiet. I started the Mercedes, wishing I had something simpler than this showy car my father had given me when I finished med school. She would not be impressed by money. That was obvious. I racked my brain trying to think of a place to take her that would break her silence, get her smiling again. I'd take her mad and shouting over this.

I backed out of the parking spot. "Are you a vegetarian or gluten free or anything?" I asked.

"No," she said. "Just don't make me eat meatloaf. Or spinach casserole."

I had to smile at that. "Not a problem."

"My mother made me eat those. I can't stand them now."

I almost told her how my mom rarely cooked but often got lost in some song she was writing until long after the dinner hour had come and gone. Then I realized I couldn't say anything personal, anything that Cynthia might have also said to her about Mom. Tina would figure it out.

Maybe I should just tell her.

The garage was dim as the light fell for evening, so I couldn't make out her expression. I had never been so nervous with a woman. Tina was hard to figure out. She made me want to know her, understand what drove these moods.

"My mom didn't cook a lot," I said, figuring that was safe enough. Many didn't. "So, meatloaf sounds like some 1950s dish prepared by a woman in a lace-trimmed apron over a house dress with pearls."

"You just described my mother."

"Really?"

Tina tucked her hair behind her ears. "She's older. I was a late-in-life baby. She was the sort of mom growing up that was exactly what you said, making dinner all dressed up. Bringing the martini while her husband read the paper. I think my mom wanted to be her. She certainly tried."

"Sounds good to me."

"Ha." Tina kicked off her shoes and propped her striped stocking feet on the dash. Now I was really grinning. She was like a teenager in so many ways.

"Picture a perfectly poised June Cleaver trying to drag a chain-smoking black-haired goth girl from a pot party with a bunch of high school dropouts."

I almost missed the garage exit and had to hit the brakes harder than I intended. "Seriously? That was you?" I wanted to introduce my father to her *now.*

"I'm just skimming the surface." Tina stared out the window as we left the garage and turned onto the parkway. "I was a wreck. A total disaster."

"Did they punish you? Were they strict?"

"Oh yeah. I left the house through my window way more than by the door. I could count on one hand the number of days in high school I *wasn't* grounded."

"But you turned out all right."

Tina turned to look at me. "I'm not so sure about that."

"You seem fine to me."

She laughed. "Well, let's see. I got fired yesterday."

"But you're back today."

Tina hesitated. "Did you have something to do with that?"

"Not a thing."

She pursed her lips. "I'm not sure I believe you."

I didn't know how much to tell her about my father. I was pretty certain he hadn't stepped in. "What happened with Duffrey?"

"He said I had made a powerful friend who would donate some unspecified amount of money — enough to make Duffrey squirm — if I was back in my classroom by the end of the day."

"Wow." I pulled up to a red light. "That is a powerful friend."

"But not you?"

"I don't have that kind of money. I don't know anyone who does." And it was true. I had a decent trust, the sort that gets you through school and set up in a nice house and lets you take European vacations as long as you are not relying on it for your income. But nothing that would impress a hospital board. Not even if I dumped the whole sum on them.

Besides, I had to save it for Cynthia. It was half hers anyway. If Dad wouldn't sign it over, I would.

Tina blew wisps of hair off her forehead. I had the intense urge to brush them aside myself. Where could I take her that I could sit close to her? Some place she wouldn't find pretentious?

She rolled down the window. "It's a nice night. We shouldn't sit cooped up in a box of canned air."

I lowered my window as well. The evening breeze blew across my face. We still had half an hour until sunset. The light turned green, and I knew what to do. "You want to eat outside somewhere?"

"Sure," she said. "Sounds nice."

A little place near La Jolla did takeout picnics. You could have the whole thing packaged in a pretty basket. Lots of people did it to propose on the beach, or for special occasions. When we first came to San Diego, I had gotten one for me and Cynthia, before she had to go back to the hospital.

I wanted her to love our new town, this new home. So, we'd done the picnic and spent the day on the beach. She was feeling good then. The blast counts were high in her blood and bone marrow, but she wasn't really sick. I remember thinking this could be the last good day for a while. She still had her blond curls, like in the picture I showed Tina. Her hair was never long, since the treatments were never far apart, but sometimes it got a chance to grow out a little.

When we stopped at the next light, I pulled out my phone and found the email where I'd ordered the previous basket. I replied with a quick message — *Can you have one of these ready in half an hour? I'll pay double.*

While I waited for a confirmation, I drove toward Torrey Pines. Maybe we could walk a bit there first. "You up for a little stroll?" I asked.

"Pretty much always," she said. She had her elbow resting on the open window, her chin propped on it.

I pulled up inside the park near one of the walking trails. If I didn't hear from the picnic place, I could find another little bistro with an outdoor section. Right now, the timing was perfect for a moment I sometimes came to witness by myself, when I got a chance, if Cynthia was doing all right and I got away from the hospital in time.

Only one other car was parked nearby. The dirt path crunched as we walked along it, through a smattering of trees, then along rough ground covered in scrubby brush.

"I haven't made it out a lot since I moved here," Tina said. "I've been to the beach a few times, but not this park."

I almost blew it again, about to mention the times I brought Cynthia when she was well enough, but said instead, "I like walking here. It's peaceful after a tough day."

The ground got a little steeper as we approached a cliff. Another couple sat on the edge looking out.

Tina hurried ahead. "Wow, oh wow," she said. "This is amazing."

The cliff overlooked a narrow strip of beach and the wide expanse of the Pacific. The sun was a yellow ball hovering over the water, spreading gold light over the breaking waves.

Tina gripped my arm. "I want to come here every day."

Her nearness was a comfort and a relief, and I began to come down from the anxiety I'd felt all day after our encounter in the surgical suite. She had her job back. She'd agreed to come with me. The hospital and its troubles seemed very far away.

The evening stretched out like a promise, as endless as the ocean below. And Tina was here.

For this moment, life was very very good.

23

TINA

This was the most amazing moment I'd had in San Diego since my arrival several weeks ago. The sunset was incredible, the ocean vast and inspiring. I wanted to paint, to draw, to take a photograph.

Instead I soaked it in, trying to commit it to memory. The slight chill, the salty breeze, the golden light on the water, and this man, tall and strong and warm, right beside me.

As so often happened when I felt overcome by beauty, I thought of Peanut. He'd be five years old, big enough to recognize the enormity of this view. A painting came to me, fully formed, this ocean, this sun, the cliff, and a mother and her boy. The woman would be three-dimensional, colorful, edged in gold. The boy would simply be a shadow, suffused in light, a memory at her side.

I would start it tomorrow. With Albert. I'd pick up some canvas, real paints. He was shaking less. He would paint too. Or help me. I surged with this. I couldn't wait. I hadn't done anything for weeks except go to the hospital and work.

I wanted to create again, fall into that heady space where vision and reality collided.

I was so excited, my hands were shaking. It became hard to stay in the moment, but then, everything I was feeling was tied to this experience, this place, and Darion.

He pulled me against him. "What are you thinking about, so serious and intense?"

I let my head fall on his chest. I felt surrounded by him, protected. What had he said in that message? *Let me shelter you.*

It had seemed so out of place at the time, overwrought. But now, it made sense. Despite how little we knew of each other, and this major secret he was trying to keep from me, we had been drawn together like a string closing a bag.

Maybe if I told him about my baby, he would talk about Cynthia.

"I had a baby once," I said, surprised, a little, to hear a tremor in my voice. I hadn't sounded so vulnerable, *been* so vulnerable, since those days.

He squeezed my arm. "What happened?"

"He was born prematurely." I realized I was talking to a doctor, so I could be more technical. "Nineteen weeks."

Darion let out a long breath. "That's early."

"His foot descended. They couldn't stop him from coming."

"How old were you?"

I looked out over the setting sun, glad for something beautiful to focus on. "Seventeen."

Another long breath. "Was he stillborn?"

"No, he lived for three hours."

"The father?"

"Took off during labor. I didn't see him again for weeks."

Darion gripped me more tightly. "I'm sorry."

"He was beautiful. So small. I could hold his little head with my fingertips, and his little butt would fit right in my palm. Not even a pound. Have you seen one like that?"

"I did a few obstetric rounds, but most everything I saw was routine. I never did the NICU."

"Babies this small don't get to go to NICU."

He squeezed me again.

"They let me keep him with me. Checked on his heartbeat occasionally. I'm not sure he actually breathed." I pulled away a bit. Darion was a doctor. One who might give me answers to the questions I never got to ask. "Do they breathe that early? Does it take a long time for the heart to stop, even without breathing?"

"He must have been getting some oxygen," Darion said. He looked down at me, and the sun reflected gold in his eyes. "Otherwise, your heart will stop pretty quickly. Within minutes. As soon as the oxygen in the muscles is depleted."

"Then he did breathe."

"If he lived three hours, then yes, his lungs had some functionality."

"Then why wouldn't they save him?"

"There's so much to it," he said, and his voice took on a softer tone. "The biggest one is bleeding in the brain. The real world is no place for babies who are supposed to be growing in amniotic fluid. We just can't replicate that perfect environment."

"Do you think that one day babies born that early will be saved?"

"We've already gotten the threshold so much younger than before. Just twenty years ago, even two-pound babies were sometimes not resuscitated. Now that would be considered robust.

One pound is the minimum."

"Peanut weighed thirteen ounces." I held Darion's gaze, as we both considered how close he had been. A couple more weeks. Just a little more time.

He knew what I meant. "How different your life would be," he said.

The sun dipped into the water. We watched it kiss the surface, then Darion said, "I don't have a flashlight. We should head back to the car before it gets fully dark."

I grasped his hand. "Thank you for bringing me here. It's beautiful. A good end to a complicated day."

It seemed the right moment for him to kiss me, and I wanted him to. The emotion of telling him about Peanut and asking my long-held questions pulled me in. I had none of the distance that usually allowed me to pull off a one-and-done.

But for some reason, he didn't. He just held me tightly and led me back down the path. As we crossed the scrubby ground, I looked back at the cliff, the water, and the sunset. I would come back here. I would not try to capture it with a crappy cell-phone camera. I would paint it. Get it right.

24

DR. DARION

By the time we got back to the car, the picnic place had buzzed me saying they had prepared the food. I opened the door for Tina, who still seemed lost in thought and practically vibrating with emotion.

I slid behind the wheel. Darkness was settling rapidly now. But the beach would be fine. All along the waterline at La Jolla, people lit fires. I had only walked along that stretch with a sleeping Cynthia in my arms, but it was the most romantic place I'd ever been. I wanted to go there with Tina.

The Picnic Bistro was not far. "Are you hungry?" I asked Tina.

"Sure. What did you have in mind?"

"I had a picnic made up for us. Have you been on the beach at night?"

"You can do that?" A streetlamp lit up her hair, gold like a halo around the shadow of her face.

"You can. It's not crowded or anything, but there will be people. Playing guitars. Sitting around fires."

"Ooooh," she breathed.

I had chosen the right thing.

The picnic place did not have a restaurant attached, although there were outdoor tables. When I pulled up, a girl ran out with the basket. I had forgotten when I forwarded the email that the previous one asked that someone meet me outside. At the time, Cynthia's ANC was zero, and her lack of immune system meant I didn't take her to public places, not indoors anyway. The risk of any infection, even just a cold, was too high.

The beach had been perfect, open, warm, and while she couldn't swim, just walking in the sand had been a great escape as we transferred from one hospital to the next. A vacation in our new hometown.

But because the email had implored them to deliver to our car, the girl came out this time as well. I opened the car door to receive the basket.

"Thank you," I said, quickly signing the bill.

"Have a lovely time with your sister," she said.

Damn. I glanced back. Tina was looking out her window. Hopefully she hadn't heard, or would assume that the woman was confused about who she was.

I set the basket in the backseat.

"Sister, huh?" Tina said as we drove away. "I guess we really are good at hiding our surgical-suite moments."

"We should try acting," I said, silently relieved she hadn't questioned the comment.

"I don't know my way around yet," Tina said. "I don't have a car. Are we close to the beach?"

"Very." I pulled out of the parking lot. "In fact," I said, turning onto the next street, "we're almost there now."

The parking lot was mostly empty. Between the onset of winter and nightfall, the families were gone. Only a few couples and a group of college kids hung out on the fringes of the parking lot.

Tina got out of the car and looked out on the inky blackness of the ocean. I pulled the basket from the backseat and checked inside. Yes, they'd packed a thin blanket for us to sit on.

I took her hand again, small and cool, and led her between the posts and out into the sand. We only walked a few steps before she paused to take off her shoes, then lifted her skirt to roll down the striped stockings.

My pulse sped a little at the sight of her bare knees as she stripped her legs.

"Will you be cold?" I asked.

"Not if you do your job," she said. "Brother," she added with a laugh.

She created a neat bundle by knotting the stockings through the strap of her Mary Janes and tied it over her shoulder. I could feel the sand filling my own shoes, but I wasn't the sort to run around barefoot while fully dressed. I'd manage.

The moon was bright and almost full. As I'd hoped, small parties were lighting logs in fire rings at regular intervals. Tina lifted her skirt and stepped gingerly toward the water's edge. When she got wet, she squealed.

"It's cold!"

"You're going to catch pneumonia," I said.

She turned and stuck her tongue out at me. "You of all people know that wet feet have nothing to do with fluid in your lungs."

I had to laugh. "You got me there. It's more a function of immune suppression when your body has to pull its warmth to your core to protect your organs."

She splashed around, kicking at the gentle waves. "Do you always talk this sexy?"

I set the basket in the sand, and before she could predict my next move, I swept her into my arms.

"Hey!" she said, laughing. "I'm going to get my dirty feet on your fancy doctor clothes."

"Someone has to save you from a terrible death."

I carried her back to the basket, but didn't set her down. Instead, I dropped down into the sand, keeping her on my lap. The dry cleaners could deal with the mess later.

"You planning to keep my organs warm?" she asked. Her hand cupped my neck, and she fingered the hair at my nape.

Had we really just met two days ago? It seemed like forever already.

"I'll do my best."

I already knew what she was wearing beneath the jacket, the silky camisole. I wanted to touch it again, to run my hands across her belly. So, I did.

"Which organs did you have in mind?" she asked.

"Your pancreas."

"What?" Her laugh was like a sprinkle of light. "Dr. Marks, you are very strange."

"I can't seem too boring." I ran my thumb along the base of her ribs. Her face was so close to mine that each of her breaths puffed against my cheek.

"I don't think I've had a boring moment since the moment you walked into my art room."

"Two days ago or two weeks ago?" I asked.

"Either one."

Her fingers slid across the edge of my ear. Now I wished we'd taken the basket someplace more private. But going slow, being careful, that was the best course.

My free hand moved behind her head to bring her to me. Her lips were cool, but they parted and her mouth was soft and warm. I pulled her in close, still on my lap. I explored the silky curve of her waist and tugged the camisole from the band of her skirt. When my fingertips reached her bare skin, she sighed against my mouth.

I took my time, grateful to be away from the hospital, able to touch her without distraction. Everything about her was delicate and small. It's what brought out this protectiveness in me. She seemed so easy to break.

Tina shifted on my lap, turning in to me, her legs on either side of my waist. I reached behind her to unfasten the bra, and now I had access to so much more. Her pert breast fit exactly in my hand, and the taut nipple rolled neatly under my thumb.

She gasped against me, her arms encircling my neck. She broke the kiss, letting her head fall onto my shoulder. I kept one hand on her body but let the other drift down to her knee, where her skirt was trapped against the sand. I pulled it free and slid my fingers beneath the heavy fabric, up her thigh.

Her panties were small, just a bit of lace. I tucked my finger inside the thin band, just above her hip.

Now Tina moved against me, slow and hard, rocking her pelvis. I knew she could feel me wanting her. Her hands gripped my arms, holding tight, sliding against me.

I wasn't sure I could take much more.

25

TINA

Whoa, Nelly. I was already moving too fast, grinding against the doctor like a dog in heat.

I knew all the terrible places sand could go. And this doctor had me so primed and ready, I was about to not care. The skirt would hide everything. I was damn near ready to rip his pants off.

Down the beach, someone was playing a guitar. The notes dipped over and under the steady crash of waves on the shore. My feet and knees were buried in sand. But the rest of me was all over this doctor, working him like a stripper in need of rent.

I had to bring this down. If my one-and-done didn't come off as solid as I wanted, I might be tempted to go for two.

And that would be disastrous.

I was about to pull away, to break this spell, when he moved his fingers just a tiny bit along the edge of my panties. He brushed against a really sensitive part, and that was it, I couldn't handle any more. I needed him. I wanted more.

I lifted away from him just enough to give him access, and he took it, slipping a finger inside the lace and into my body.

It accepted him greedily, and I clutched his shoulders, my head still buried against his neck, as he began to work inside me.

Lost. I was lost. Maybe a doctor knew all the good spots, or maybe he was lucky, but I was spiraling up so fast that there was no way to stop things now. I was whimpering, ready to beg, and shifting against him. But he got it, he knew the speed and the pressure and just how to curve his finger.

I quit caring what we might look like to spectators, locked together in the sand, and let the tension build, let him take me where I wanted to go. His breathing sped up alongside mine, as I tightened around him.

Then it all released, my muscles clenching and letting go, the pleasure coursing through me. I managed to stay quiet, to keep my voice below the crash of the water and the filtered notes from the guitar. But Darion heard me. He held tight to me, one hand steadying my back while he cupped me from below with the other.

I settled back down and he withdrew, holding my quivering thigh until I calmed. I hadn't done this sort of thing before. Usually the conquests were streamlined and simple. We meet. We go out. We bang. Then I quit taking his calls.

But here I was with this doctor, fooling around in empty rooms, and now this moment on the beach.

What was I doing? Stalling? Stretching it out? Maybe I knew if I didn't do the deed, I wouldn't have to give him up after.

And I had told him about Peanut.

My belly heaved with a tightly held sob. I tried to pretend I hadn't, but we were locked together, and Darion noticed. He squeezed my leg and turned his face to press his lips into my hair.

I remembered, all those years ago, sitting in the garage

apartment my parents set up for me and Arnie after we told them about the baby. Arnie had loved to lie behind me, and run his hands over the fat bump of my belly.

I always thought it was so cool, here he was eighteen years old, and he got it. He knew how special this was. It was a *thing*. A thing to recognize and hold on to. I thought he was so into it. That we were on this road together.

I believed that he loved me and that he loved Peanut. But he didn't. He just liked the attention, and the idea that we were rebelling in the most potent way possible. We got to be kids acting like grown-ups. When we actually had to *be* grown-ups, he blew.

He left me to manage it all by myself.

"What's going through that complicated mind of yours, Tina?" Darion asked.

I didn't want to let us get any closer. I didn't want to be the tiniest bit more vulnerable than I already was. So, I said, "That people suck."

He released me, taken aback, I'm sure. You don't get a girl off, then expect her to act all bitchy. But I was good at that.

I lifted my sand-encrusted leg from the ground and rolled off him. "Are we going to eat this fancy food or what?" He'd probably paid some ridiculous sum for the gimmick of a picnic.

Yeah, I was on a roll now. Poor doc. I opened the basket and yanked out the blanket. "That would have been handy," I said.

Darion didn't say anything, just sat there with his elbows on his propped-up knees. I wouldn't look him in the eye. I already knew he was halfway out of my life. We'd do the deed, probably some other night, and I would move on.

It just didn't matter.

26

DR. DARION

The next morning, I sat in my car a little longer than necessary before going into the hospital. I didn't know what to do with Tina after last night. She had become a whole different person after our emotional encounter. Like she was a sullen teenager stuck with some boring grown-up who didn't "get" her.

I took her home and didn't go in. Didn't let anything progress. It seemed wise to punt and try again a different day.

I couldn't dwell on it. Today was Cynthia's chemo day. I had pulled strings in Houston and gotten her in the trial of a new drug. We couldn't even attempt a second stem cell therapy for months. I had to get her in remission. Had to. She didn't have time to wait.

I walked inside the hospital and paused at the desk to check her morning stats. ANC was still low. No fever, thank God, so nothing had gotten to her despite her running around the hospital with no white cells to fight infection.

Still an alert on her urine. Damn. I had ordered a PET scan, but it wouldn't be until after her treatment. If she had an adverse reaction, she wouldn't even make the test.

I drew in a deep breath. Pretend she's someone else. Don't think about her expressions or her pain or her upset. Just worry about the treatment, the test results, the response to the medication, and take one problem at a time.

"Dr. Marks?" A woman I had never seen before waved at me from the other side of the desk. She was in her forties, friendly looking, like a den mother for a Boy Scout troop. I glanced at her badge. She was from administration. That explained the street clothes.

"I had a question about one of your patients going into a clinical trial today," she said.

My senses went on alert, but I played it cool. "Jerry Fresno?" I asked.

"No, a girl, a pediatric case." She glanced at her folder. "Cynthia Miller."

I kept my face very neutral. "What was your question?"

"The consent forms aren't all filled out. No mother or father."

"Her mother is deceased."

"And the father?"

"She has no father of record."

"Is there a birth certificate available?"

I shrugged. "I don't know. I'm not in charge of records." I gave her a quick smile.

"Who is her legal guardian? I can't even make out the signature here."

"Would you like me to handle it? Since I'm supervising the administration of the trial?" I held out my hand for the file.

"I can talk to the family." She held on to the folder.

I expected this. "I believe she has an aunt with her. Amy or

Angela or something. She's been signing the documents."

"Perfect. I'll take care of it." The woman nodded at me and took off down the hall.

Damn it to hell. I'd carefully gotten all the documents in order so no one would look too carefully. I needed to get a medical proxy for Cynthia to handle these things, but I had no one, and I had hoped to have Angela around for a while before I could be certain I could trust her.

I could not let her trial be jeopardized. This drug was a breakthrough, a whole new way of fighting lymphoblastoma.

I pulled out my phone and texted Angela. "Busybody en route. Just smile and sign."

This was the worst part. Lying. Involving a paid person in a lie. Relying on someone else.

I'd step up as her brother before I let them take away this trial.

My hospital phone buzzed. I was late for rounds. I had to get my head together. At least with all this going on, I had no time to think of Tina. In fact, I'd stay away from her hall entirely. Once I had Cynthia through the chemo round and she had gotten her PET scan on the kidney, I would think about my own life again.

I was fine. I would be fine. I could handle this. I had to.

Despite this fine proclamation inside my head and my razor focus as I met with three patients and their families, when I had to walk across the hospital to the pediatric ward, I couldn't help myself. I took the hall that held the art therapy room.

I slowed down as I approached the wide window that allowed visitors to see the patients at work. Tina had a group of very small children right then, all under five. Two aides helped corral the kids and keep them coloring. One little boy kept tugging on Tina's sweater, and she smiled patiently down at him, putting the fat crayon back in his hand.

She seemed like her normal self again, happy and busy and willing to help. I didn't know what to do to keep from upsetting her again. She didn't seem to want anyone to get any closer than she allowed. I hadn't even intended to let the evening get so emotional and passionate.

Or maybe I had. She had me in knots, that was for sure.

I realized I had stopped in the middle of the hall and was just staring at her. I had to go, or she would see me. And that wouldn't help matters.

But I was too late. She turned toward the window, and I knew the minute she saw me. Her hand pressed against her chest. She must have made some sound, as two of the kids and one aide turned to follow her gaze.

I didn't wave or anything. I just stood there like a big stupid statue. I didn't even smile. She shook herself and bent down to the kids again. I waited a moment to see if she would glance back my way, all the time knowing that the aides were getting curious, but she never did.

27

TINA

This had been the crappiest day ever. I rushed out during lunch to pick up painting canvases for me and Albert, struggling with the oversized bags on the bus. And then Albert had been too sick to come. I got a message from the nurses that he wasn't well.

I asked if I could visit him, and they said no. And wouldn't tell me what was wrong. I wasn't family. I didn't have clearance.

Then of course Cynthia wasn't in her group. I remembered Darion had said that she had chemotherapy today. I expected him to drop by the room, say hello. I wasn't sure how to talk to him after last night. I knew I had behaved badly. Some things I still didn't do very well. Almost all of them involved men.

But he had just stood in the window, staring at me like I was a display in a zoo. *Homo sapiens.* Female. Prefers the wild. Gets vicious when trapped in emotional corners.

I wasn't sure what to do about Cynthia either. I wanted to separate my relationship with her from the one with her father, or whatever he was.

But I knew going to her room was a risk. Doing anything that involved him was a risk. I sat at my desk and just stewed, shoving all the social work paperwork around.

I couldn't explain to him what I was going through. I knew I was a mess. I couldn't do anything about it. We all had histories. We all had baggage.

The room was stuffy, so I pushed up my sleeves. Then I saw the scars again and shoved them back down. I didn't need any reminders of how screwed up I was.

The form "Consent for Psychological Evaluation" slid off the desk. I reached down to pick it up. This one scared me. They'd probably rule that I was too crazy to be a therapist. Then all this would be for nothing. The Big Rich Honcho would have to deal with me not working at the hospital, and Duffrey the jerk wouldn't get his fat payday.

I should go work at the coffee shop. So much simpler.

But when I closed my eyes, I could hear the waves and the guitar. The sand crunched beneath my knees, and Darion's hand worked its magic. My blood ran hot again, and I pushed the papers out of my way to lay my head on my desk. I just needed to get this over with. If I could just do the one-and-done, I'd be better. It always worked. I could shut all these feelings off. It had never failed me before. See the guy. Do the guy. Leave the guy.

In fact, we'd do it now. I'd find him, drag him to Surgical Suite B, and we'd just get it all out of the way. Bone in. Fade out.

I glanced at the clock. Six p.m. That's when he left yesterday. He was bound to be in his *daughter's* room. Uggh. Liar. He should fear me, really. I could cost him his job. Maybe his license.

I jumped up from the desk and snatched a set of markers I'd picked up at the art store when I got the canvases. I thought

Cynthia might like them. If you crossed one ink over the other, it created an entirely new color.

I had a plan. See Cynthia. Give gift. Get doc to suite. Bang him against the wall. Walk away with a clear conscience.

This felt better.

I picked up my bag and closed up the art room. The halls were quiet, and I began to calm down. I actually looked forward to our moment. I'd never had sex in a hospital before, and certainly not with a doctor. It would be a great story to regale Corabelle and Jenny with over boxed wine.

Yes, this was exactly right.

When I knocked on Cynthia's door, no one answered at first. I wasn't sure what to do. I knew she was still there. Her art covered the door. Tons of pictures of a woman I assumed was her mom, and Darion, with herself between them. Sometimes she drew herself with hair, sometimes not. I figured this was probably significant. Maybe once I started classes in psychology, I would learn why. The hospital was right. I needed training.

I knocked again.

Finally the aunt opened the door. "Oh, Tina!" she said. "I'm sure Cynthia would like to see you. I'm just not sure…" she trailed off, glancing back at the bed. "Come in."

I felt a little anxious going in. The woman was rattled.

Inside, a nurse stood over the bed, where Cynthia was curled in a ball on her side. "I've put on a temperature monitor so we can watch this fever," the nurse said, pointing at a little sensor stuck to Cynthia's head. "Let us know if she gets worse, starts vomiting, or has any swelling in her hands or feet. This is a new drug for us. I'll let Dr. Marks know how she is doing."

The nurse glanced at me. "I would keep as few people in here as possible. Her infection risk is very high."

I backed away to leave, but Cynthia saw me. "Hi, Tina," she said. She was shivering, and her eyes were rimmed with red.

"Hello, sweet Cynthia," I said.

The nurse left, and I turned to Angela. "Should I go?"

"No," Cynthia said. "I want you to see a picture I made."

I set my bag on the floor and pushed up my sleeves to scrub my arms and hands at the sink harder than I ever had before. Now that I'd seen the girl, I was shaking myself. She looked terrible, in such misery. It wasn't right that children had to go through things like this.

I had to pull myself together.

I tossed the paper towels in the trash and mustered a solid smile before I turned back around. Angela was arranging gel packs against Cynthia's back. The monitor next to her read 101 degrees.

"I brought you something," I said. I pulled the package of markers from the bag. "It's a special kind of marker. You can cross two different colors to make a third color."

Cynthia looked over at Angela, and they shared a smile.

"What?" I asked.

"Dr. Marks brought us those markers too," Angela said. She opened the drawer of the cabinet next to the bed and showed the package. "Great minds think alike."

"You'll be set up for a long time, then," I said. "You won't have to worry about running out of red."

"Or purple," Cynthia said.

I kneeled down on the floor next to the bed. "That's right. Purple is your favorite color."

"Your favorite color is black," Cynthia said.

"That's right. You remembered," I said. I now regretted saying it. I should have shut my old goth mouth and said something normal, like pink.

"You're funny," Cynthia said. "Nobody picks black."

"You're right," I said. "Maybe you can help me pick a new one."

"My mother's favorite color was blue."

"That's a good one," I said.

"She said it was the color of forever. That's why the sky and the ocean are blue. They go on forever, just like she would." Cynthia squeezed her eyes shut. "But she didn't."

My chest tightened so hard, I could barely breathe. "But you still draw pictures of her. You still remember the things she said. That's one kind of forever."

Cynthia opened her eyes. They seemed duller today. "I want the other kind. The kind where you don't go away."

A little beep went off on a monitor. I looked over. The monitor read 102 degrees. Angela moved some of the cooling packs from Cynthia's back to her belly. "I'm going to call for a gel blanket," she said.

"I made a picture for you," Cynthia said. "Since I missed art class."

"What did you do?"

"It's on my table." She tried to roll over, but Angela held out her hand to stop her.

"I'll get it," she said. "Let me talk to the nurses real quick." She punched the button on the remote and asked for a gel blanket.

When that was done, Angela pulled an oversized piece of art

paper from beneath a pile of crayons and colored pencils. "Here you go."

Cynthia tried to reach her hand out, but she began shivering violently, so she tucked her arm back against her body. She tried to smile. "This part is not fun," she said. "I'll be better later."

I wondered how many rounds of chemotherapy she had done, how many times it takes for something to become so routine that being violently sick is just "this part" and not something extraordinary or rare. This girl had more strength than pretty much anybody I'd ever met.

I took the picture from Angela. "Let's see what you've got here." I angled it so we both could see. "There's the hospital," I said, pointing at a big building with a medical cross on it. "Is this you in the window?" A figure was lying on a bed.

She nodded. Her eyes were barely staying open now.

Above the building were several people. One was in a lab coat. "Is this Dr. Marks?"

"Yes."

"And Aunt Angela?" The funny glasses gave that one away.

Cynthia nodded.

"Is this me?" A girl with pigtails and striped stockings hovered over the hospital.

"Yes."

Next to me was a woman with wings. "And this, is it your mom?"

"Yes."

"Your mom had red hair?"

"Yes." She tried to say something else, but the words all ran together.

The monitor beeped again. 103. Angela got on her phone. "I'm calling Dr. Marks. It might be time for you to go, Tina. I'm sorry."

Cynthia opened and closed her mouth a few times. Her eyes rolled up, then to the side, like she wasn't seeing anything. Angela moved the gels around and hit the nurse button again. "We're spiking," she said. "We need some help."

I stood up. Cynthia no longer seemed to know I was there. "I'll come back tomorrow, check on her."

Angela nodded in acknowledgement, but she was busy working over Cynthia, sponging her body with a wet rag. I felt a terrible sense of panic that something would happen to the girl during the night and I wouldn't know.

But I had Darion's number. I could ask.

I moved to the door just as Darion dashed in. He saw me but didn't pause. "Where are we now?" he asked.

"103. It's rising fast."

"Vomiting?"

"None."

I backed to the door. Cynthia was rolling her head back and forth on the pillow. I worried about Darion. How could he manage? This was his daughter!

He began to examine her, then two nurses entered the room. I had to go. I shouldn't be there. I moved into the hallway, but couldn't go any farther. It was too much. I was too frightened. I had to see if she was okay.

I leaned against the wall, my heart hammering. I could hear Darion's voice, strong and unfazed, telling the nurses a medication to give her, and how much. He seemed calm and in control. I didn't know how he could do it.

One nurse left, and another one came, holding a big silver blanket.

They would take care of her.

I waited another fifteen minutes, anxious. A few other staff members came and went. I asked one how she was, but she asked, "Who are you?" so I let it go. I knew hardly anyone on the evening shift.

Darion came out finally, tapping on his iPad as if he'd left any regular patient.

"Darion?"

He stopped and looked up. He seemed shocked to see me. "Tina? You're still here?"

"She looked so terrible. I was so worried."

"She's all right. We got her fever down. She'll sleep now. She's okay. She'll be okay."

"Will you stay with her?"

Something crossed his face, maybe regret. Maybe concern that I knew his secret. "I'll probably stay close by. It's an experimental drug. We have to watch her closely since there isn't a lot of data to go on."

We were talking like two colleagues, as if last night had never happened at all.

"Darion — I'm sorry about the beach."

A nurse came out of the room and walked between us.

He motioned for me to follow him down the hall. "Let's talk about this someplace quieter."

"I know you have other things to worry about. I just wanted to say I was sorry. Sometimes I forget that there is a bigger picture."

He moved us into a small waiting area with a few cushioned

chairs. It was empty. "It's fine. We all have things. Tough things."

"Will you let me know how she is? Later tonight? Text me or something?"

His eyebrows drew together. Maybe because he knew I cared about her too. I wished he would confess. Let me know that she was more than a patient. Maybe soon.

"I will."

I wanted to kiss him. I really did. The urge was so intense, I almost did it. But we were right in the middle of everything, a nurse walking by every few minutes. "Okay," I said. "Good night then, Darion."

He swallowed, his Adam's apple bobbing. "Good night, Tina."

His lab coat flared a little as he whirled around to stride away. I'm sure he intimidated his coworkers with that "Don't mess with me" posture, as though what he was doing was far more important than anything they might try to stop him to ask about.

He needed to relax.

I needed to grow up.

We could each stand to be a bit more like the other.

28

DR. DARION

It had been a long night.

I didn't leave the hospital at all, but I had anticipated this and packed a change of clothes. I napped in the lounge, and once on a gurney in Surgical Suite B, surrounded by memories of Tina and the lingering smell of the custodian's cigarettes.

Cynthia leveled out by late evening, and we reduced the drugs in her system and removed the coolants. Angela was exhausted, I knew. We all were. I realized I might need to hire a second nurse so we could have someone around the clock. This was ludicrous, though, really. We were in the hospital. She already had 24-hour care.

I showered downstairs next to the gym and checked on Cynthia before I was even supposed to arrive on shift. She was still sleeping, but her vitals were fine. Temperature still up a bit, but 100 was nothing like 105, where we'd topped out before getting it down.

We were out of the woods. She was going to get better now.

I walked down Tina's hall late morning, intending just to wave.

She had been kind and calm on the phone when I managed to call last night. We talked of Cynthia, and the coincidence of the double gift of the markers. She didn't bring up the beach night again, and neither did I. It seemed understood that we were past it. And I knew her a little better now. I realized she had some triggers.

But when I got to her window, she was alone inside. Instead of just walking by, I poked my head into the room. "Got a second?"

Tina stood up from the box of markers she was wiping down. "Sure." She tweaked her ponytails, a gesture that made me smile. When she wasn't all upset, she was damn cute.

The big window made us super visible, so I stood by the door. "I just wanted to see you."

"How is Cynthia?"

"She's stable. Low-grade fever, but nothing like yesterday."

Tina relaxed her clenched hands. "Good, I'm so glad. I was so scared for her."

"We've had worse, actually."

"I don't know how you stay so calm."

I leaned against the door. "That's what we have to do." I wanted to hold her close, pull her into me. I thought about asking her down to the surgical suite, but that seemed self-indulgent.

Tina tugged on the bottom of her sweater. She had this bohemian chic look today, a fitted ice blue cable knit over a deliberately wrinkly skirt. And the stockings, of course. Blue and beige stripes. I couldn't help but wonder if she was wearing a bra.

"Come here," she said, and headed toward the supply closet.

I glanced back at the window. As soon as I stepped away from the door, I would be visible.

"I won't sully your sterling reputation," she said. "Well, not on purpose."

She opened the door, but the closet was not a walk-in, just a set of shelves.

"I don't think I'll fit," I said, but she grabbed my hand and pulled me behind the open door.

Now I got it. We fit in a triangle of space formed by the corner of the room and the open door. No one could see us now.

I pulled her in tight. For just a moment, I let the stress and fear over Cynthia flow through me. I could feel it, actually allow it to penetrate. Jesus. How did families without the resources I had manage this? Even though I could control every aspect of her care, I still felt helpless. So much of how a disease progressed was left completely to chance.

I rested my cheek on Tina's head. She gripped me around the waist, her face buried in my lab coat. Something surged in me, a protectiveness I'd felt for no one but my sister. Damn. She was getting to me.

My finger lifted her chin so she looked up at me. "Can I see you later?" I asked.

She nodded. "Meet me down here when you get free."

I leaned down to kiss her. Her mouth was paradise, soft and pliant. I intended to keep it simple and light, but within seconds I felt hungry for her. I held her head with both hands and pressed her into me, diving between her lips, tasting her, spearmint and coffee.

I felt lost, running my hands along her body. The sweater was soft and textured. I desperately wanted to know about the bra, a little secret to carry with me through the day. I ran my hand across her breast and felt the nipple harden beneath the sweater. None today. I smiled against her mouth.

Just one touch. One brush of her skin. My hand slid down her side and up under the sweater. I bumped across each rib as I moved up her body. My thumb rested at the base of her breast, rounding the curve. When my palm cupped her, she exhaled against my mouth in a sigh.

Too much. I wanted her so terribly. I had to pull myself away. Get control. I withdrew from her sweater and ran my hand through my hair.

She straightened her clothes. We looked at each other a moment and burst out laughing.

"You're insane, Dr. Marks," she said.

"I just suspected you weren't performing the recommended breast self-exam, Ms. Schwartz," he said. "I have to look after my patients."

She pushed me against the wall and pressed against me. "How about testicular exams? Should we add those in? I'm not very skilled, but I make up for it in enthusiasm."

God. I was rock hard. Thank goodness for the lab coat. "I can't get enough of you," I said.

Tina's expression was soft and easy, a gentle smile. "We'll meet up later."

I pushed away from the wall. "I look forward to it."

She peeked around the door. "All clear." She pushed it back around until it closed. "Thank you for your concern about my mammary health."

"Anything that keeps you proactive." I couldn't stop smiling as I headed for the hall. Then I stopped and turned around. "I might have to send you text messages reminding you of the body parts you should take particular care with, or I will need to examine them."

She sat back down at the table, resuming her marker cleaning. "Then I just might have to tell you which of my body parts should be at the top of the list."

I swallowed hard. I was done for with this one. And the way Cynthia felt about her too — I had never been this involved, ever. And we'd been on one date. One mostly failed date.

I opened the door to head back to my rounds. But I'm pretty sure a big part of me stayed behind.

29

TINA

The doctor had me snared. I'd have to run with it for a bit. That was the problem with getting involved with someone at work. You couldn't just walk away and never see them again.

I was in trouble with this one.

I put the markers away and got out the canvases I'd bought for my time with Albert. I had called the psychiatric ward to ask after him, but he'd been transferred out to a regular hall. No one was sure where just yet.

I would be ready in case he came.

Meanwhile, all I had to do was wait and brood over Darion. I had planned all along to do this one-and-done, and then I had stalled to avoid having to dump him before I was ready.

But now I could tell that neither was going to happen. I wanted to see where this was going to go, and I was fairly sure I wouldn't leave after.

Yep, I was done for.

I pulled out a sheet of construction paper and began the rough sketch of the painting I had planned after seeing the sunset at Torrey Pines. The water line, the cliff, the mother, the shadow of the boy.

I realized the boy was too tall and erased him and tried again. Even with just an outline, I felt a wave of grief as I outlined his sleek hair, his shape, the bulge of a sagging sock. I knew none of those things about Peanut. If he would have been tall or short. Curly haired or straight. Pudgy or a weed.

My wrists ached like they sometimes did when I thought of him. It was psychosomatic. I knew this from the quack docs I'd been forced to talk to after I got out of the hospital. Thankfully the social worker for my case decided that I could go to a pregnancy loss support group instead.

Those women had been great. I sometimes talked to Stella, the leader. She still ran the group even though she was long past having babies, and never had one herself. They had gotten me through a really rough time. When I was on the suicide talk circuit, lots of times I'd pull up things they told me to pass on to people who were hurting, or thinking of hurting themselves.

The right person seemed to come along when you needed them. You just had to open your eyes and see that they were there. Then open your ears and listen.

Both of those things were hard to do when you were buried in pain, though. I understood that too.

The door opened, and an aide in pale pink scrubs wheeled Albert in. I was so relieved to see him, I wanted to cry.

Albert waved. He wasn't in his usual jeans and flannel anymore. He had on pajama pants and a hospital gown. His arms were exposed below the short sleeves, and the angry gashes on his wrists stood out like someone had stitched them with garish thread.

"I missed you yesterday," I said.

"Mr. Al got moved to a new room," the aide said. "He's on six now."

"That means I can visit you!" I said.

Albert looked up at the aide. "See, I told you. All the women are going to show and keep me up at night."

The aide patted his shoulder. "I bet you're right, a fine catch like yourself." She headed for the door. "I'll be back for him in an hour."

"What are you working on, Miss Tina?" he asked. "I see you've graduated to real canvases." His shaky finger pointed at the stands.

I turned the sketch around so he could see it. "I went to a cliff the other night and saw this scene. Well, I saw the sunset. I imagined the scene."

Albert examined the sketch. "Very nice."

"It's not right somehow."

He nodded. "You're using one-point perspective here." He pointed at the woman and boy. "The point of view is another human behind them."

He picked up a blue pencil from the table. His tremor was noticeable today, but he sketched anyway. "If you shift to three-point, the bird's-eye view, then it becomes another vision altogether."

Now, instead of the woman's back, we also saw the top of her head, just the tip of her nose. And the shadow was even more pronounced as different from her.

"It's God-like," I said.

"Exactly. But not really God, necessarily. Just viewed from a broader point of view, something more all encompassing."

"I was terrible at three-point in school," I said.

"Never let a technicality stand in the way of doing a painting the way it demands to be done. Learn what you need to know."

I pulled out a fresh piece of paper. I sketched the scene again, but this time, when I got to the shadow of the boy, he was no longer just an outline filled with shadow. He became three-dimensional too.

"I'm losing my idea," I said.

Albert shook his head. "No, you are finding the truth in your work. Start again."

I set aside that sketch and pulled out another piece of paper.

This time I brought the view back down, somewhere in the middle between directly behind, as though I was standing at their backs, and above, as if I was flying over their heads.

"Fill in a bit of the scene they are looking at now," Albert said.

The cliff was more pronounced from this angle. The rocks were craggy, and the ground below was visible, unlike from the other view, which focused on the happiness and light of the sunset.

I looked up at Albert, astonished. "I wasn't just supposed to draw the beauty of the sun, but also the danger of the fall."

He nodded. "Now you see the true power of bringing together your technical skill and your artistic vision."

The sketches spread before me. Not in four years of college had I learned something so important so fast. Who was this man? And why was I meeting him now, when it was almost too late?

My own thoughts from earlier rushed right back at me.

People came along when you needed them.

And, I amended, *you should learn from them.*

30

DR. DARION

Cynthia was sitting up and drinking a little broth when I visited her again at the end of the day.

"Hey, Dary," she said. "Did you find the Pokémon for Andrew?"

"I did." One of the volunteers had picked it up for me since I hadn't been able to get away.

"Did he like it?"

"I don't know. I left it with his nurse."

"Dary!"

"I'll ask."

"Can I go back to art tomorrow?" Cynthia asked.

"Are you feeling like throwing up?"

Cynthia frowned. "Maybe a little."

"Well, we'll see how you feel when it's time tomorrow, okay?" I pressed a hand against her forehead. She was a little warm. The monitor read 99.6. "Angela, can you take her temperature manually in a bit?" I pointed at the screen. "I don't trust these things."

Angela nodded. "Will do. You going home tonight finally?"

Cynthia's eyes got big. "Did you sleep here?"

I sat next to her on the bed. "I slept in the operating room," I said. "I used the little blue paper sheets for a blanket."

"You did not!" she said.

"Did too!"

Angela laughed. "You two kids are something else."

I patted Cynthia on the shoulder. "You call me if you need me, okay?"

"I will."

It wasn't easy leaving. But I did have to go home, at least for a while. I needed clothes.

Plus, I was going to see Tina.

I stopped at the desk to see if Cynthia's blood test results had come in. Once again I had to separate the clinical side of myself from my feelings as I pulled up the report.

WBC less than 0.1 (out of range)
Hgb 11.2 (out of range)
Platelets 32 (out of range)
Lymphocyte 73 (out of range)
Monocyte 14 (out of range)
Eos 13 (out of range)
ANC 0 (out of range)

I didn't expect anything to look normal. We were just establishing a baseline. I'd order her a transfusion for her platelets and a G-CSF to boost her white blood count. Hopefully her ANC would bounce back this time. She'd been immunosuppressed for so long.

I scrolled to the second page. This was more telling, if there were still cancer cells in her blood.

No atypical or immature lymphs detected.

No blasts in her blood. No cancer. I let myself relax, just a little.

I wouldn't order a bone marrow aspiration for a while yet. I didn't want to put her through it until I was certain her cells were rebounding. Nothing was more discouraging than a hypocellular draw, which told us nothing.

But this was a start. No blasts. The cancer was not circulating.

We would beat this thing.

I powered down the iPad. Fatigue threatened to set in, but I pushed it aside, something I had mastered during my first residency. I pulled off the lab coat, and laid it over my arm. Official duties were done for the day.

Now I could see Tina.

When I arrived at the window, she was partially obscured by a large canvas on a wood frame. I could only see the back of it, propped on a metal stand. On the table, she had mixed a rainbow of reds, pinks, oranges, and yellows in a palette.

I rapped twice on the door, then opened it. Tina looked up at me, her gray eyes standing out from her pale face. She had a small smudge of pink on one cheek.

"You're working," I said.

"Having fun." She stuck the paintbrush between her teeth as she squeezed a bit of white onto the palette. When she took the brush in her hand again to blend it in, a touch of orange transferred from the handle to the tip of her nose.

"I am almost at a stopping point," she said. "Just let me get this last color down." She dipped the brush in the white and added it to orange until she achieved a pale melon. When she touched the brush to the canvas, I walked around to see what she was doing.

Along the top third of the canvas, the colors of a sunset radiated across a translucent sky. The center was almost pure white, moving to a yellow gold, then shifting to all the colors from orange, to pink, to a dusty red.

I let her work, admiring the set of her jaw, the concentration in her eyes. She moved the brush smoothly across the canvas, dipped and mixed and blended, then cut through one color with the other.

She stuck the brush in her teeth again, an endearing habit. I sat next to her and picked up a clean brush. A piece of unused children's construction paper sat at the end of the table. I slid it over.

I had never taken formal art classes past high school, when my father stepped in to ensure that my education would veer back toward premed. But dipping the brush into paint had a sensuousness I always appreciated. And the slide of color across the textured paper felt like a caress.

At first I mimicked the sunset of Tina's, then ventured off, realizing the pinks and pale oranges had the appearance of skin kissed by a late afternoon sun. The strokes took on more shape, a waist and a hip. I had filled the page with the lines, so the form was close up, an indentation of a belly button, a hint of a shadow of the thigh propped up. The knee disappeared up beyond the page, but I brought in the darkest color to shadow in behind a calf as the leg came back into view.

Now the image began to emerge. A woman, lying on her back, her leg bent.

I chose a pale color, imagining the light coming from near her head. The tension of the day began to unfurl as I took a chance and painted the woman's arm across her face, revealing a breast. Only after I had touched the brush into a pale pink and swirled in a delicate nipple did I realize I was painting Tina.

I set down the brush.

Tina had stopped working, watching me. When she realized I had stopped, she looked up at me with wonder. "I didn't know," she said.

I wasn't sure what she meant exactly. That I could paint. Or that I had this image of her in my head, sensual and naked.

Her hand slid over mine, her fingers barely grazing the surface of my skin. "You have more secrets than I would have guessed."

This made me tense up a little, but as Tina continued to run her palm over the back of my hand, encircling my wrist with her fragile grip, it dissipated again. I should tell her about Cynthia, soon, before it became too big a lie. Before she sensed it and felt alienated by my lack of trust in her.

I glanced up at the viewing window. The halls were quiet, but the evening staff would still walk by occasionally.

"Where should we go?" Tina asked. "I assume you have a place?"

Filled with images of Cynthia and our family, I thought. But here Tina was, making this move. I remembered her on the beach, so passionate, so lost in the moment before she withdrew. What would she do this time? And if she got angry with me again, what could she do with my secret? To Cynthia?

"I do. It's not close, though. Is yours?" She might have a roommate. If so, I could take her to a hotel. We could be decadent.

"It's not far," she said. "Just don't get eaten by the Pink Monster."

"Are you referring to your —"

"No!" Her eyes got big. "Oh my God." The spell was broken, and Tina became more of herself, laughing instead of intense. "Although I do like the thought of my girl parts as a force of destruction."

She let go of me. "Maybe you can paint those next time, all flowery like Georgia O'Keeffe." She stood up. "Or go full-on Gustave Courbet."

I didn't know Courbet's work, but I could guess. "That sounds like a fascinating idea. You'll model for me?"

She sat back down, mostly obscured from the hall window by the canvas. She lifted the edge of her skirt slowly, up the striped stocking, above her knees, past the elastic edge, and finally revealing a long expanse of thigh. "You choose the lighting," she said.

I was going to have to put my lab coat back on.

31

TINA

He painted.

He painted.

The whole drive to my apartment, this wouldn't leave my head.

He was an artist.

Who was this man?

I still felt in a fog as we walked up to my door. Then I remembered the furniture. As I unlocked the door to my apartment, I turned to Darion. "I wasn't kidding about the Pink Monster."

"Really?" Darion asked. "Is it like Godzilla or more Oscar the Grouch?"

"Worse than either."

I stood back to let him in.

He held the pizza box over my head as he passed. I knew the moment when he saw the fuzzy sofa, because he said, "Good God."

I closed the door behind me. He was here. In my apartment. Well, Corabelle's. I texted both her and Jenny while Darion paid for the takeout pizza, warning them to stay away.

"The doctor is making a house call," I told them.

Corabelle responded with nothing but exclamation marks. Jenny said, "Time to break in the Pink Monster!"

Darion ran a hand over the fur. "Is this your usual style?" he asked.

I had to laugh. "Are visions of tackiness dancing in your head?" I dropped my bag and keys on a side table and plopped down on it. "My friend Jenny has this bizarre boyfriend who keeps buying her stuff. This is one of her castoffs."

Darion lowered himself gingerly onto the sofa. "I'm picturing bodily fluids mixed in the fur."

"Are you now?" I took the pizza box from him and set it on the coffee table. "Is it disturbing your sense of sterility?"

"Are you telling me you haven't thought about it?"

"I've only had the sofa for two days."

He ran his hands over the surface. "I've definitely never seen anything like it."

"Let's imagine pizza grease on it first." I popped open the box. "I'll get some plates."

I dashed into the kitchen, then peered around the cabinet. I still couldn't get over it. Dr. Darion was sitting on my pink sofa.

I tightened my ponytails. Why was I nervous about this? I wasn't exactly a virginal teenager. I pulled a couple of Corabelle's plates from a shelf.

I peeked around the corner again. "You're not a knife-and-fork guy, are you? With pizza?"

"Not a chance," Darion said. He leaned back on the sofa and surveyed the room. I saw his gaze land on Albert's mermaid.

I returned to the sofa. "One of my patients made that," I said, then remembered when he'd insisted I didn't have patients. "Well, one of the hospital patients. I guess they aren't mine."

Darion frowned. "I'm sorry I said that. I shouldn't have."

I shrugged. "It's okay. I know what I am." I plunked a piece of pizza on each plate. My half was just cheese. Darion had gotten all sorts of junk on his. Sausage and anchovies and peppers.

"I'm so glad to be away for a little while." He took a bite and leaned his head on the back of the sofa.

"I bet. Do doctors often sleep at the hospital?"

"During our internship and residency, sure."

"Aren't you a staff doctor now?"

"I'm a little unusual. I completed a residency in oncology, but now I'm also working in pediatrics. I have another year to go on that. But technically, yes, I'm staff, not a resident."

"I'm trying to figure out what program to do for the hospital. Be a social worker or a therapist."

"Very different things," Darion said.

"What do you think?" I set my plate down. I wasn't really hungry. Having him here put me off balance. "For, you know, a lazy artist type."

Darion rested his plate on the pizza box and turned me around to face him, my legs draping across his lap. My heart sped up a little as he ran his hands along the stockings.

"That's a tough call. I don't see a lot of places where social workers can do art therapy, though. You probably want to go the psychology route for that."

Darion's fingers slid up the bump of my knee, pushing my broomstick skirt out of the way. I kicked off my Mary Janes and let them fall to the floor.

He made it up to the elastic band at the base of my thigh and ran his finger inside the edge. "I like these," he said.

"Everyone thinks I should give them up," I said.

"Why?"

"Be a grown-up."

He shrugged. "People want everyone to be like everybody else. I say just be you."

Cool air hit my skin as he tugged the stocking down. His fingers traced the indentations in my skin from the elastic. "I've always found it fascinating how skin is so easily altered, and how quickly it corrects itself."

I realized with no small panic that too many lights were on, and that my skin had not corrected itself at all on my wrists. The scars would be very visible. Time to get this show on another road.

I dropped my legs to the floor. "Let me put the pizza away," I said.

He watched me get up and take the box and plates into the kitchen. Dang it, I should have planned better. I thought about the lighting. Maybe we should just go to the bedroom now.

No, that seemed too fast. But if the sweater came off, and it was going to…crap.

I flipped on the kitchen light. The box went into the fridge, and I dumped the plates in the sink. Now to just get the main light in the living room off. Without weirdness.

I walked back toward Darion. "Let me get the light in here," I said.

His eyes followed me as I moved to the door and turned off the overhead. The room dimmed considerably, lit only by the distant light of the kitchen.

I sat back on the sofa. "I assume you know your way around a body and don't need surgical illumination."

He leaned toward me, his mouth on mine. He must have been holding back before, as he crushed me against him, pushing us both back on the sofa. His body was solid and muscled, braced above me. His lips took mine hungrily, the kiss deepening.

I could barely catch my breath. One of his hands went beneath my head to pull me in more tightly. The other moved along my body, breast to hip, and beneath the sweater. I knew it made him crazy that I didn't wear a bra. I kept pulling out my thickest sweaters so I could do it again.

His palm reached a breast, and my hips pressed up against him. I could feel him erect between us. I wondered what sort of lover he would be, sensitive or passionate, slow or fast.

He braced himself on one arm and pushed the sweater up over my belly. I had been right, this was the first to go. But the light was way too low for him to see the faint scars. I would tell him eventually, but not now, not yet. Normally I didn't have to worry about it, one-and-done. But this was going to be different. It already was.

He broke the kiss to pull the sweater over my head. I shivered for a second from the loss of warmth, and Darion pulled me against his body. His shirt was rough, the buttons pressing into my skin. He kissed along the curve of my neck and along my shoulder. I quit thinking about anything but his mouth and hands.

He made his way down to that territory we covered in the surgical room, his lips surrounding a nipple and drawing it in.

Blood pounded through me, sending waves of heat in its path. His tongue took its time learning every curve. One of his hands moved lower, pushing the skirt out of his way.

His hand shifted my knee farther out, giving him access. My breathing sped up as he felt his way up a thigh and his fingertips brushed against the lace edge of my panties.

I clutched at his head. He moved from one breast to the other, taking his time. He cupped me between the legs, holding me gently at first, then letting one finger slide against the folds, still covered by thin fabric.

I writhed beneath him, wanting more, wanting it faster. He knew what did it for me after that time on the beach. But he was patient, slow, and only after long agonizing moments where I pressed up into his hand did he slip a finger inside my panties and into me.

I could barely hang on. Despite our beach moment, it felt so long since I'd fallen into a hot encounter like this. Sometimes my exit strategy weighed on my mind before we were even done. But this time, I had none.

Darion lifted his head and whispered against my cheek, "I think I sent you a message about this part."

He had. A very hot, very sexy text about the Courbet painting and what would happen when I struck that pose.

His body shifted down, and the finger moved out of me to the edge of the panties and pulled them down my legs. My skirt was gathered in a bunch around my waist. I ran my hand through his hair as he made his way down.

"I think I might have mentioned something like this." His mouth landed on me, my knees on his shoulders, and now my neighbors were going to know who I was because I cried out without any control.

Darion didn't start slow, or take his time. Everything went into it, fingers, tongue, his lips. Pleasure crashed through me, blasting out like a dynamite strike. I clutched at the furry pink cushion, utterly lost, out of control. I couldn't hold anything back even if I wanted to.

He never hesitated, never slowed down, not waiting on my rhythm, but creating it, controlling my response.

The sensations began to pulse, like a heartbeat, like breathing, and then it all let go, the orgasm blossoming out from my body, surrounding him, engulfing his mouth and hand.

I relaxed against the sofa, the world spinning. Damn. Even if I had wanted to cut and run from him, I wasn't sure certain parts of my body would have come with me. They already belonged to the doctor.

He kissed his way back up my thigh, across my hip, and skipped the bunched-up skirt to find my belly. He gazed up at me, his eyes dark in the low light. "I love every sound you make," he said.

My face burned hot. I didn't trust my voice yet to reply.

He sat up on his knees and closed his grip on the waist of the skirt. "This is in the way," he said, and yanked it down. He tossed it aside. He smoothed the one loose stocking back into place. "These can stay." He nipped my skin just above the elastic band.

His hand went back into me, and I was shocked to find that I still had so much need inside. Darion seemed to want to pillage me over and over again, his hands and mouth everywhere, never stopping, stroking, sucking. Little red marks bloomed across my belly as he made his way over my body.

"I hope I don't need a physical exam anytime soon," I said.

"Mmmm hmmm," he said, landing low again. My head fell back. God, I was going crazy with it. This time he kept stopping each time I got close. My hands were worn out from clutching his shoulders.

"Please," I said.

He grinned up at me with an expression I would never have imagined on his face. "Please what?"

"Get naked."

"I live to serve," he said.

He loosened his cuffs and a few top buttons, then whipped his shirt over his head. The T-shirt beneath was tight and hugged his ribs and abs. I ran my hands along the warm cotton, then grabbed the bottom edge.

"And this," I said, yanking it up.

I couldn't reach all the way, so he pulled it off. His chest was hairless and toned. I fitted my thumbs in the indentations of his belly, my throat thick. He was damn beautiful.

He unlatched his belt and slid it from the loops. I lay back to watch as he shucked his pants. A boxer boy, the fitted type. His shoes rolled away, and the black socks. Now it was just the navy underwear.

I reached for him, sliding along his length, straightening him until he peeked out the top. I couldn't wait anymore and grasped at the waistband and jerked them down. He sprang at me, powerful and long.

Darion kicked the boxers away. "We really are going to break in the Pink Monster, aren't we?"

"Yes," I said, reaching out for him again. "Yes, we are."

He braced himself over me, and I got hold of him, grasping at the base and sliding my fingers to the end. He sucked in a breath, his eyes closed, and I kept working it, rearranging myself beneath him so my stocking-covered knees were outside his legs. I wasn't letting him get away this time.

His face dropped to my neck, burying itself there. I worked him until I felt a tremor in his arm. "My turn to say please," he said into my ear.

"Condom?" I asked. I'd been on the shot forever, plus I had an IUD. I had no intention of accidentally getting pregnant ever again. But still, no use taking a risk for anything else.

He nodded against my shoulder and reached for the discarded pants. I kept my hands on him while he fumbled with his wallet and tore open the package.

"I'll do the honors," I said, and took it from him.

He groaned a little as I touched the circle to the tip and slowly rolled it down his length. He was trim but not bare at the base.

Darion didn't dive in immediately, but reached between us. "I have been thinking about this for weeks," he said.

"Weeks? Since that first time you asked to see me?"

"Yes."

"But you never came back."

He stilled a moment. "I had to leave town suddenly," he said. "I had no way to contact you."

"It was fine." We shouldn't have this conversation now. "Come here." I grabbed his bulging shoulders and brought him down closer. "Show me how sorry you are for standing me up."

He plunged in then, and I nearly screamed. God, it had been forever. He split me wide open, and I couldn't do anything but hang on as he set the speed and rhythm. His breath puffed against my neck as he worked. I locked my ankles around his back. After a moment he sat up and brought me with him. I straddled him, sitting high, and he held my waist to assist as I moved up and down.

I felt dizzy, lost, like I wasn't sure which direction was up or down. I held on to his shoulders, letting everything course through me, the splintering pleasure rising up, the burn in my thighs, the ache in my belly from need.

He slowed me down, letting each stroke get long and deep. I cycled against him, clutching his head against my chest. I could do this forever, truly forever.

But he reached between us to work that little nub. And I found that I needed to move, to pick up the tempo, to work it again. My legs were on fire, and I must have quivered, because Darion knew, and dropped me back on the sofa again.

His finger never left me, and now his strokes were powerful and fast. I couldn't keep up with him and just let him take over, let him take me. I could hear us both, his groans, my faint gasps. I could feel the keen edge he balanced on, and so I just let go, stopped trying to control myself, and the second orgasm blasted out with more intensity than the first.

My ears were ringing with my own cries when Darion grasped my hips and pulsed against me, letting out one elongated groan.

I could barely breathe, my chest heaving. I wanted to cry, feeling so damn emotional. I tried to remind myself that this was just an act, just sex, but something had come over me. I couldn't rein anything in, I couldn't laugh it off or coat it with disdain. All the things that let me blow the guy off at the end were well out of reach, carried off in the tidal wave.

Normally I would push the guy away, throw on my clothes,

and leave, never returning another call.

But we were here, at my place, and I didn't want him to go. Even if we only ever did this one, I was far from done.

32

DR. DARION

Something hard-core was going through Tina's mind. Even in the low light coming in from the kitchen, I could see that her eyebrows were pressed toward each other. She seemed pained.

"Are you all right?" I asked gently. "Does anything hurt?"

She opened her eyes, baring just a flash of vulnerability, then she laughed. "You are such a doctor. No, nothing hurts."

I dragged her against me. We were still pressed tightly together. I had spent the last hour worrying about crushing her. Sometimes I swore she was nothing more than feathers and vellum paper, so light and delicate.

But tough. Tina was a set of extremes I'd never seen in a woman.

"You'll want to get that," she said, looking between us. "Let me find a box of tissues or something."

She slid out from under me, her body pale and gleaming above the stockings. Now that would be something to paint. She had hidden my earlier work in the art closet, but I could start another one. Her lithe little body, the striped legs. I stirred again just thinking about it.

I didn't know what she would want now, for me to leave or stay. I needed to check on Cynthia, but I had to be careful about logging in with Tina so close. And to go to my place. Damn, my mind was already buzzing. I didn't want that. I just wanted to be right here.

Tina returned and passed me a box. I crushed the condom in a tissue and reached for her. "Come here," I said.

She sat beside me, but I pulled her onto my lap again. I wanted to keep touching her. I could not get enough. "Let's just be for a while," I said.

She nodded.

I pulled her down on the fuzzy sofa, facing me, and I cradled her against my chest. She tucked one knee between my legs, and I held fast to her. Her heart hammered, a little fast. This was good. She was engaged with me. I had this fear that she would kick me out, that she would be unaffected and want me gone.

But her own pulmonary response gave her away. I ran light fingertips along her neck and up around the base of those pigtails. Such a girl-woman. She built this whole way of protecting herself, but it couldn't last. She felt things too deeply. I would take care with her.

We stayed like this for a long time. She slept a little, and I listened to the sounds of her apartment. A faint drip of a faucet. Doors slamming in other apartments. Cars coming and going in the lot.

I wanted to memorize her. I couldn't stop looking. When she woke a little while later, I ran my hand along every curve I could reach, gently. I wanted her again, but I wouldn't push for it, just wait and see.

"These are probably hindering circulation," I said, tugging at the elastic of her stocking.

"You're talking sexy again, doc," she said.

"Do you sleep in them?"

"Not usually."

So, I pushed one, then the other, over her knees. They got loose, and I tugged them down. "Now I get to see the rest of you," I said.

"Are you one of those puritans who gets hot for ankles?"

I trailed my fingers across the bump of her ankle bone. "I do for yours."

Maybe I would press. I was rock hard now. I shifted so she could feel it against her belly.

Her eyes got wide. "I can work with that," she said. "Too bad there isn't a gurney close by. That one thing you were doing when I was sitting —"

I couldn't take any more and silenced her with a kiss. I nudged her knees apart with my thigh. She seemed fairly flexible, so I lifted her leg and locked her ankle on my shoulder.

Now I had all the access I wanted. I thumbed her little nub, and her breathing immediately sped up. God, I loved her reactions to this. Two fingers in, her body warm and wet and ready, and she was making these little gasping noises again.

I could not get enough of her. I keyed her up, working until she moved with me, until she clutched my arms.

I felt around for my wallet. I'd better buy more condoms. Thank goodness I had two. I wasted no time on this round, lifting her onto me as I sat on the sofa, back to the cushions. She reached on either side of me to hold on to the sofa, her pert little breasts right against my face.

She slid over me easily, and I clasped her hips, driving up into her until she cried out. I worked her hard and fast until I could tell she was close. I made sure she had solid contact with me and grinded against her until she began to tighten against me.

Then I unleashed, controlling the strokes, holding her in just the right place as it all let go, tight, then loose, relaxing, coming down. She shuddered against me and rested her forehead on my shoulder.

Damn, this girl had gotten under my skin. I no more finished one round when I was already thinking about the next.

I knew she had to be tired. It was late. I scooted forward on the sofa and brought her legs around my waist. She weighed next to nothing, so I was able to stand up with her on me.

I held on to her back and walked down a hall that I assumed led to her bedroom. It was seriously dark back here, but I spotted the illuminated numbers of an alarm clock and headed for them.

I could make out a pillow, then the bed.

I bent over, laying Tina down on it. As much as I wanted to curl in next to her, I knew I couldn't. I needed to log in at the hospital, check Cynthia's last vitals. Pick up clothes at my apartment. Shower.

Life. Work. So much getting in the way.

"I'll stop by the art room tomorrow, okay?" I said.

"It's Saturday, doc. We're off."

"Not for residents. I have to do a pediatric run."

"Kiss Cynthia for me."

"I will." I squeezed her hand and let go.

Back in the living room, I got dressed and found a trash can for the tissues. The kitchen was bright and lit up, mostly empty. On the wall was a small framed photograph in black and white. I walked up to it. A premature baby, less than twenty weeks' gestation by the look of it, photographed against a white sweater.

This must have been Tina's. I thought for a moment about watching Cynthia slip away and realized, *Tina has already lived through it.*

I was never going to be as strong as her.

33

TINA

I woke up to soreness in all the right places. I peeked under the sheet. Yep, still naked. I vaguely remembered the good doctor tucking me into bed.

I pulled the covers to my chin. Whoa. I should have added more doctors to my list. I had a feeling I wouldn't be scouting around for one-and-dones for a while.

Had I really just thought that?

I sat up and peered at the numbers on the clock. Good God. Morning was half over. Darion had probably already seen a dozen patients, saved three people, and cured some obscure disease. AND painted a picture.

I flopped back on the pillow. Who was this man?

I had to know more.

I leaned over the side of the bed and pulled my laptop out from under the side table. I propped it on my knees and fired it up, heading straight for Google.

I typed in the search box. *Dr. Darion Marks.*

I got some easy hits at first. His graduation from med school.

A couple hospitals' press releases when he joined their staffs. His LinkedIn profile.

But nothing about a wedding. No dying wife. I found his father pretty easily, though. Dr. Gerald Marks, on the medical board. Hmmm. I wondered if he was the mysterious benefactor that got me my job back. But Darion said he didn't know anybody with that kind of money. I took him at his word on that.

He was thirty-two Good to know. Nine years older. A largish gap, but not unreasonable. I clicked on a strange link that I felt probably wasn't related to him but looked interesting.

Then sat straight up. The doctor took his art more seriously than he let on. While he was in medical school, he actually had a show of his work at a small gallery.

I clicked through the images. They were not unlike the one he had knocked out in my art room, almost impressionistic images of people, very close up, faces filling the canvas, or hands, or legs. No nudes, not like the one he had done of me. This made me a little happier than it should have.

I closed the laptop. I couldn't think of anything else. Darion. Darion. Darion. Had he written me while I was sleeping?

I jumped from the bed and dashed into the living room. When I saw the Pink Monster, I couldn't help myself, but dived right onto it, naked skin and all.

I buried my face into the fur, squealing a little as I remembered him braced over me.

I wanted him back. I wanted him right then.

My bag was under the table, so I bent over the arm and snatched it up. My phone had three text messages.

Two were from Darion.

I fell back on the sofa, clutching the phone to my chest. God, I was like a lovesick teen.

For the first time since I had been a teen.

I refused to go down any dark path. The third message was from Corabelle, so I pulled it up first. That way I could build a little anticipation for what Darion might have said.

Don't forget the bachelorette party tonight! We'll be by to get you at 8!

Damn. That was going to be so fun. But what if Darion was free?

I took a deep breath and scrolled back to pull up his first message.

You looked so beautiful sleeping there. You made it hard to leave. I'll message you later, when you're up.

I pressed the phone to my skin again. He definitely knew what to write a girl.

Then the second message.

Cynthia is doing well. It's been a good day. I wish when I walked by the art room, you were there. Let me know when you are up.

I checked the time stamp. The second message was at 8:30 a.m. Ha, we were not a good match on sleeping in. But I could have guessed the doctor was an early riser.

I could cure him of that in a hurry.

What to say back? Please come back here and do everything again?

I laughed out loud. So much for one-and-done. I was practically begging him back.

Besides, we'd gone for two in the same night.

I held my phone directly in front of my face as if it could tell me what to say.

Finally, I figured it out.

Feeling pretty sheltered this morning. Off to buy more condoms.

He didn't answer right away, which I would expect since he was at the hospital. I decided that rather than sitting around to wait for a break in his day, I would shower and get myself together. I had a long night ahead.

I tapped off a quick note to Corabelle about the bachelorette party, asking her what to wear, and stepped into the shower.

I could not stop thinking about Darion. His hands on me. His mouth. I stuck my face in the spray, trying to shake off the memory. I had to get on with life.

But I didn't want to. I wanted to stand there and relive every minute.

And I wanted to do it again.

My phone chimed a couple of times from the counter, but I forced myself to take my time washing my hair and wait to see who it was. Probably just Corabelle and Jenny. They were super fired up about tonight. We were going to have dinner at some Italian place, then head to a party hosted by Jenny's director guy. Supposedly the whole cast of some movie would be there.

Gavin was meeting us. I wondered if Darion could go.

Good grief. I wanted to introduce him to my friends already? What had happened to me?

I toweled off and picked up the phone. Corabelle had told me to wear something sensible, since it would be a long night. Ha. Her definition of sensible and mine were probably not in the same universe.

Jenny had also written, telling me to ignore Corabelle and wear the skimpiest, most daring outfit in my closet and I could probably end up with three hot hookups before the night was over.

Oh, that Jenny.

I ran my fingers over the third name. Darion. He must have been watching for my message.

If you're buying the condoms, I'm going to go lobby Duffrey to get you a raise.

I smiled and typed in another one.

Off to a bachelorette party for a friend tonight. What are you going to be up to?

He was clearly between patients or on break, because he answered immediately.

Pining for you in Surgical Suite B. On the clock until midnight.

I glanced at the clock. Did I dare? I could do what Jenny said, put on my trampiest outfit, and then show up at the hospital. I felt a little rush as I typed my next message.

Tell me when to meet you, and I'll see you there.

34

DR. DARION

I checked on Cynthia just before my scheduled break at 6:30. She was sitting up, practicing her card tricks again. After her little friend Andrew got the Pokémon I sent him, he had sent her another special deck. I was glad she had found another child her age to relate to. I hoped her immune system would bounce back soon so she could see him more easily.

"Are you and Andrew going to run around taking money off the staff?" I asked her. "Because I wholeheartedly approve."

Cynthia shook her head at me. "Dary, I'm not a cardsharp. I'm a magician!" She held up the fanned-out deck. "Take a card!"

I reached out, then pulled back. "From anywhere or a special place?"

"Anywhere!"

I pulled a card out.

"Look at it, but don't show me!" she said.

I took a peek. Ace of spades.

"Now put it back in," she said. "Anywhere."

I stuck it back in the fan.

She awkwardly shuffled the deck, catching an errant card that popped out. I pretended not to notice it was the ace of spades. Finally she fanned the deck out again. "Pick any card."

I pulled another one out.

"Is it the ace of spades?" she asked.

I held it out. It was indeed. "Very good," I said. "You're getting better."

She took the card back and held the stack close to her chest. "Yes, I am." A card slipped out of her grip and landed on her lap. Another ace of spades. I pretended to look at my iPad and held in a laugh.

I glanced at the clock in her room. 6:30. My crotch tightened. Tina would be arriving.

I squeezed Cynthia's arm. "I'll be back again in a little while," I said. "Angela, you'll be here until eight?"

The woman nodded.

The halls were fairly quiet as I made my way through the ward. Saturday night. I had definitely spent more weekends in hospitals than out with friends. Even in med school, when we all knew our free time was about to end, we didn't party much. By the time you got there, the majority of the wild kids were elsewhere. The med students had to blow off steam, certainly, but they didn't tend to do it with raucous weekend parties.

I buzzed into the surgical wing. The hall was empty. A few rooms were operational farther down, probably lengthy surgeries, the type that took twelve or more hours, a few late-afternoon scheduled ones, and possibly an emergency or two. But most routine work was long over.

I paused in front of the door to Surgical Suite B. I assumed

Tina's badge would get her access back here. If she wasn't in the suite, I'd go back out to catch her and get her through.

The door lever clicked as I pushed it down. I let my eyes adjust to the lower light, scanning the room to see if Tina had made it in.

Then I saw her.

She lay on her side on one of the gurneys, her head propped up on one elbow. Her outfit wasn't like anything I had seen her in before, or would have even imagined. Very short black leather skirt. Spike-heel boots to her knee, leaving plenty of leg in between. A top that could best be described as a crisscross of straps. I expected any movement to reveal something delicious.

Her hair was down, crinkly instead of sleek.

"Hello, doctor," she said. "You might want to lock the door."

I whirled around and twisted the latch. I took a second to get myself together and turned back to Tina.

She was sitting up now, one leg crossed over the other, the black boot swinging. "You're way over there," she said.

I headed for her, trying to take normal, measured steps, but I wound up hurtling in her direction, and the second I made it, pressing my mouth to hers like a dying man.

I ran my hand along the crazy shirt, fingering the straps. Built inside were little cups that acted as a bra, but that was nothing to pull away. I shoved them aside and leaned down, that naked exposed breast in my mouth as fast as I could get it there.

She arched against me, and I remembered all the exquisite sounds she had made the night before.

I pushed her legs apart so I could get closer. My hand closed over a naked knee, then up.

Another luscious surprise. Nothing in the way there.

My fingers slipped inside her. She was wet as hell already. Her face pressed into my neck, keeping her from crying out.

I had a good feel for what worked for her, and I plumbed every bit of that knowledge. She tightened against me, her hips moving with me. She was so close, her breathing fast.

I withdrew, and she let out a tiny squeal. I jerked her forward, closer to the edge of the gurney. She got it, and reached to unbuckle my pants. I groaned as she reached inside the boxers and the cool air hit my skin.

She scooted even closer, tugging a condom from inside her shirt. She ripped the package open and rolled the circle along the length of me.

I could barely stand it, so anxious for her.

Tina surveyed her work and sat back a little, wrapping her legs around my waist. I pushed her skirt up and out of the way and just dove in with one sharp plunge.

She gasped, leaning back, propped on her hands, one sweet breast exposed between the straps of her shirt. I felt completely out of control, trying to hang on as I held her hips, working inside her. I reached between us and circled the nub.

Tina closed her eyes, keeping our rhythm, but I could feel her muscles closing around me. She tried to keep quiet, but little sounds escaped. When she started to orgasm, I knew the difference in the pitch.

As she gripped the mattress on the gurney, I let go and released into her, breath ragged. Jesus. She sat up and held on to me, rocking against me as our bodies pulsed together.

I clasped her, letting our heart rates settle at the same time. I was still inside her, and didn't want to withdraw, to move on with the work shift. For the first time since I became a doctor, I wanted to blow everything off and do what I wanted. Normal life. A regular job you could just skip for a mental health day.

"Your patients, doctor. They'll be waiting," Tina said, her breathing back to normal but her voice still catching.

I squeezed her. People had told me this could happen. A girl could just snare you. I would never have believed it until now. I pressed my lips into her hair, loose and wild. "Can I see you after my shift? Will you be up?"

She laughed a little and pulled away. "At midnight? I dare say the party will just be getting started."

I nodded. "Tomorrow, then?"

She ran her thumbs along my cheeks. "Let me know when you leave here. We'll figure something out."

I kissed her again, long and deep and thoroughly. We were still joined. I didn't want to pull away.

But Tina dropped her legs and moved back. She produced a tissue. "I thought of everything," she said.

She had. Except for how I was supposed to concentrate after *this*.

35

TINA

I took a taxi to the restaurant to meet Jenny, Corabelle, and a couple of her friends. I almost went home to change my outfit before going out. I had worn a hooded jacket through the hospital so nobody would recognize me in this crazy getup, left over from my goth days.

But I didn't really have time to stop, nor did I want to spend the extra money to go out of the way. So, I headed straight to Romeo's.

The restaurant was boisterous and full of amazing smells. I spotted the girls at a big table in the back corner and threaded through the patrons all trying to talk over one another.

"She made it!" Jenny said, passing me a glass of wine. "And look at those boots! Mama mia!"

I unzipped the hoodie and flashed them the shirt. They all erupted in a chorus of hoots. "Wow, Tina!" Corabelle said. "Have you come out of your shell or what?"

I slid into a chair next to Jenny. "No shells around here. I've just been a respectable working girl since I've been in San Diego," I said.

"Must be the doctor's influence bringing you back around." Jenny elbowed me. "You'll have to tell us what happened on the Pink Monster."

The other girls looked confused. Corabelle explained about the sofa. She introduced Melody and Kate. The conversation turned to the menu, and I was relieved not to have to give a blow-by-blow of Darion's visit. I wanted to keep him to myself for now, like a luscious secret.

"Hey, Cora," Jenny said, "tell us about the honeymoon. Where are you and Gavin going?"

Corabelle blushed a little, which I found amusing. Gavin was crazy all over her whenever they were together. Jenny and I had discovered them in a tangle on more than one occasion.

Both the girls were very open about their sex lives. I wasn't used to tight girlfriends. I had friends here and there. And we went to clubs and partied and hung out, but there was nobody I'd call particularly close. Some of them were weirded out over my refusal to be in a relationship. And eventually they'd all pair off, and having an extra single girl around wasn't fun.

But Corabelle and Jenny were fine with whatever. Jenny in particular was a man-hopper, so she and I saw eye to eye on that.

Work had been enough. And now there was Darion.

Corabelle described their plan to take a cruise down the coast into Mexico. "Turns out it isn't expensive at all to do that, and my parents are paying for it," she said.

Ever practical, that girl. "How's Manuelito?" I asked.

"He's good. I think his mom will end up working stateside soon, and it will get a lot easier."

Jenny swirled her wine glass. "I still don't see how you can stand having her around."

Corabelle shrugged. "Sometimes you have to accept what life hands you."

I wished I could confess my suspicion that Darion was Cynthia's father to the girls, but like our moments in Surgical Suite B, it seemed better to just keep it to myself.

"You girls are getting waaaay too serious," Jenny said. "We are here tonight to parTAY before Corabelle gets all tied up in the land of mortgages and minivans."

She lifted her wine glass. "Here's to all of us banging man-meat as hot as Gavin."

Everyone laughed as we clinked our glasses together.

After dinner, Jenny jumped up and announced she had a surprise. Her director boyfriend had sent a limo to fetch us to his party.

"We haven't paid the check," Corabelle said as Jenny pulled her from her chair.

"Already taken care of," Jenny said. "Let's GO!"

I downed my glass, wondering what sort of insanity Jenny was about to drag us into. I hadn't gotten any messages from Darion, but he said he'd be on shift until midnight. I figured any hospital would be pretty crazy on a Saturday night.

The sleek limo waited outside the restaurant. Jenny crawled in first, then the other girls. I wondered if I should skip this part. I felt distracted and anxious to see Darion. But Jenny reached through the open door and dragged me inside.

The seat wrapped around the perimeter. Everyone was cast blue from a twist of neon on the ceiling. Corabelle handed me a glass of champagne. "Here we go!" she said.

Jenny leaned in excitedly. "All right, everyone has to confess the craziest place they've had sex." She set the empty champagne bottle on the floor and spun it. It landed on Melody.

"I'm a virgin," Melody said

"What!" Jenny said. "WHAT?" She glanced around. "We've got to do something about that!"

"Jenny!" Corabelle said. "Some people wait for the right guy!"

Melody nodded. "Just hasn't happened."

Jenny looked outraged. "The right guy is the one with a functional penis!"

"It'll happen," Kate said.

"Don't tell me you're a virgin too!" Jenny said. "I'm going to schedule an intervention!"

"Not everyone likes sex with strangers like you do," Corabelle said.

"But it's good for your metabolism!" Jenny said. "It's the fountain of youth! The magic elixir! It's the meaning of life, the universe, and everything!"

"Nope, I'm quite sure that is 32," Melody said with a giggle.

"42," Corabelle corrected.

I sat back and sipped the bubbly. Jenny was really on a roll. "Give us yours, Jen," I said. "Craziest place for you."

Jenny stared up at the neon. "There are several contenders," she said. "Could be on a water tower."

"No way!" Melody said.

"I'm not afraid of heights," Jenny said. "But it might have been on the Pirates ride at Disneyland."

Corabelle covered her face with her hands. "Please tell me

there were no kids on the boat."

"We were alone," Jenny said, "and the ride broke down right in the middle of the cannonball fight." She spun a lock of pink hair around a finger. "Works great for covering up other noise."

We all cried out in a chorus of "Noooo."

"But," Jenny said, holding up her glass, "what might take the cake would be the time I got caught with a boy in the locker room in high school and we were sent to the principal."

"You did it in a locker room?" Kate asked.

"Oh, sure, lots of times," Jenny said. "But this time we finished up in the principal's office."

"You didn't!" Corabelle said.

"Oh, yes I did," Jenny said. "Didn't get caught either. High school boys, you know." She looked around the room. "Kinda quick on the draw."

"I did it at a funeral once," Kate said. "Nobody I knew. My boyfriend's second cousin."

Jenny cast a quick glance at Corabelle. She and I both knew Gavin had left Corabelle four years ago during their baby's funeral. We didn't want to bring down the evening.

"Now that's something," Jenny said. "You didn't worry about lightning striking?"

"Oh, no," Kate said. "Mainly we worried that someone would figure out we were the ones who broke the communion cup. We were in the sacristy and knocked it right off the rail."

Everyone laughed at that, including Corabelle. Jenny relaxed. "All right, Corabelle, cough it up. We know you and Gavin are like rabbits. I've seen both of you naked so many times I could probably claim alimony as a sister wife."

Corabelle sipped her glass innocently. "I don't know what you're talking about. I'm wearing white at my wedding!"

Another chorus of laughter.

"You're not getting out of this one," Jenny said. She took away Corabelle's champagne, prompting an unhappy "Hey!"

Jenny held it away. "You'll get your booze back when you tell us where you've most nefariously done the deed."

Corabelle's black hair was loose and wild, a chaos of curls. It was rare I saw her without it tied back in a ponytail. "Well, it might have been on the fifty-yard line at our high school stadium."

"Turf burns!" Jenny yelped, handing her back the glass. "Or it might have been…"

"In an emergency room after Gavin broke his arm."

"What!" Melody cried. "There had to be dozens of people right nearby."

"Indeed," Corabelle said. "Just on the other side of the curtain."

"Wait," Jenny said. Headlights coming through the window cut across her face. "Let me get this straight. He breaks his arm. He's in some pain. And so you two decide, oh, let's get busy?" She leaned toward Corabelle. "That's crazier than me."

Corabelle sipped her champagne. "We had too long of a wait to get discharged," she said demurely. "He was a little looped out on pain meds."

"You took advantage of him!" Jenny toasted her. "Now that's my kind of story!"

She turned to me. "So, Tina. You and the doctor are on the move. Surely you can trump Corabelle's ER story."

I'm not sure what came over me, if it was the booze or all the talk, or missing Darion, or not having breathed a word about him this whole time, but I found myself saying, "I just straddled the good doctor an hour ago on a gurney in Surgical Suite B."

The resounding squeals could have shattered glass.

36

DR. DARION

I was fairly certain Tina was really, really drunk.

By the time midnight came around and I made one last check on Cynthia and got out to my car in the garage, her texts were making very little sense. I scrolled back through to the last few.

Did you see that movie about the girl who does something crazy and then runs away and meets that boy?

That narrowed it down.

Then, *I better not take off this hoodie or I'll get cast in a bad movie.*

Had to laugh at that one. Then,

I think I just saw sombuddy famousish.

She had texted me the address of the party before she got too toasted. I sat in my car for a moment, trying to decide what to do. I was bone tired. A night at the hospital, then up late with Tina, and now another long day. I was off tomorrow, at least.

I backed out of the spot. Did she really want me to meet her friends already? Did I want that?

I plugged the address into my phone. Fifteen minutes away.

I should do it.

***

The place was actually a mansion, the gates thrown wide. I parked in the grass and walked across the circle drive past a fountain to the front door. I could hear a faint pounding of what sounded like a live band in the distance.

I was just pondering whether I should knock or go in, when a man in serving attire opened the door. "Welcome," he said.

I wasn't sure what to expect, something elegant with fancy food or crazy debauchery that could get me arrested. The house was stately and impressive, so it seemed the party could go either way. It also seemed fairly quiet, no hint of a crowd.

"I'll show you to the back," the man said.

We walked along an entryway, through a formal living room, and into an enormous sunroom looking out on the backyard. Noise began to penetrate as we crossed it, the thump thump of a bass guitar.

Colored lights on wire crisscrossed through the trees and arced over a pool. A few souls were actually swimming in it.

Naked.

I guess I had my answer.

A quick scan as we headed toward the door told me that Tina was not one of the people in the water. I didn't realize how tense I'd gotten as I looked. I really didn't know anything about her outside the hospital.

The door opened, and the music hit full force. Laughter, talking, glasses clinking.

I wasn't going to know a soul other than Tina. And if she was as impaired as she seemed, she could be throwing up in a bathroom somewhere by now. She was very small. It wouldn't take a lot. I scanned the crowd for drunk, high, and potentially about to be ill people, especially the ones in the pool, where they could drown. I noted flushed faces, anyone showing signs of distress.

Then I made myself stop the damn party triage.

You could take the doctor out of the hospital, but you couldn't take the hospital out of the doctor.

I wandered through the clumps of partygoers, trying to spot either Tina's blond head or a black-hoodie girl covered up. I paused to tap out a quick message to her: *I am here.*

A waiter passed by with a tray of champagne and stopped to offer me one. I almost waved him off, then decided to blend in. I could at least hold the glass. I took one.

Then I spotted her.

She was still wearing the hoodie, but it was unzipped, revealing the front of the strappy shirt. Still, the effect was definitely muted, nothing like seeing her bare shoulders and arms and the swaths of revealed flesh.

She patted her pocket for her phone, probably reacting to the buzz of my message. A beefy tricked-out twenty-something guy in a leather jacket was talking to her, looking down at her shirt. He had his hand on her shoulder. She swayed a little. She had definitely been drinking. I could see it.

These people were closer to her age, more her style. I was this uptight doctor with a horrid schedule and a seriously ill sister. She should be partying like this, not sneaking in random hours with me between my very pressing responsibilities.

I began to back away.

I bumped into a girl. I turned to apologize. Her wild black hair blew every direction.

"Sorry!" she said. "I couldn't zig away from your zag!"

"My fault," I said.

She squinted her eyes at me. "You seem familiar." Then she laughed. "Everyone does. Most of the people here are actors."

"Are you?"

She shook her head. "I got dragged here by a friend." She glanced at the pool, then looked away. "It's a little wilder than I could have ever imagined my bachelorette party being."

Bachelorette! "You know Tina, then?"

The girl stared me in the face again. "I knew it! You're the doctor!"

She grabbed my arm and started dragging me toward Tina, who was trying to subtly look at her phone while the guy, probably the star of some movie I didn't have time to see, kept chatting her up.

I dug my heels in. "I think she's busy with that other fellow."

That made the girl stop. Then she started laughing. I could tell when she got past the point of no return on it, because she held on to her belly and her hair started to fall in her face.

"Are you all right?" Maybe she'd had way too much to drink. I held on to her arm. "You don't want to hyperventilate." I leaned over her. "Try to relax."

The girl began gulping air.

Tina apparently had spotted me, as I heard her say, "Darion's still on duty."

I looked up. She was smiling at me, not seeming to notice that the movie stud had followed her.

"Did you get her started?" the guy asked. "Because it can be seriously hard to turn that giggle box off." He circled Tina to get to the other girl. "Sometimes I like to fuel the fire." He grasped the girl by the waist and began tickling her.

She burst into a renewed fit of laughter.

"That's Corabelle," Tina said. "And her groom-to-be, Gavin. They have these sort of epic tickle fights."

About three tons of weight rolled off my shoulders. Corabelle was the girl who had given Tina the apartment. And the guy talking to Tina was the fiancé.

Tina took my hand in hers, surprising me. "I'm glad you came." She leaned on my arm. Yes, a little tipsy, no doubt about it.

Another girl with bright pink hair came up behind her and leaned over her shoulder. "About time you got here," she said to me. "I thought about three of these hot actor guys were going to throw your girl over their shoulders and make off with her."

I squeezed Tina's hand. "Would this be Jenny of the Pink Monster?" I asked.

"The one and only," Tina said.

Jenny got between us, draping an arm around both of our necks. Her face got very serious. "I hear you got the first shot at popping the Pink Monster's furry cherry. It's all yours."

And just like that, she disappeared again.

"Did you get to meet the director?" I asked Tina. She had mentioned Jenny was secretive about him.

Corabelle was gasping now, trying to break the chain of giggles. "No! That's the crazy part." She sucked in a few more breaths of air, elbowing Gavin in the ribs when he threatened to start her up again. "We're here, at his PARTY, and he's nowhere."

"Really?" I glanced around. "That's pretty odd."

Tina said, "We're starting to think she and Frankie are actually the same person. They've got the same taste."

"This isn't his house, then?" I asked. Nothing was pink or tacky inside.

"Oh, no," Corabelle said. "It's the producer's." Her face was finally returning to a normal shade after her giggle marathon.

A huge splash in the pool made us all turn to look. A fully dressed man surfaced and dogpaddled his way to the side.

"That's a lot of naked chicks in the pool," Tina said.

I pulled her closer. "Thinking of getting in there?"

She lifted her gaze to mine. "What would you do to me in there, in front of everyone?"

And there went the crotch. And no lab coat. I pulled her in front of me and fitted her body against mine. "Use this, maybe?" I whispered in her ear.

"I think they're worse than we are," Corabelle said to Gavin.

"Dude, word to the wise?" Gavin pointed into the far corner of the massive yard. "Cabana house. Back fence. Unlocked. Lockable."

"Is that where you two disappeared to a while ago?" Tina asked.

Gavin yanked Corabelle up against him. "Maybe."

Tina glanced down at the full champagne glass in my hand. "You're not drinking that."

I passed it to her. She was having fun. I hadn't been around a lot of alcohol-impaired people in a while. I was fine with it as long as no one left. The car accidents were the worst in the ER. Then seeing those BAC levels and knowing it was all preventable.

I tried to shake it off. This was a party. Nobody had to go

anywhere, and that's what taxis were for.

"Something cooled your jets," Tina said. She whirled around to face me. "Maybe I need to get naked in the pool after all." Despite the night chill, she pulled the hoodie off and laid it over her arm. I remembered how easy it was to peel that shirt away from what I wanted. Her friends seemed easygoing, so I leaned down and kissed her, and not gently either. Hard and long, until she pressed her body up against mine.

When I released her, Gavin and Corabelle had moved over to a long table filled with food.

"Get drunk with me," Tina said. She stopped a waiter, downed the champagne I gave her, and set the glass on his tray. Then she took two more. "You need to get a little crazy for once."

"I think we might have done that last night," I said.

"Mmmm," she said, passing me a glass. "But now we're going to get crazy here." She took my hand and led me through the party to the corner Gavin had told us about.

Another splash meant someone else had joined the group in the pool. The band finished out a number, and the singer said into the microphone, "Either that water is heated, or you're all crazy drunk."

"It's heated," Tina said to me. "Jenny warned us that this party would get a little wild."

"And yet you stayed."

"Corabelle's two nervous friends left half an hour ago. We stayed around, hoping to catch this mysterious director."

"Gavin crashed the bachelorette?"

"We brought him to get us all home. Corabelle's more fun when he's around. She feels safe."

We arrived at a line of small outbuildings. "What about you?" I asked. "Do you feel the need to be safe?"

Tina whirled around. "I figured out a long time ago that nothing's safe." She grabbed the front of my shirt and pulled me toward one of the cabanas. "And that goes double for men like you, dear doctor Darion. You look safe, but oh, you are not."

She opened the door to the building. The inside was dark and warm, lightly illuminated by a small space heater.

"Nice," she said. "You might want to lock the door."

I did so. My heart was revving up. I knew what she was up to, but I didn't have a clue what she'd do next.

A narrow bench on one wall held a few towels. In the center of the cabana was a pair of outdoor chairs with high backs. She drained her champagne and pointed to mine. "Bottom's up, doctor."

I did as I was told. She took the glass and set them both on the table between the chairs.

"When I met you earlier in Surgical Suite B, did you have anything particular you didn't get to do?"

She made me so crazy. My blood was pumping now. Heart rate 120, easy. "Maybe," I said.

"So, why don't you do it now?" she asked. "And don't be nice about it."

I yanked her against me, and seared my lips into hers. She arched against my body. I'd spent a lot of time wondering about her, and what she liked. I had a good idea now. But now she wanted something rougher.

I could do that.

I yanked the shirt over her head. The pale light from the space heater exposed the pink lines the straps left on her body. I bent down, capturing a breast in my mouth while squeezing the other with my hand.

She moaned and clutched at my shoulders. "Yes, baby," she said.

My free hand went beneath the skirt, a little surprised to find panties this time. Screw that. I yanked at the elastic and snapped the thin band in two.

"Well, then," she said. "Don't let anything get in your way."

My hand went up inside her, showing no mercy. She gasped, then writhed against me, and I worked every inch of her, so slippery. God. But as soon as she started to tighten against me, I pulled away.

"Shit, Darion," she said. "You're killing me."

I walked her over to the wall and turned her away from me. I reached around and got to her from that angle. She pressed against me, gyrating, her hands bracing her.

"Bend over," I said in her ear.

"Yes," she said.

I felt like I'd lost my head. I was driven by this need of her, how she prodded me. I yanked my belt open and pushed my pants and boxers out of the way. The khakis had hit the floor when I remembered the condom and dragged one out of my wallet.

The boots made her taller, and as I came back up from locating the package, I could see up her skirt. Instead of going straight for the endgame, I twisted beneath her, spreading her feet farther apart and pressing my mouth between her legs.

"Oh my God," she said, and shifted against me, pressing down.

She was so damn wet. I licked between the folds, then reached to open her wide. Now there was no stopping her, and she pulsed against my mouth, crying out, her muscles quivering as the orgasm crashed through her.

Jesus, she was hot. I felt like this part of my life had just opened up and sucked me in, this whole other dimension I had forgotten existed.

"I can't get pregnant," she said. "I do both the shot and IUD. I'm clean."

I tossed the condom across the room. "Me too."

"Dump it in me," she said. "I want that."

I don't think I'd had an erection that hard in my life. I stood up and got behind her. She was so ready. I eased inside her like sliding into a hot bath, enveloping and warm.

"You can't hurt me," she said.

I held on to her hips. I didn't think I'd ever wanted to plow into someone as badly as I wanted this. She pushed back against me, and I just unleashed. The faster I pushed it, the more she cried out with yes, yes, more, harder.

I grabbed her hair and held it fast, and then I could tell she was going to come again. God, this was something unbelievable, addicting. I reached for her, circling that hot nub, and now she was crying out, pushing against me, and I just let it go, emptying into her. It was such a different feeling, and I had to think if I'd ever done it like this before, skin to skin. If so, I didn't remember it.

She was sucking in air, gulping, and I could sense something had changed. She was emotional, touched by something. I pulled out of her and turned her around, holding her tight. It was like that night on the beach, when she'd gotten defensive and pushed me away. I needed to figure out a way to prevent that this time.

I backed up and sat in one of the chairs, dragging her onto my lap. She curled up on me, breathing fast, making little sounds of distress.

"Hey, hey, I'm here. I've got you." I wrapped her up in my arms, holding on tight. I feared the worst, that she'd shove at me and stomp out, no shirt and all. That one of these times she'd decide enough is enough and just quit.

I held on to her, smoothing her hair. She wasn't crying, just making these noises, and breathing. Post-traumatic stress, maybe? I had to stop diagnosing her. Just be.

The chair swiveled, so I rocked us back and forth until she began to quiet down. I tried to stay relaxed. I wanted to see her through this to the end. She would not push me away this time.

Gradually her breathing slowed. After a while I realized her respiration was even, so I dared to look down. Her hair was everywhere, and her eyes closed. The alcohol, I thought. It had done its job. She was asleep.

I shifted a little so that we rested together more comfortably. The party was still loud outside. This was just about the craziest thing I'd ever done, sex with a girl I had known only a little while at a stranger's house.

But Tina was nothing like anyone I'd ever known. A set of total opposites. Tough. Bitter. Unorthodox. Sexy. God, the way she'd wanted it so rough.

But then also vulnerable, sensitive, gentle.

I was going to fall so damn hard for this girl.

37

TINA

I hadn't counted on a hangover to beat all hangovers when I volunteered to babysit.

Gavin turned from the mirror. "Tina, I have to say it. You look terrible."

Unlike me, he looked pretty stunning in a black tux, even if the pants trailed over his white socks.

"Thanks, mister. You look awesome."

Manuelito sat in my lap, licking a lollipop. Corabelle was working today, and Gavin had his three-year-old son. I told them I could tag along to help out while Gavin got fitted for the wedding. I hadn't thought about how it would be the morning after the bachelorette and I might not have my head on straight.

"Dude, you're rockin' that!" Gavin's friend Mario came out of his dressing room. "But not as good as me!"

Mario twirled in his tux. He was the best man. His dark skin offset the black even better than Gavin's. Too bad he couldn't last two dates with a girl. I hadn't quite pegged the problem yet.

"Tia Tina?" Manuelito showed me his lollipop. He grabbed his tongue. "Hurt."

I took the sucker from him. A tiny piece of the wrapper was still on it, creating a little bump in the surface. "Wrapper," I said. "Let's just get a new one." Concentrating on trying to pry a tiny piece of paper from a half-eaten sucker was way too much for my pounding head.

I pulled a new one from my bag, unwrapped it carefully, and handed it to the boy. Normally we would color or build Legos. But today I could barely hold myself upright.

"You need to rehydrate," Mario said, laughing. "I should have gone to that party. Especially in this." He spun around in front of the mirror.

"Those actresses would have spit you out like three-day-old gum," Gavin said.

"Nah," Mario said. "I'd be on the cover of some salty tabloid." He ran his hand through the air with each word of his headline: "Rich movie star elopes with hot garage mechanic."

I stifled a laugh. "Mario, you do dream big."

Gavin punched him in the arm. "You find a date for the wedding yet?"

"Someone will come along," Mario said.

The seamstress, an energetic girl who couldn't be much over twenty, came in. "Anyone ready for a hem?" she asked. Her sleek blond hair was tied up in a bun.

"I'm ready for anything with you," Mario said.

And that's when I got it. Too eager. Too pushy. Only a narrow swath of girls would go for that, and they weren't interested in long-term stuff. One-and-dones.

The gospel I had once preached. Look at me now. Four times

with the doctor in 24 hours.

I closed my eyes. I was way over the top on this.

Manuelito tapped my leg. "Tia Tina?"

"Yes, sweetie?"

"Play game?"

"Sure." I turned him around on my lap. "I Spy? Practice your words?"

He nodded. Manuelito had grown up in a bilingual household, but we liked to work on his vocabulary. "You go," he said.

"Okay. I spy…" I looked around. I usually kept it easy. "Something tall."

"Papa Gavin?"

"Nope."

He looked around. He saw the mannequin but probably had no way to describe it, so instead he said, "*¿Puerta?*"

"Si, Manuel," I said. "But it's a door."

"Door," he said.

"You know that word," I said, tickling his belly. "Silly boy."

He laughed his loud baby-boy laugh. I tried not to think about how he was only a little over a year younger than Peanut would have been. I just held him close, dodging the sticky lollipop, and was glad that he was such a sweet kid since Corabelle had to manage him in her life.

Manuel's mother lived in Mexico. She had an odd relationship with Gavin, and never even told him about his son until this year. It had been a rough road for Corabelle to learn about it, even if they had been split up all that time.

Gavin's vasectomy meant his ability to have kids with Corabelle was a big question, if a reversal ever worked. Their situation was tough, but they'd found a sense of harmony with it that I envied. And now they were getting married.

"Book?" Manuel asked. I guessed we were done with I Spy already.

The seamstress pinned both the boys' pants and sent them back to their dressing rooms to change. My head was still pounding, but I pulled a book out of the bag Gavin brought and read it to Manuel. *One Fish, Two Fish, Red Fish, Blue Fish.*

By the time we got through it twice, the boys had come back out. Mario took off, but Gavin sat in the chair next to me. "Thanks for watching him," he said.

"Not a problem," I said. "He's easy."

Manuel hopped off my lap to jump up on his father. Gavin swung him up in the air and brought him back down to rest on his knee.

I rubbed my temples. I needed to take something.

"What's the deal with that doctor? Corabelle didn't want to leave the party without you, but you totally disappeared."

"We spent the night in that cabana you told us about." I didn't really want to say anything more. Half my hangover was emotional. I totally fell apart after that crazy encounter with Darion. He'd been unlike anybody I'd ever been with. What I asked for, I got. In spades.

I couldn't figure out which was the bigger mistake. Doing the one-and-done all these years. Or stopping now. My life was in upheaval. I couldn't stay snarky and distant.

As if they knew I was doing something ill advised, my wrists began to itch beneath the sleeves of my sweatshirt. I didn't really need the reminder. God, I told him to bareback, even. I hadn't lied about the doubled-up birth control, but still. Such a couples thing to do. We were strangers.

"He's getting to you," Gavin said.

"Maybe a little."

"You don't like that."

"I wasn't expecting to get involved with anyone."

Gavin locked his hands behind his head. Manuel dug another book from the bag and flipped through the pages.

"He seems uneasy. Like he's got a lot on his mind," Gavin said.

I shrugged. "He's a doctor. He'd just come off a long shift."

"Is everything on the up-and-up with him?"

"What do you mean?"

Gavin adjusted Manuel on his lap. The boy leaned back against Gavin's chest, the sucker stick hanging out of his mouth, and flipped through *Pat the Bunny*.

"I recognized that look he had. That distraction. I just want to make sure you aren't setting yourself up."

I pressed my fingers against my temples. "I think he's got some stuff he isn't telling me," I said. "Probably everybody does."

"You tell him about your history?" Gavin asked.

"He knows about Peanut," I said.

"But not the rest?"

I tugged on my sleeves. I didn't go around confessing about my scars. Although all Darion had to do was Google my name to see my old suicide talks. He probably had. He was probably waiting for me to tell him.

Probably wondering why I wouldn't.

Maybe hesitating to tell me about Cynthia, waiting until I told him about my past.

The more I thought about this, the more I knew it was true. I jumped from my chair. "Thanks, Gavin," I said. "I know what I need to do now."

He looked taken aback. "Not sure what I did, but no problem."

I kissed Manuel on the head. "See you soon, little man."

The boy didn't even look up from his book.

Time to call the doctor.

38

DR. DARION

Things were blowing up in my face.

Angela was up at the hospital, dealing with some weekend social worker who was insisting on something more substantial than an illegible signature on the paperwork for the clinical trial of the new drug.

This could not be happening now. Cynthia was doing so great. Despite the spiking fevers that first day, she hadn't been sick at all, and her blast levels were zero. No circulating cells. It was the best drug I'd seen, ideal for her situation. We were supposed to go back for another round in five days. I could not let anything get in the way.

I might have to confess. I knew I should have gotten that medical power of attorney squared away.

If only my father wasn't such an idiot, this wouldn't be an issue. I knew my mother hadn't been with anyone else. I was in my early twenties when it all went down. I was perfectly aware of her situation.

And if he really thought about it, he knew it too. But he'd gone off half-cocked when he finally came home from Oxford after a freaking thirteen-year absence.

And then that stupid paternity test. The worst part about it was that the same blood test reported that Cynthia didn't belong to my mother. And THAT was clearly ludicrous. The mutated gene sequence had clearly caused the test results to fail.

It was a known medical fact that it could happen. Nobody knew that better than my father.

I wanted to punch him. Daily. Until he got past his stupid hatred of all the artists and creative types that had nurtured Mom in ways he never could.

I riffled through the files in my study at home, pulling copies of the reports. I stuffed everything in a folder and headed to the hospital.

When I got to the room, Cynthia looked much better. She pushed her IV around the room, skating on her fuzzy socks. She must have worn the nonskid nubbies right off.

"Dary!" she cried. "Look what I can do!" She spun in a circle with the IV pole on its casters.

"It's like she's on speed," Angela said. "Been running around like she's never been sick a day in her life."

"I'll have them run her blood counts," I said. "She might not need the platelets anymore. Has she eaten?"

"Some. A grilled cheese. Ice cream. She does have mouth sores."

"I'd expect that."

"They don't hurt," Cynthia said. "Not like last time."

"Just nothing spicy," I said.

"We're on it," Angela said.

I leaned against the wall, watching Cynthia twirl around the room as though the IV stand was her dance partner. "If her ANC is up, she can walk the halls, go in the courtyard," I said.

Angela nodded. "She'll like that."

"Is Tina here today?" Cynthia asked.

"It's Sunday," I said. "She's at home."

"Like you should be," Angela said. "They're going to wonder why you're here."

I held up the folder. "But the family of one of my patients felt threatened that they were going to lose access to the trial."

"They can't do that now that we've started," Angela said. "It would be unethical. I just wanted you to know they were still questioning it."

"I'm not going to risk it. We have to jump through all sorts of hoops to get those chemo bags."

"What are you going to do?"

Cynthia stopped buzzing around the room.

We shouldn't be discussing this in front of her. "I'll just make sure it's taken care of."

"That lady is already gone."

"I'll go down there tomorrow, then. I wanted to check in anyway." I tucked the folder back under my arm. "Should I bring you something special for lunch tomorrow?" I asked Cynthia.

"A cheeseburger!" she said. "A real one!"

"Done," I said.

"When do I get to go home?" she asked.

"I'm not sure, Cyn. That fever was pretty bad, so they'll want you here to do the treatments just in case."

"I don't even remember it," she said.

I wasn't surprised. She'd been completely delirious by the time we started getting her temperature down. Among scary things, it hadn't been the worst. But it was up there.

My phone buzzed, so I checked it. Tina, asking if I would come over.

I'd dropped her off at home in the wee hours, after we'd slept a while in the cabana house. The party was actually over when we emerged, the tables cleared off, the pool empty. There were still quite a lot of cars parked haphazardly out front, but the owners must have all been tucked away in the wings of the house, as the living room had been empty as we passed through.

I tried to convince Tina to drink water and take aspirin to head off a hangover, but she'd crashed as soon as I got her in her apartment. I had gone home and slept a few hours myself before getting the first text from Angela.

"I'm going to head out," I said. "Let me know if anything else happens."

Cynthia skated over to me and wrapped her arms around my waist. "I can't wait to go home," she said.

"Me too," I told her. I knew the better she felt, the more she would start to fight having to stay. Maybe if the second treatment went smoother, we could check her out in between.

I tapped off a note to Tina as I headed out of the hospital.

Things had certainly been intense. That first night, followed by the surgical suite — I felt my blood surge just thinking about it. Then last night.

We probably needed a little bit of normal. Maybe we could have a quiet dinner somewhere.

A cold front was blowing in. The temperature dropped

noticeably in the time I drove from the hospital to her apartment. The wind howled as I took the path up to Tina's door.

She must have been watching for me, as she opened it before I could knock. I hadn't seen her quite like this before, in jeans and a loose sweatshirt, her hair pulled back in little clips.

We sat on the Pink Monster, and she leaned into me. "Have you looked me up online?" she asked.

This was unexpected. "Hadn't thought to. Is there a criminal record I should know about?" I tweaked her nose.

"None of the bodies have ever been found," she said. Her fingers traced the pattern of my sweater across my belly.

"If I ever need to dispose of someone, I'll know who to call."

She glanced up at me. Without mascara, her lashes were pale and delicate. "I Googled you as soon as I knew your name."

"Mine's a boring story," I said, grateful, as I had been for years now, that my mother's obituary had never been public, linking both Cynthia and me as her surviving children. Dad hadn't been listed at all.

"It was, actually," Tina said. "You're squeaky clean and doctorated."

"I take it you're not?" I felt a trickle of apprehension. What was she about to tell me?

She hesitated, plucking at her sleeves. "I do these talks, or I used to," she said. "When I was in college. It was how I made money. It's what got me the job at the hospital, actually."

"What kind of talks?"

She paused. When she finally spoke again, her voice wavered. "About suicide."

My chest tightened. "Is it something you're familiar with?

Someone in your family?"

Tina pushed up the sleeves of her sweatshirt, revealing pale scars from wrist to mid-forearm. Years of experience helped me hold in any reaction to them. I reached out and encircled her slender wrist with my fingers. "How long ago?"

"Same time as everything else. When Peanut died."

"Was it postpartum depression?"

She laid her arm on her lap. I kept my hold on her. "I don't think so. I didn't even do it with the thought of dying. Just to be scarred. I felt like somehow I needed to be permanently marked by what happened."

I ran my thumb along the lines. "You didn't realize how dangerous it was to do?"

"I kinda knew. It just didn't really hit home until I'd already done it."

"Razors?"

"Nice sharp ones. Part of my art tool chest."

"You got help after?"

Tina snorted. "More than I wanted. I thought I'd never get free of the social workers." She snorted again. "And now I'm going to be one. That's a lark."

She pulled her sleeves down, forcing me to let go. "Is it too freaky for you?"

I wrapped my arms around her and tucked her in a little closer. "Not too freaky." Truth be told, this didn't surprise me at all. The signs had all been there from her history. I wished she hadn't had to go through it, though.

She relaxed her head on my shoulder. "I have five people who attempted suicide coming to my art class. Four teens and an older man. So much hurt in the world."

I definitely agreed on that.

She got quiet, as if she was waiting for me to say something else.

"It's part of who you are, Tina. It's all right."

But this didn't get her to relax.

"Is there anything you want to tell me?" she asked.

I tensed a little. Was that what this was about? A secret for a secret?

Had Cynthia spilled something?

I had to go face the whole mess tomorrow to make sure she got her chemotherapy. I couldn't jeopardize it right now.

Tina began to pull away. Damn it. I needed to do something. Maybe I was wrong. Maybe she just expected me to say something else about her history.

"I'm not spooked by it," I said.

She stood up. "I'm not normally the sort of girl who dates anybody long term," she said. "I don't even know how to do this."

I got up too. "There isn't any one way. I think we're doing fine." I tried to squeeze her shoulders, but she shrugged me off.

"You don't think there is anything in your history I should know? A marriage? Anything?" She wouldn't look at me.

"I've never been married, Tina. Did the Google search maybe point you in the wrong direction? Or is someone telling you something about me?"

"No. No one knows anything about you."

"You've asked?" I tried to keep my voice even.

She whirled around at that. "Not really. Everyone thinks you're this obstinate, coldhearted machine."

"I can't help the impression people get of me."

"Of course you can!"

"Tina, what do you want me to be?"

She walked toward the kitchen. "I don't know! Honest with me, maybe?"

"What do you want to know?"

She leaned against the wall, facing away. I had no idea how to manage her moods. She was so hard to figure out.

"You don't have a daughter?" she finally asked, quietly.

Where would she get that idea? "No, I do not have any children," I said. "I've never been married."

"I see," she said.

I stood in her living room, not sure what else to say. I knew it was probably time to explain about my sister, but she seemed more worried about my marital status. I had no idea where that was coming from. As upset as she was acting, bringing up Cynthia seemed like a bad idea.

"I'm still tired and hungover," she said. "Can we just call it a day?"

"I was hoping to take you to dinner. Do something simple."

She hugged herself, still not looking my way. "Maybe tomorrow."

"I have a twelve-hour —"

"Right," she said. "That's fine."

I walked toward her, but she held up her hand. "Tomorrow," she said. "That'll be better."

I wasn't sure what else to do, so I just agreed with her. "Okay," I said. "Tomorrow."

But I had a feeling that this was the wrong answer.

39

TINA

I couldn't think about anything but Darion, Darion, Darion during all my art therapy sessions the next day. Had he straight out lied about Cynthia? I didn't think so.

But he wouldn't tell me anything either.

This wasn't good. He had been completely unmoved by my confession.

He wasn't the right guy.

The aide wheeled Albert in, and my excitement over getting to see him was immediately squashed by his haggard appearance.

He slumped in his chair, holding tight to the arms as though if he let go he would simply fall out.

"I didn't want to bring him," the aide said, "but he insisted."

"Pshaw," Albert said. "You guys are always making me out to be sicker than I am." His eyes sparkled as they always did when he winked at me. "If I get well, who will they flirt with?"

The aide wrote a number on a piece of art paper. "Page me directly if you need me," she said.

When she was gone, I said, "You were doing so well on

Friday."

"Easy come, easy go," Albert said. "The whole thing is one step forward, two steps back. Tricky when you've got one foot in the grave."

He held up his hands, and the shaking was so pronounced that even holding a brush was probably impossible, much less using it.

I tried to think of something we could do, but Albert was shaking his head. "Stop worrying about it. Let's work on yours."

"And here I thought you just came down to escape all the unwanted attention of the nurses."

He laughed weakly. "You have me all figured out."

I turned my canvas around to show him the colors I'd done so far.

"Very nice," he said.

"I'm not sure how realistic I want to make the mother and son," I said.

"Your hand will decide," he said. "Have you done enough work over the years to find your style?"

"I don't think so," I said. "I've been kind of all over the place."

He waved at the painting. "Then you'll do this image many times in your life before you get it right. Consider it a trial run. Don't get too attached to this one effort."

I laid the canvas flat on the table. No one had said anything like that to me in art school.

A movement in the hall window caught my eye. Darion walked by, slowly, looking in. It wasn't the first time I'd caught him doing it.

Albert noticed and turned. "An admirer?" he asked.

"Something like that."

"Ah, a love affair."

I waved at Darion and turned to face Albert. "What gives you that impression?"

"You changed when you saw him. Even the air around you was different. Suffused with this magnetic charge."

I folded up the easel. "Time to reverse my polarity, then."

"Trouble in paradise?"

"I don't think there ever was any paradise." Not true, I thought. Most of it had been amazing. But it was the same as the one-and-dones, only it had just lasted a little longer this time. Encounters. Nothing more.

Probably for the best.

"You should draw him," Albert said. "I found I could unknot most of my women problems by putting their image on paper." He drew a face in the air. "Always, the answer was right in front of me."

That was an interesting idea. Draw Darion.

Then add horns and a tail and cast him into hell.

40

DR. DARION

That hadn't gone well. I had to stop walking by Tina's room. She seemed downright annoyed with seeing me.

I stopped by the nurses' desk to pull up the day's labs.

And felt like dancing.

Cynthia's bloodwork was spectacular. ANC at 1000! We hadn't seen that in weeks. If it weren't for the clinical trial protocol, I would have been sending her home for a few days.

I ordered a bone marrow aspiration, certain she wouldn't be hypocellular. If we were very very lucky, this new drug was the thing we were looking for. Something to knock this cancer into remission so Cynthia could go back to the business of being an eight-year-old girl.

I began to think ahead. I could enroll her in school instead of using tutors, which I hadn't even bothered with since we'd been here. She had been too sick.

But now, I felt positively giddy.

My hospital phone buzzed. Odd. It wasn't a patient code. Duffrey himself wanted to see me in the admin offices.

I glanced through my schedule. I might as well do it now. I wouldn't have another free moment for hours. I couldn't imagine what he wanted me for.

Unless it was Tina. Or Cynthia.

Either choice was bad.

I girded myself as I wound through the maze of halls to Duffrey's office. I didn't much care what happened to me. But Cynthia. And Tina. Both were vulnerable.

Duffrey's dour secretary waved me on by as I approached. I didn't knock on the door, just pushed through.

Duffrey was perched on the corner of his desk, talking on the phone. He motioned for me to sit down.

"Must run, love," he said. "Meeting. Love you." He set the phone down. "Mrs. Duffrey number three," he said. "Trying not to piss this one off."

I was still standing. I didn't particularly care to sit for whatever was about to transpire.

Duffrey walked around his desk and picked up a file. "Do you have any idea why you're here?"

"I can think of twenty reasons."

Duffrey chuckled. "Good." He held the folder up. "Pretty good snow job you did on this."

I glanced at it. The colored labels at the top didn't match St. Anthony's system, which was mostly electronic anyway. This was an old file from somewhere else.

"Birth records," Duffrey said. "Of one of your patients, a girl named Cynthia Miller."

I kept my face carefully neutral. This was it.

"I know her. Pediatric leukemia, tough case, responding well to the NCI trial. We're working with M. D. Anderson on it."

He waved away my summary. "I noticed something in her file."

My heart hammered, but I didn't react. "What's that?"

"A paternity test."

"She has no father of record."

"But the man who took the test is your father."

Where the hell had he found that out? Time to shut up and listen.

"When I saw that, I looked up the mother. Sandy Miller, mother of Cynthia Miller and Darion Marks." He glanced up at me. "I'm sorry for your loss."

So, it was out, then. "She was a spectacular lady."

"And now you've brought your sister to my hospital for a clinical trial."

Time to play it straight. "I have."

"And you're violating our rules on the treatment of immediate family."

"She's got no one to look after her."

"And you for damn sure aren't going to be now."

My jaw clenched. "My care of her has been perfectly in order."

"And it's been transferred to Clements. All your current patients will be."

"What?"

"You'll be taking a four-week leave of absence. We'll convene again at the end of it."

"What about her drug trial?"

"She'll remain on it. No reason to discharge her over this. She's our patient. It's you with the problem. You violated our protocols from the beginning, covered up your relationship, altered records."

"Nobody was harmed in it," I said.

"Which is why this is just a leave of absence. I expect you to obey visiting hours."

"Parents of pediatric patients are allowed to visit anytime."

"Don't make me call in CPS to reassign her guardianship."

"You wouldn't dare."

"Be a normal parent," he said. "Do normal parent things."

Duffrey hesitated before he said the next thing, and I wondered if the hammer was coming down about Tina too.

"What's the deal with your father?" he asked. "He took a paternity test with his own wife's child."

"You'd best stay out of that one," I said.

Duffrey held up his hands. "Works for me. I don't tangle with the personal lives of men on the medical board."

"He won't appreciate my leave of absence."

"You going over my head on this? With Dad?" His voice was a challenge.

Of course I wouldn't. I would do everything I could to make sure my father didn't even know. But Duffrey could sweat it out for all I cared.

I turned on my heel and headed for the door.

The office doors were a blur as I headed through the halls. Damn it to hell. I'd only been at this godforsaken place for two months. A four-week leave! At least I hadn't been escorted off the premises like Tina.

Tina. I wanted her with a fierceness I had no intention of denying.

I tore through the corridors. She would see me. I would make her.

41

TINA

Darion looked like he was ready to blow his stack when he stormed into my room. I was cleaning markers with antibacterial wipes. This was my longest break in the day, lunch and a prep period.

"Come with me." He took my arm and pulled me to standing.

I resisted, jerking free of him. "What has gotten into you?"

"I just tanked my career. Will you come with me already?" He stalked to the door, then turned to see if I was coming.

I refused to follow. "What are you talking about?"

"I'm out. Four-week leave of absence." He yanked the door open. "Will you come?"

I glanced around. Everything was mostly ready for my next session. "I only have an hour."

"That's enough for me."

I followed him down the hall. He was walking a hundred miles an hour, shucking his lab coat as he went.

"You going to tell me what's going on?"

"Not here."

We took the elevator down. Darion stood angry and silent,

glowering at the numbers as if he could make them move faster.

I relented a little and reached for his hand, squeezing it. He held on to it, and even when the doors opened, didn't let go. This surprised me, but I didn't pull away.

We headed toward the exit, and I realized nobody cared about us. We were just two people in regular clothes heading for the parking garage, like any visitors.

When we got in his car, he didn't start it right away. He turned to me, and pulled me in close, hanging on to me across the console.

I had a million questions, but I let them go for the moment. His grip on the back of my neck was intense. He definitely was not the stoic guy I was used to seeing in the halls.

"Did you just want to talk here?" I asked.

He pulled back. "No, we'll go somewhere." He started the car.

"You want lunch?" I asked.

"Are you hungry?"

"Not particularly."

He backed out of the spot and we left the garage, flying down the side street. After a couple turns, I knew where he was headed.

The cliff.

Torrey Pines was different in broad daylight than it had been just before sunset. The scrubby bald landscape seemed bleak. A cold front had blown in the day before, so it was considerably colder. I should have grabbed a jacket.

We picked our way along the path to the cliff, Darion leading. The winter day was bright and clear. When we reached the edge, the Pacific spread out in blinding white blue, the waves sparkling like they were newly sprinkled with pixie dust.

It was still magical to me. I looked down at the narrow strip of beach that edged the water, taking in more details for my painting. In the light of day, the drop seemed more treacherous. You could see every outcropping, every sharp rock.

Darion plunked down, sitting with his legs dangling over the edge like he was considering a jump. That seemed too close to me, as the dirt was crumbly on the rocks. I pictured Albert's painting of this scene, the ground dropping away below the oblivious circus.

But I sat next to him anyway. The danger of it made my belly buzz. We were completely alone. Between it being Monday and the frigid wind, no one was in the park. Nobody walked the beach below either.

We were the only people as far as either of us could see in any direction.

Darion stared out at the water for a while. I waited for him to talk. Maybe now he would say all the things I'd asked about yesterday. Maybe it was tied to what happened today.

"Cynthia is my sister," he said finally.

Suddenly everything made sense. Her mom was his mom. He was taking care of her now that she was gone. And he couldn't lose her too. God. How difficult.

I moved closer and laid my head on his shoulder. "Is she doing okay?"

"Fantastic, actually. Everything is going perfectly with the new drug."

"But —"

"I lied to the hospital. Scrubbed any family references from her records before they were transferred here."

"Why?" I shivered, and he drew me against his body, blocking the wind.

"It has to do with my mother. How she was cared for. And the mistakes the last hospital made with Cynthia. She lost a kidney because of them."

God, no wonder he lied. "You wanted to be in control."

"I changed my whole career path, my whole life, so that I could."

I let my hands wander along the path of his ribs, although I couldn't feel them for the muscle. "And now it was all for nothing."

"Maybe not. If this drug works, and it looks like it is, I can discharge her. Well, Clements can."

"And try it all again somewhere else?"

He sighed. "No. Hopefully have a normal life."

"They didn't fire you, though, right?"

"No. Just put me on leave. But that's a big deal."

"It's four weeks to spend with your sister. No long shifts. No work stress. That's a win."

He lifted my face up to his. "How do you do that? Make everything seem like it was supposed to happen exactly as it did?"

I choked out a short laugh. "Don't be calling me Little Miss Sunshine. I'm all about the doom and gloom. It's just obvious this time. Cynthia is better. You got busted. Now you can have a normal life for a bit."

He pulled me onto his lap. This had become a familiar place.

"I'm sorry I didn't tell you," he said. "I should have."

Yes, he should have, I thought. But I said, "I'm just the girl you were banging in Surgical Suite B."

"You're the only thing I've looked forward to for a long time."

He hand moved along the sweater, feeling the curves of my body. I wasn't cold anymore.

"I should have had dinner with you yesterday," I said. "We wasted a day."

"And a night," he added.

His mouth came down to reach mine, just a whisper of a kiss.

I responded, but upped the ante, my tongue on his lips. He deepened the kiss, and now we were crazy, falling into it.

I shifted over on him, and bits of dirt fell off the end of the cliff to the beach below.

"Maybe we should move back a little," I said.

But he didn't let me, lifting me so that I straddled him like I had on the beach. He pulled the skirt out from between us so that it settled around our bodies like a cloud.

His hands went beneath the sweater. When he reached my breasts, he groaned against my mouth. "Your lack of bras drives me insane."

His thumbs on the nipples sent sparks flying through me. Outdoors. Public park. Broad daylight.

He was my kind of boy.

Darion reached beneath the skirt and tugged on my panties. "Should I just tear them off again?" he asked.

"I'm too poor to keep buying underwear," I said. "And you're temporarily unemployed."

He fingered the slender strap. "I think lingerie is the perfect use of my trust fund," he said. And with that, he snapped the waistband.

Before I could even chastise him for ruining another pair, his fingers were inside me, and my mind was erased. My forehead dropped to his shoulder. God, he had this figured out.

His breath puffed warm against my ear. "I didn't bring a

condom," he said.

I reached for his belt buckle. "I think we dispensed with those in that cabana."

He sucked in when the cold air hit his newly exposed skin, but I didn't leave him that way for long. I slid over him, reveling in the feel of each inch entering my body.

The wind blew his hair around, but mine was neatly tied in pigtails. His hands moved to my hips and lifted me up and down.

I was lost. Occasional pebbles rolled off the cliff and fell to the rocks below. The sky was bright white, and between breaths I could hear the waves crashing against the shore.

I'd never done anything quite like this. But the doctor was already familiar, and he knew me too. When I started to tighten around him, he increased the pace, moving me over him. I clutched his shoulders, thighs working, driving me up and down. There was no stopping this, and I cried out against his neck, the orgasm blasting through me like a tidal wave.

He gripped me tightly around the hips and held me steady as he pulsed up into me, hot and wet.

I started giggling immediately.

He started laughing too, even as he said, "You can give a guy a complex this way."

"Oh…it's not…that," I said, gasping. "I'm just trying to picture myself later, no panties, trying to manage art therapy, after…this…stickiness."

"Oh," he said. "Right. I think I have some duct tape in the trunk."

I smacked his shoulder. "You're going to make me duct-tape panties?"

"No! I mean to fix the strap I broke."

"So, panties *mended* with duct tape."

"You'd rather leak on the floor?"

I pressed my cheek into his. "Oh my God, we somehow went from new lovers to crazy old couple in four days."

He gathered his arms around me and held me close. "Perfect. I want to be a crazy old couple with you."

"With duct-tape panties."

"Exactly."

And that was how I ended up teaching the rest of the day with silver duct tape up my skirt.

42

DR. DARION

I sat in the parking garage a solid half-hour after Tina went back into the hospital, wondering what to say to Cynthia. I needed to do it sooner rather than later, before Clements came in and introduced himself as her new doctor.

My phone beeped. A message from Angela.

Who is this new doctor? Where are you?

Too late.

Just go with it. I'll explain later. Buzz me when he's gone.

I'd let them talk for a moment, then I'd go up as a random visitor. I had no idea who knew what had happened. Clements, obviously. Whatever nurse was on shift with Cynthia. The charge nurse, surely.

My patient load was too big to dump on Clements, no matter what Duffrey said. It would be split between other oncologists. I thought of Harriet. I wouldn't be there when she got discharged from ICU. Hell, I wouldn't even be able to log in to check on her.

Cars passed behind me, other doctors coming in for rounds. The hospital routine would go on. But unlike in the main wards, the subspecialty clinic had fewer workers, so patients were used to getting to know their caregivers.

I had to let it go. I'd done this thing.

Maybe Duffrey could be swayed. I hadn't even argued my case.

I could involve my father.

My phone buzzed. Another message from Angela.

All clear.

Nobody paid much attention to my stroll through the ward, as if without my white lab coat I wasn't anybody anymore.

I opened Cynthia's door.

Marlena, the nurse friend of Tina, was inside, removing the IV. I froze up for a second, then forced myself to relax. "No more platelets?" I asked, trying to sound casual.

"Dr. Clements said her numbers were good," Angela said. "I wrote them down." She glanced at the nurse. "In case you wanted to see them."

"I saw them this morning."

Marlena cut her eyes at me, then away.

Cynthia waited patiently for her to take it all away. "Almost time for art!" she said. "And I don't have to take the pole!"

I sat on the end of the bed. "That's great!" I could see the question in her eyes about the new doctor, but she knew not to say anything in front of the hospital nurse. I guess if there was one good thing about the new arrangement, she wouldn't have to lie or cover for us anymore.

When Marlena finally left, Cynthia and Angela started talking at the same time. "What happened? Who is that doctor? Where have you been?"

I said that I was officially on vacation.

"Can we go to Disneyland?" Cynthia asked. "It's really close!"

Why the hell not? "Let's see how your second treatment goes," I told her. "Then, yeah. Let's go to Disneyland."

"Can Tina come too?"

I tilted my head, watching Cynthia. "What makes you think Tina would come?"

"Because she likes you."

I froze. "How do you know that?"

Cynthia picked up the image I had drawn of Tina as a princess in front of a castle. "It's right here." She pointed to Tina's face. "Anybody can see it."

She was right.

***

I waited by the curb in front of the hospital for Tina to come out at the end of the day. It felt strange to not be inside, working until late, fighting exhaustion. I hadn't been this free since undergrad. Cynthia and I had spent the whole day making Brother Pix.

Tina popped out through the glass entrance, immediately spotting my car. When she opened the door, the winter air came with her, fresh and cool. She leaned over to kiss me lightly, like it was an everyday thing for me to pick her up from work.

I could get used to this.

"I have a kept man," she said. "I think I should keep you tied to the bed to await my pleasure."

I dropped the car into gear. "I think I like this new lifestyle."

I didn't know what she'd think of where I lived.

When we moved to San Diego, I was more or less in crisis

mode with Cynthia, her stem cell transplant having failed and then her kidney removed. Since my father was familiar with San Diego and I didn't have the time or energy to look around, I let him choose a place.

Of course, he completely neglected Cynthia's needs, as he refused to acknowledge her existence, and we ended up in a high-rise with no place for her to play. I'd made up for it with jaunts to Torrey Pines and the beach.

When we turned into the valet circle, Tina said, "It's close!"

I remembered that night we first went to her apartment, when I had said it wasn't.

"I'm sorry. I lied." I realized all the ways I had messed up with her.

But she laughed. "I don't think I'd trade that first night on the Pink Monster for anything."

The valet opened our car doors. Tina stood looking up at the grand covered entrance to the building. She seemed so small and uncertain. With her hippie clothes and pigtails in front of the marble facade, she appeared to have been transported from some other place, a stranger from another land.

But it wasn't the girl that was wrong. It was the place. We should have a house. With a yard. And a furry dog.

I was remembering home with my mother.

"This is fancy," she said as I took her hand.

"I mistakenly let my father pick it out."

"Not great for kids."

"Exactly." A doorman nodded at us as we walked inside. "He always liked these modern skyscrapers. Mom always wanted rambling houses with scratched-up wood floors and rosebushes by the porch."

"I hadn't really thought about it," Tina said. "Both seem nice."

We rode the elevator up.

"You're not one of those penthouse people, are you?" she asked.

I shook my head. "Not even close."

The carpeted hall was silent. Tina leaned in to whisper. "It's like a hotel."

I laughed. "It sort of is."

I unlocked the door and stepped back to let her inside.

Her head swiveled as she looked around, stopping to take it in. Then she turned to me. "Darion!"

I closed the door and tried to see the living room through her eyes. It was the one thing I had spent time on during the hours I was here alone.

The ceiling was vaulted and lit from within, creating a bright white sky. Additional recessed spotlights aimed at the walls. Pretty much every painting I'd ever made was in this room, carefully jigsaw-puzzled together to create a riot of color and images.

"Are all these yours?" she asked with something close to awe.

I clasped my hands behind my back, pleased that I had managed to actually impress her. "Yes."

She began to walk the perimeter of the room, dodging the neutral sofas and chairs, all chosen to avoid distracting from the art.

"I saw you had a show once, in college," she said.

"Then you did Google me."

"I can't believe you've managed to keep evidence of your sister completely off the internet."

"No Facebook, no blog, no Twitter. It's not impossible to go off the grid."

She paused in front of an enormous painting of a two-year-old Cynthia, my mother before she was sick, and our old dog, Sparky. Cynthia was beaming, her cheeks pink. My mother was laughing at Sparky, who was sniffing at a neighbor's kitten.

"Is this from a photograph?" she asked.

"A composite of two of them," I said. "Sparky, the dog, nudged the kitten with Cynthia. I added my mother to the scene."

"She's very pretty," Tina said. She sat down on the sofa and continued to stare up at it. "I am not good at straight portraits. I'm far more abstract."

I slid in next to her. "I am not very imaginative. I stick with the world as I see it."

"Tell me about her," Tina said.

I took her small hand, still marred with marker smudges. "She was a free spirit. She sang all the time. ALL the time. Always said it took the edge off any task, no matter how bitter."

"Cynthia sang one of her songs for me once."

"Yes, the one about my father leaving us."

"You were the baby boy with gray eyes." She stared at me. "I should have guessed that."

"There was no way to know. She changed her name back when my dad pulled the nasty stunt about Cynthia."

"What happened?"

"He had been working at a county hospital where we lived. I was twelve. If you ask him, he'll tell you how much pressure his own father put on him to move up, something he couldn't do at that small facility. My grandfather got my father a position in Oxford at the med school. A huge step up."

"Why didn't your mother go?"

"Her own mother had just died, and she couldn't see taking the only grandchild away from her father. Plus she was close to Grams, her mother-in-law. She had no clue my father would be gone for thirteen years."

"In the song, you were a baby."

I grinned at her. "Poetic license. Makes a sadder tale of woe."

"Then he came back."

"He visited a couple times a year. We made one trip to England while I was still living at home. Mom was almost swayed by how lovely it was. Then her father got sick."

"I don't understand why your father doesn't claim Cynthia as his."

I leaned back on the sofa and stared up at the ceiling. "Mom was always very hippie. With my father gone, she didn't even try to be normal. Even though we had a house, we spent summers living in communes. My father didn't understand that world at all. He pictured men with a dozen wives, young girls taken advantage of."

"And your father decided she was cheating on him."

"If she did, I never knew it. She was wild, and men were always interested in her, but we always stayed together in rooms. I was a teenage boy. I would have noticed, I think."

"We're always blind to our parents' love lives."

"Maybe. My father came in unexpectedly to interview for a position in California. He'd already forced me to switch to premed."

Tina sat up. "And you did it?"

"Yes."

"You let him bully you?"

"He was right."

"No!" She jumped up and waved her arms at all the paintings. "Look at this! You could have been great!"

"So, you're saying art isn't great unless it's in a museum? It can't be great right here?"

She got quiet. "No. It's great here."

"My father is a smart man. What he said stuck with me."

"What was that?"

"That I can be a doctor who does art for the love of it. But I can never be an artist who doctors on the side."

She sat back down. "I hate parents who are right."

"He was. I love being a doctor. And I love painting. I get to do both."

I curled her into me. "Mom got pregnant right as I was starting my internship. She was totally shocked since she was deep into her forties."

"Had your father been home?"

"Yes, for those interviews. He got the position and went to Oxford to settle his affairs there. Mom waited until he was home to tell him, as a surprise. She had no idea what was coming."

I closed my eyes, reveling in Tina's closeness. "He insisted on a prenatal paternity test. Mom was really hurt and refused until the baby was born. He took this to mean that it might not be his. She just didn't want the risk of the needle."

"But she did one later?"

"Yes, and it didn't come out with enough markers. Said it wasn't his."

"God."

"The thing is, after I found out about it all, I did a test with

Cynthia and Mom, and it said she wasn't the mother."

"Was there a switch?"

"No, Cynthia is definitely ours. When we tested my tissue markers, she and I were a match. That's how I donated stem cells."

"Doesn't your father know?"

"He won't listen to me. And now that he's gone eight years insisting that Cynthia isn't his, he'd never back down."

Not that I'd make him. He didn't deserve her.

"Poor Cynthia," Tina said. She snuggled her head into my neck. "Come here."

She began to unbutton my shirt.

I stroked the fine hair of her head, sleek in the pigtails. "You know we've never even done anything on a bed?"

She paused, thinking. "You're right. Pink Monster. Pink Monster. Surgical Suite B." She bit her lip. "That was crazy."

"Cabana," I finished. "And cliff."

She moved to my lap, picking up one of my arms to place under her knees. Then she clasped her hands around my neck. "Take me to your bed, Dr. Marks."

I had no problem doing that.

43

TINA

The hospital seemed strange without Darion in it. I left the art therapy room to deliver the paperwork to the main office. I had decided to go the psychology route.

As I crossed the main entry, I spotted a man who looked so much like Darion, I almost called out to him.

He had the same no-nonsense stride, a strong jaw, and their mouths were identical. But then, I saw the crinkles around the eyes. And his hair was receding just a bit.

He was headed the same direction as me, to administration, so I followed, picking up my pace to keep up.

The man stopped beside the evil secretary's desk. "I'm here to see Duffrey."

"Do you have an appointment?" she asked. "You can sit over there." She pointed to the hard-backed chair of doom, and I stifled a laugh. I hid behind a corner, pretending to shuffle papers while I watched.

"I do not NEED an appointment," he said.

"Everybody needs an appointment," she said. "Dr. Duffrey is a very busy man."

"So am I."

I so wanted to giggle.

"What's your name?" she asked.

"Dr. Gerald Marks. California Board of Medicine."

My head popped up. Darion's dad! Holy shit!

"You can have a seat, Dr. Marks," she said.

Dr. Marks glanced at the chair. "I'm going in," he said.

The secretary stood up, looking more energetic than I'd ever seen her as Dr. Marks pushed through Duffrey's door. She followed him in, saying, "I'm so sorry, Dr. Duffrey."

But she was clearly waved back out, as she returned to her desk and angrily stuck a pencil behind her ear.

I decided now was not a good time to turn in my late forms.

I dashed back to my room and typed out a quick message to Darion.

Your dad is at the hospital! Just bullied his way into Duffrey's office!

He wrote me back right away, saying he was on his way.

I'd never be able to concentrate on art therapy with this going on. I glanced at my schedule. The toddlers were being visited by some puppet troupe, so I wouldn't see them. Thankfully, the only thing for the next couple hours was Albert.

Whew. Good.

I got out my painting of the ocean sunset and Albert's last drawing, in case he was up for working on it. I wondered if I had time to make another run down to the office, to be there when Darion's father came out.

Probably not.

I picked up Albert's image, the circus scene on top of the

crumbling cliff. That top clown still really bugged me. I knew I had seen it before.

I had about ten minutes. I searched my phone for the shot of the clown I had taken and loaded it into Google image search.

And suddenly everything became clear.

Tons of hits. The clown on oil paintings. Posters. Mugs. Calendars. Coffee-table books. Two entire galleries devoted to it. Of course. I'd seen it a million times.

I pulled up the Wikipedia article, and there was an image, clearly of Albert, although a much younger version, his crazy curls brown instead of gray. But the artist was named Claude Van du Seaux.

I couldn't believe it.

Claude Van du Seaux. He was ubiquitous in art circles and had invaded pop culture in the 1970s. There was no mention that this was an assumed name, but of course, if they'd listed Albert before, I could have found it the first time I searched. And if I'd found Claude, I would have recognized Albert immediately.

I scrolled down the article, then stopped with shock.

It said he died three months ago.

I scrolled back to the top. I'd missed that. 1937–2014.

I scanned through the headlines of the related articles.

"Famous artist commits suicide at studio."

"Studio a bloodbath after artist slits wrists, says assistant."

"Image of blood-splattered clown goes viral after famous artist suicide."

I remembered this now. It happened right before I graduated. I was still talking on the self-help circuit, so people had forwarded me the links.

But he wasn't dead.

Was Albert his brother, maybe? They looked so much alike.

Not possible. I'd seen him draw that clown with my own two eyes. Plus, the scars on his wrists.

Had he faked his own death?

I paced the room, waiting for him to arrive.

The time came and went. He didn't show.

Darion texted me.

I'm in Cynthia's room. All seems fine here.

I wrote back.

I'll be there when I can. Class now.

Except I didn't have class. No Albert.

I called up to the nurses' desk to ask about him. The phone rang and rang with no answer.

I slammed it down. Forget that. I checked my roster. He was on level six. I'd go find him.

My heart hammered as I ran up the stairs, too worried to wait on an elevator. What if he had *really* died? When did they update my list? Would anyone tell me?

Tears pricked my eyes. No, I wasn't going to let that happen. Not today. Not with everything else going on.

No one was at the desk, so I stopped a nurse. "How can I find one of my patients' rooms?"

The woman glanced down at my badge. "Ask the desk nurse."

"She isn't there."

The soft voice of the paging system called a code. I had a sudden terrible feeling that it was Albert. "I need to find Albert Cisneros," I say, my voice breaking.

"Oh." She pointed down the hall. "He's right in there. 614."

"He's okay? He didn't come for therapy."

"I wouldn't know about that."

I hurried in that direction. I knocked a couple times. No answer.

The door was only partially closed, so I pushed it open. "Albert? It's Tina."

Albert lay in bed, staring out the window. His hands trembled on top of the sheet.

"Albert?"

With great effort, he turned his head. "Tina," he said, but his voice was strained and soft.

I rushed over to him. "Albert? What's going on?"

"New drug is a bust," he said.

I took his hand. He didn't have the Fall Risk bracelet anymore. I guess they didn't expect him to try to walk at all now.

"Are they going to try something else?"

He stared at me, his eyes milky. "I think I'm done here."

"You have to help me finish the image! The cliff!"

He clasped his other hand around mine. "You already know what you're doing."

"I don't!"

He smiled. "But you do. What did you paint first?"

I thought about the oranges and pinks on the canvas. "The sunset."

"Not the drop? Not the danger?"

"No."

"See? What would you have painted first before?"

He had me there. "The rocks. The fall."

"What does that mean?"

"I've changed."

"Exactly."

Was Darion the change? Or was it me?

"Are we supposed to change? Do artists change?" I asked.

He coughed weakly, and said, "All my life I was known for these dark images."

I thought of the clowns. Yes, they had a definite sinister look.

"But for a while, I drew unicorns."

I couldn't hide my surprise. "Unicorns?"

He laughed until he gasped. He let go of my hand to press his palm to his chest. "I know. But they were gorgeous."

"Did you paint them as Claude?"

He dropped his hand to his lap. "So, you know."

"I figured it out just ten minutes ago. It was the clown on the cliff."

"My silly redundancy," he said. "I never could get that face out of my head. They said to paint your demons until they had no power. Never worked for me."

"Maybe you are what you paint," I said. "And not the other way around."

"That would be nice, wouldn't it? I should have stuck to unicorns."

"What started the unicorns?"

"A little girl a lot like you. Blond. Dramatic. Her own person."

"Your daughter?"

His face scrunched with emotion. "She was. Her mother was a true psychopath. Viciously disappointed that I hadn't 'made it.' Drove the two of them into a lake when she was six. They both drowned."

"Oh my God."

He swiped at his eyes. "That was long, long ago. I switched to sinister clowns. Only then did I become the artist she had always expected me to be. Funny how it works. Or not funny. Satirical, really."

"The world thinks you're dead."

"Ah, yes. When I lived, my assistant was embarrassed for saying I was dead. I pay a boy to edit the Wikipedia entry if it gets changed. I like being dead. In fact, the world lamenting my demise was one of the things that kept me going after I botched my own real death."

I reached over. "I thought I was what kept you going," I teased.

"And the doctor keeps you going. You still haven't drawn him, have you?"

I shook my head. "No."

"There's your assignment. Your trouble in paradise with three-point perspective."

He relaxed into the pillow. "And don't let Duffrey bully you into being a therapist OR a social worker if you don't want it."

Had I told him about that?

He closed his eyes, and I rose slowly from the bed.

"I'll be by tomorrow," I said.

He unlaced his hands and lifted one shaky finger but did not open his eyes. "With a draft!" he said.

"With a draft."

But as I wandered back to my room, I realized something. I had NOT told him about the new position. I referred to my one-day absence only as an administrative hiccup.

And then it dawned.

The wealthy powerful man funding my position.

Was him.

44

DR. DARION

Cynthia and I were deep into a cutthroat game of Go Fish when two orderlies arrived with a gurney.

"Where is she going?" I asked. When I sent Angela home, she hadn't mentioned any procedures.

"For a bone marrow aspiration," they said. "We have the papers here, signed yesterday."

We put down her cards. Right. I had ordered it myself, assuming I'd be doing it. "Have they done the PET scan on her kidney?" I asked.

They stared at the paper. "Not listed."

Damn it. They were already dropping the ball. I'd have Clements paged.

"Are you coming with me?" Cynthia asked.

"You can walk with her until we get to the room," they said.

Cynthia clutched my hand. "You won't be there?"

"Not this time, Cyn."

Her eyes got wet. "But you're always there."

I tried to muster all my sincerity when I said, "You're in good hands."

The orderlies helped her move from the bed to the gurney and locked the side rails into place. I walked with her as we rolled down the familiar halls. We were buzzed into the surgical hall, and I glanced over at Surgical Suite B.

The orderlies pushed Cynthia into another suite. Inside, two nurses I didn't know were waiting.

"Hello, Cynthia," one said. "You ready for this?"

She nodded.

"You've had this done many times, right?"

"Yes," I said. "Many times."

"Lay on your side for me, okay, sweetheart?"

Dr. Hammonds, a pediatric oncologist I worked with often, came in. He stopped short when he spotted me. "I didn't expect to see you," he said.

I took him aside. "She's my sister."

His confused expression told me everything. The staff knew I was on leave, but not why.

"Time for you to wait outside," one of the nurses said.

"How about you let me stay with her?" I asked Hammonds.

He hesitated. "I think you should wait in her room. We'll have her right back." He turned to Cynthia. "Hello, Cynthia!" He gave his usual silly introduction that he did with pediatric patients.

One of the orderlies held open the door. "This way," he said.

The nurses watched me. Probably ready to give a report.

Be a normal parent, Duffrey had said.

I hated to go. I didn't want to go. But I did.

I went straight to the admin offices. When Duffrey's secretary saw me, she jumped straight up. "Not again!" she said.

"Pardon?" I knew she was confusing me with my father. He must have caused a scene.

"Oh," she said. "You looked like…someone else." She sat back down. "Dr. Duffrey isn't in at the moment."

"When will he be back?"

"I had to cancel everything until midafternoon," she said. "Didn't exactly make MY day."

I backed away. For all I knew, he was at lunch with my father, plotting my next career move. He was probably striking some sort of deal I didn't need or want.

I went back up to Cynthia's ward to wait in her room. I half wished I hadn't sent Angela home. I might be needing her still.

At the last minute, I veered down Tina's hall. She had a group of teen girls with her, but she waved when I passed.

That was pretty much the only thing going right at the moment.

And thank God for that.

When I got into Cynthia's room, it wasn't empty. My father was sitting in the rocking chair, staring at his phone.

"Fancy seeing you here, Dad," I said. "I thought Cynthia didn't exist in your skewed little world."

"Hello, son." He tucked his phone in his pocket. "Didn't realize you'd resort to involving your supervisor in our little family matter."

"What are you talking about?"

"Duffrey. He faxed me Cynthia's file. Including your bone marrow HLAs. You should have told me you were a ten-point match."

"It's not my fault you were a blindsided idiot."

My father jumped out of the chair. "If you discovered that you two were one-hundred-percent siblings, you should have told me."

"I always knew. She's been fine without you for eight years. And you turned out not to be worthy of my mother. Why would I give you my sister?"

He whipped around to face the window. "Your mother was living in communes, staying at artist colonies. No telling who might have fathered that child."

"The only father that mattered was you."

"The paternity test was negative."

"It happens. You should have figured it out for your own damn self."

"Where is she?"

"Getting a bone marrow aspiration."

He sighed. "I flipped through her file. Are you going to do another stem cell transplant?"

"We're not eligible for another three months."

"Have you contacted Mayo? St. Jude's? M. D. Anderson?"

"Yes. M. D. Anderson had the best match for a trial."

"You took it?"

"Yes. I pulled a thousand strings, but I got her on it."

He turned back around. "What's the prognosis?"

"I'm not sure you deserve to know."

"Damn it, Darion. I'm trying to do the right thing here."

The door pushed open, and an orderly bumped the gurney through. Cynthia lay on her side, sleepy from the sedative.

"Dary, I think I see two of you," she said.

I had no idea what to do. I couldn't exactly introduce him as her father. Not after all this time.

"I think you should go," I said to him. "This is not a good time whatsoever."

The orderlies carefully transferred Cynthia back to her bed.

"Is this your friend, Dary?" Cynthia asked. "I have seen his picture in Mommy's photo books."

"Yes, Cynthia, it is. His name is Gerald."

"Hi, Gerald," she said.

"She looks like your mother," he said.

"I know."

"Were you friends with Mommy? What was she like before I was born?" she asked. She could barely keep her eyes open.

My father glanced at me, then pulled the chair closer to her bed. "Your mommy loved to sing," he said.

The orderlies left us. I backed against the wall, so full of rage I could punch a hole in it. He could not just walk right in here. He could not mess with her now. He didn't deserve her.

"I remember," Cynthia said. "I know her favorite song."

"What was that?"

She yawned, but still she managed to sing a few lines.

I spent my life in old Kentucky.
Moved to Cali when I got real lucky in love.

I knew exactly when my father realized the lyrics were about him. His jaw clamped down.

Then you found a whole new love to make you happy.
T'weren't another woman but a job overseas.
You traded workin' for my love.

Cynthia's voice faded out. My father sat there a minute, then he said to me, "Your mother wouldn't come with me."

"You asked too much of her."

He stood up, his voice charged with emotion I had never heard in him, not when his own mother died, and certainly not when he left mine.

"I can't have this conversation now," he said.

And he walked out.

Again.

Big surprise.

45

TINA

When I finally got free of my therapy sessions to get to Cynthia's room, I wasn't prepared for what I saw.

Cynthia was sitting up, coloring on her pad. And Darion was fast asleep in a chair, leaning over her bed with his head on his arms.

"Shhh," Cynthia said. "He's sleeping." She giggled. "I don't think doctors are supposed to sleep in the rooms."

I wasn't sure if I was supposed to let on that I knew they were brother and sister.

Cynthia turned the pad around. "Dr. Darion wanted me to make you green, but I said you weren't an ogre."

The drawing was of me, dressed as a princess. Darion had drawn it. I could tell by the sweep of the lines. "That's very good," I said. "I'm glad I'm not green."

"I missed art class," she said. "I had to get an aspiration."

"That doesn't sound very fun."

"They stuck a needle in my butt."

"Did it hurt?"

"Not really."

I wanted to reach over and run my fingers through Darion's hair. He really was out. "Does he do this often? Fall asleep in your room?"

Cynthia opened her mouth to answer, then changed her mind. "He's just my doctor."

I decided enough was enough. "He's also your brother."

Her eyes got very big.

"It's okay that I know," I said. "I'm a friend now. Not just the art teacher."

Cynthia set the drawing pad down. "I'm not supposed to tell anyone."

"I probably wasn't supposed to tell you!"

She giggled. "We have secrets!"

"We do."

"You want to draw with the new markers?" she asked. "I've been saving them."

"Sure."

She reached over carefully to the table by her bed and opened the drawer. I saw a twinge of pain cross her face, but it didn't stop her. She pulled the package out.

She took out the purple. "This is my favorite color," she said. She set it in her lap. Then she pulled out the black. "Here's yours."

I regretted my choice so much. Stupid goth phase. Dumb reflexive answer. I could see it for what it was. Rebellion. Anything to stand out, impress the other antisocial kids.

But I took it.

"Let's see what color they make," she said.

I opened the cap. "I'm not sure the black one works like the others. I think it's just for making edges. Maybe I should take a different one. I think I have a new favorite color."

"Oh, no," Cynthia said solemnly. "You can't change your favorite color. That would be like changing your mom."

I wouldn't have minded that either.

"Let's just try it," she said. She drew the shape of a butterfly and colored it in. "Now you make the dots," she said. "Make them shaped like hearts."

"Okay," I said, smiling at her. "But it might be a funny butterfly with black hearts on it."

"I won't mind," she said.

We both watched as I drew the first heart.

It turned blue.

"I knew it," Cynthia said. "Another favorite color!"

"Is blue Darion's favorite?" I asked, actually surprised the black ink could change.

Cynthia shook her head. "It was my mother's."

Now I remembered her telling me that before. The color of forever.

My hands shook a little as I closed the cap on the marker. Just a coincidence.

Darion woke up then, startled. When he saw me, he smiled sleepily. "Am I dreaming?"

"No!" Cynthia cried. "She's here! And purple and black make blue!"

Then she leaned toward me and whispered loudly, "Can we tell him?"

"Tell me what?" Darion yawned, pushing back a lock of errant hair.

"That you should sleep more," I said.

"Tina!" Cynthia said.

I leaned back near her. "Tell him what?"

"About what you know," she whispered.

"Maybe we should wait until he tells me you're his sister, and then it won't have to be a secret." Our whispers were so loud, they could probably be heard in the hall. I was trying not to laugh.

Darion's gaze switched back and forth between me and Cynthia. "Tina," he said, trying to keep his face serious. "I need to tell you something. It's been a big secret."

"Yes, Dr. Marks?" I replied.

Cynthia clasped her hands tightly, like this was a big moment. "Don't be mad, Tina," she said, then giggled.

"Cynthia is my sister. There, I said it."

I pretended to gasp. Cynthia giggled so hard she fell backwards on her pillow. Markers rolled off the bed and scattered everywhere.

I leaned down to pick them up. "Dr. Marks, I'm so shocked!"

"I knew you would be," he said. "But now you know."

"You're very very silly," Cynthia said to me.

"This is a serious matter!" Darion said. He rolled Cynthia over to him. "So serious that I have to tickle you for making me tell!"

I held on to the markers, knowing I needed to clean them before giving them back. But watching them made me forget where we were, what a fight we were still waging, for Cynthia's health, with her real father, and with the hospital over Darion's job.

For a moment, we were just people having a good time.

This was quite possibly the happiest I had ever been.

46

DR. DARION

My father had been trying to reach me for three days, but I didn't care. I called my lawyer to ask if my guardianship of Cynthia was in danger.

"Not right away," the woman said. "That paternity test would hold up in a preliminary hearing. If he wants to bring in medical experts to discount the paternity test, that would be a bigger deal."

"But he could do it."

"Yes. We could delay him. Throw up blocks. Get time. We'd want to establish abandonment. But still. If he can prove paternity, you will lose. No judge denies parental rights without due cause. Work with him, Darion. Keep this out of court."

"But I can't let him take her."

"Give an inch so you can keep the mile. Don't force his hand."

I hung up the phone, disgusted. All this was happening because of me. If I hadn't changed the records, gotten on Duffrey's radar. If Cynthia wasn't so sick. If we hadn't had to use my stem cells and established my match.

I flung the folder across my bedroom. I would not lose her. I would not let him mess her up. He was not to be trusted with another tender heart. His career always came first. Next time it could be anywhere — Switzerland, New York. If he had her back, he could take her far away from me.

My doorbell rang. What now? Tina was working. Nurse Angela had never been here. Nobody even knew where I lived.

I flung open the door, prepared to buy off some kid selling cookies.

But it was my father.

"Don't slam the door," he said.

I ignored him, shoving the heavy door in his face.

My father's hand flew forward to block it.

Damn it. Keep it out of court, the lawyer said. How was I supposed to do that?

Give an inch.

I took a step back. "All right. What do you want?"

He pushed the door open and walked past me into the living room. "Now this is something," he said, gazing at all the paintings.

"Make your point."

He turned around, tugging at his tie. "I know you've seen Cynthia through a lot."

"You mean your abandonment?"

"I was laboring under the impression that she wasn't mine." He held out his hands, palms up. "I take my responsibilities seriously."

"Right. Which is why you left for thirteen years."

"Those thirteen years got me where I am. Put me in a position to help you." He lowered his arms and straightened the cuffs to his suit jacket.

"I didn't need your help."

"Who do you think got you on at St. Anthony's? After all that waffling on your resident specialty, Mayo wouldn't touch you."

Well, hell.

"And for the record, I did call Duffrey about your lady friend."

My head snapped up. "Really?"

"Yes. There was an ungodly fifteen-million-dollar endowment attached to her. She didn't need my help."

I sank onto a chair. "Really?"

"Some artist set it up. I did convince Duffrey to send her back to school rather than make her a glorified secretary."

My throat felt thick. "She's going to be a therapist."

"Good." He sat down on the sofa, and his gaze fell on my life-size painting of Mom and Cynthia with the dog. His jaw ticked again.

"You left her," I said. "Pregnant."

He leaned forward and stared at his polished shoes. "What do we do about it now?"

"You didn't come to her funeral."

"I didn't have it in me."

"Cynthia really could have used a dad. I was doing my residency. I had a terminally ill mother and a baby sister."

"You wouldn't even talk to me, if you remember."

I gripped the armrest. "I hated you."

"That's fair." He tapped one of his shoes against the carpeted floor. "What do we do now?" he asked again.

"You will not take Cynthia from me."

"You said yourself she needs a father."

"You're a workaholic who puts his career before his family."

He met my gaze. "And you're a workaholic trying to fill two staff positions at the same time."

"Except I'm on leave right now."

"I can fix that."

"I don't want it fixed. Stop manipulating people, Dad. It's not right."

"You call it manipulation. You'll eventually learn it's just business."

I stood up and walked the perimeter of the room. Looking at the paintings calmed me. Give an inch, the lawyer said.

Only if I could also take a mile from my father.

"She's my daughter," he said.

"She's your daughter," I said. "Prove you're worthy to be her father."

He stood next to me. "How do you want me to do that?"

I knew the mile I wanted. "Resign from the state medical board. Devote your time to family."

He exploded. "Do you know how long it took me to get that position?"

"I do!" I shouted back. "The thirteen years you deserted me and my mother."

The room echoed for a moment, my voice ringing off the walls.

He stared back up at the image. "The two of you seemed happier without me."

"And Cynthia wouldn't be?"

This got him. "I won't make the same mistake twice."

"Then resign from the board. Until then, you can visit her, but you WILL NOT tell her who you are."

"But if I resign, then we can tell her?"

I snorted. "That'll be the day."

He couldn't tear his eyes from that portrait. "I'll submit my resignation this afternoon."

I stood there, frozen with shock, as he strode through the living room and showed himself out.

47

TINA

Today was a big day.

I led Manuelito through the park by the hand. Corabelle had class, and Gavin had to work, and I'd offered to take him rather than send him to the drop-in day care.

Cynthia was coming home from the hospital today, and I felt like having another child around would be fun for her. He was holding a purple sucker to give to her.

The park was one block from the hospital. We were killing time, waiting for the text from Darion that she was coming down. Her second chemo had gone perfectly two weeks ago, and according to Darion, she was responding to treatment. I was beginning to pick up the lingo. No blasts. ANCs bouncing back. Good platelets.

He was right. The more people in Cynthia's corner, the better off we all would be.

Darion's father sat on the bench closest to the hospital entrance. This was also part of the plan. He looked completely different now that he wasn't working, jeans and a sweater. He had a bouquet of flowers for Cynthia. And, I knew, something else. A locket that had belonged to his mother. Today he'd be telling her that he was her dad.

Big day.

My phone buzzed. I had snapped an image of Darion to use for reference in my first portrait of him, and it came up as his icon when he messaged me. It popped up now, his hair tousled. Imperfect. Better that way.

Coming down, it said.

I waved at Gerald for us to head that direction.

Darion's leave of absence had been shortened once everything was sorted out. Gerald recommended Duffrey for the open board position. We didn't know if it was intended to be a political maneuver, but it had worked as one.

Darion was reinstated, and despite his residency status in pediatrics, he had been given normal staff hours. No more crazy workweeks. The hours were still long, but at least there was time each day to spend with Cynthia, and me.

I laughed to think I had intended a one-and-done with him. I was impossibly snared now.

"Is Sintha coming?" Manuelito asked.

"She is," I said. Gerald walked alongside us. He looked nervous.

"It'll be fine," I told him. "Cynthia is very loving, and she's gotten used to you."

He clutched the flowers. "I know."

His manner with her still wasn't easy. He didn't tickle or play or act silly. But they found things to do together. Card tricks. Board games. Lately they had been learning to make balloon animals.

Cynthia liked delivering them to other kids on the ward.

"There they are," I said, pointing to Darion walking with Cynthia. Several of the nurses had come down and were waving to her. She turned and blew them kisses.

She was wearing a funny hat with kitty ears, a gift from Nurse Angela. Darion had parked close in case Cynthia got tired, but she was a bundle of energy, skipping down the sidewalk as though the open air alone was healing her.

When she saw us, she ran ahead. "Are you Manuel?" she asked.

He nodded, suddenly shy at this bigger, bolder girl. He held out the purple lollipop.

"My favorite!" She took it and gave him a little hug. "Is there a playground here? I want to swing!" She stuck the sucker in her pocket.

"I think there's one a little farther up the path," Gerald said.

"Let's go!"

She and Manuel trotted ahead. Gerald followed behind. Darion took my hand, and we took the path more slowly.

"When's he going to do it?" he asked.

"When they get to the swings," I said.

His breath came out in a whoosh. "All right."

"He's done everything you asked. Exactly as you've said."

"He has."

I bumped into him with my hip. "It's going to be all right. He changed. You asked him to change, and he did."

Like me and my goth phase, and my one-and-dones, I thought. And Albert and his clowns. Another new drug had come along, and like the last one, it was working for now.

We madly painted unicorns in art therapy, when I wasn't

working on the portrait of Darion. Another woman had arrived on the ward and came with Albert, an older lady. If I wasn't mistaken, a few sparks were flying between them.

He was doing okay. We were all doing okay.

We were almost at the swings. I hurried ahead to help Manuel, as they were too tall for him to reach. Cynthia grasped the chains. "Darion, come push me!"

But as we'd agreed, Darion lagged behind.

"I'll do it," Gerald said.

But instead of going behind her to push, he kneeled in front of her.

"Are the flowers for me?" Cynthia asked.

"They are," he said, and handed them to her.

She touched her toes to the ground for balance and brought the flowers to her nose. "They smell pretty!"

"I have something else for you," he said. He pulled the locket and chain from his pocket. "It's a very special necklace." He showed it to her.

"Ohhh," she said. "It's a grown-up necklace."

He slipped it over her head. She handed him the flowers back so she could hold the charm, a dove flying through a silver circle. "It's pretty," she said.

"It belonged to my mother, your grandmother," Gerald said.

Cynthia looked up, confused. I glanced over at Darion. He had stopped by a tree several yards away. "My nanna died a long time ago, before I was born," she said.

"This is your other grandmother," Gerald said. "My mother is your grandmother."

"But that would make you my dad." She looked at Darion.

"That's right," Gerald said. "I am your brother Darion's dad, and your dad too."

She clutched the necklace. "Are you the love who left Mommy? In the song?"

I stopped pushing. Darion stood ready to step forward and intervene.

"I am." Gerald looked at her steadily.

Cynthia sat staring at the necklace, breathing in and out. "Why did you do that?"

Gerald took his time answering. "I made a mistake. I thought it was important to go away for my job. But I was wrong. I should have stayed."

"But then she wouldn't have written that song," Cynthia said. "It was her favorite song."

"I think she might have written a different song then," Gerald said, "and liked it best."

Cynthia shook her head. "No. Mommy always said that the things you sing about are important. You can't change them. You just have to learn from them." She settled back in the swing, lifting her feet. "Did you learn from it?"

"I did," Gerald said.

Cynthia nodded thoughtfully. "Will you push me now?"

He pinned the flowers beneath his elbow and moved behind her. "I'd be delighted to."

Darion caught my eye. Neither of us assumed it was over, that Cynthia would just accept this without question.

But we'd crossed another hurdle.

And life was nothing if not a whole lot of leaps of faith.

48

TINA

The day was perfect. Cool and breezy, but not cold. Sunshine. Everyone had warned Corabelle that an outdoor wedding in November was just about the worst idea ever.

But this was California. Good weather was almost guaranteed.

I waited at the back of the smattering of chairs for the music to mark my entrance. Manuelito was making his way up the aisle slowly, carefully holding the white pillow with the rings tied to it.

Darion and Cynthia and Gerald were seated somewhere in the middle. There were only a few dozen guests. Gavin waited at the front. The way he looked past me, expectant, dying to see Corabelle, made my heart squeeze. I knew what a miracle this day was for both of them. After the loss they endured, their seven-day-old baby dying when they were still in high school, finding each other again in college was the sort of story movies were made of.

The song changed, and I took my first step forward. Darion watched my every move. Cynthia seemed in awe of everything — the bows on the chairs, the little flower arch on the shore. Behind the minister, the ocean waves pounded the sand.

Mario clapped Gavin on the back. Behind him, Bud, Gavin's boss, served as the second groomsman.

I took my place opposite the boys and turned to watch Jenny come up the aisle. A whoop came from the bride's side, and her director boyfriend, Frankie, stood up to video her. Tacky, yes. But also endearing. I was glad he had showed. We had all begun to wonder if she was running up credit cards and pretending he existed.

Gavin sucked in a breath as Corabelle appeared to wait her turn, her arm through her father's. The boy controlling the music switched to the last song, and everyone stood.

She looked radiant, her black hair blowing around her face. Gavin was antsy, anxious for her to make it to the front, rocking back and forth on his heels.

Manuel stood in front of me, bouncing up and down with excitement. Finally he couldn't contain himself, and said, "It's Corbell!"

Everyone laughed. I laid a hand on his shoulder. He stood up straight again, holding the pillow out.

Gavin's family was not there. I knew Darion had talked to him about it, but Gavin would not relent. He didn't even want them to know about it. Corabelle's parents, who still lived opposite the alley from them, had been sworn to silence.

I glanced at Darion again. Cynthia was standing up so she could see. When she saw me looking, she waved.

Corabelle arrived at the front, and her father passed her hand to Gavin. He leaned in, and I could hear his whispered "I'm the luckiest man in the world."

For a jaded goth girl, I was more choked up than I cared to

admit as they spoke their vows. I found myself glancing back at Darion over and over again. When it was time for Manuel to bring the rings, I pushed him forward.

The ocean kept beating against the shore. Not so long ago, Corabelle had walked into it, not intending to come out. Gavin had saved her. And now here they were.

Albert's assistant had saved him, even if the world still thought he was dead. And Darion had saved his sister.

I had saved myself. I glanced down at my wrists, covered in white elbow gloves. I had purposely chosen a cold climate to live in after I escaped home, where I could wear long sleeves year-round. I had bared my secrets only in the dark.

And now I was here, in sunny California, and soon it would be spring and I wouldn't be able to hide my past. My scars would be out for everyone to see.

The minister pronounced them man and wife. The small group cheered, and Gavin kissed Corabelle, bending her backwards. Manuelito covered his eyes, making everyone laugh. The photographer snapped the shot.

I glanced up. Above us was a cliff, not the same one I was painting, but this was the same shore, the same landscape, the same world. Albert was right. I was finding my place in it, as an artist and as a healthy person, full of hope. I hadn't found my style yet, my medium, my voice on canvas.

But I was here. And there was so much to say, to paint, to experience.

I was more than ready to get started.

Epilogue

TINA

We had arrived at the happiest place on earth on the happiest day of the year.

Cynthia looked up at the massive Christmas tree just inside the gates of Disneyland with something akin to rapture.

I glanced over at Darion. He couldn't take his eyes off her.

She had a fuzz of hair now, as blond as a corn husk. Her last treatment was almost two months ago. Otherwise, looking at her, you'd never know that anything had ever been wrong.

"It's the most beautiful Christmas tree in the world!" Cynthia said. "Take my picture!"

Darion snapped what was probably already the twentieth shot, and we were barely inside the gates. It had been his idea to come to Disneyland on Christmas Day.

Cynthia ran back between us, taking both of our hands. I remembered all the pictures she had drawn of us like this when she was in the hospital, a little family with her at the center.

Until I saw the painting Darion had made of his mother with her long red hair, I didn't know that the woman in all those images was me. While he and I mucked around and did our best to screw things up, Cynthia had known all along.

"Hold up!" Darion's father caught up, holding a pair of Mickey Mouse ears. "No visit to Disney is complete without one of these."

Cynthia stood in front of him and let him place the hat on her. She still wasn't quite certain what to make of this man who looked like her brother and said he was her father. But she was kind and accepting of him.

The psychology book I was reading to prepare for my coursework said that children understood more than we gave them credit for. Though Gerald was eager to get close to her, Cynthia still knew he was responsible for so much sadness for her mother.

And so, she did not take his hand easily, or show him the affection she had for Darion. But we had all established a truce of sorts, a working relationship. It made me wonder if I shouldn't call my parents. I never went home for Christmas. Some years I didn't even take their call.

But maybe sometime today, I'd take a cue from this eight-year-old and talk to them. And actually listen. Not understanding someone was not the same as hating them. And having nothing in common did not mean we could not find some things to say.

We strolled up Main Street, all decked with holly and lights. I had never been to a theme park, and it was magical. Even my jaded goth-girl soul was moved by the music piped through the speakers, the palpable joy of the kids dashing excitedly along the sidewalks, and the holiday spirit.

"It's the princess castle!" Cynthia said. She let go of our hands to run a little bit ahead.

We followed along as the little mouse ears bobbed, aiming for the archway of the castle.

"I'll catch up with her," Gerald said.

Darion took both my hands and spun me in a circle. One of the park photographers approached and snapped a shot of us in front of the castle.

Darion's gray eyes glittered as we whirled around. The weather was ideal, slightly cool but not cold. We both were wearing light sweaters and jeans. His hands gripped mine solidly, then all of a sudden, he just stopped.

"Time to go find your dad and Cynthia?" I asked.

Darion shook his head. "Not yet." He pulled a box out of his pocket. "I wanted to give you your Christmas present here."

Then he got down on one knee.

The crowds walking around us stopped to watch. My hands flew to my cheeks.

He opened the velvet box. "I know you totally intended to ditch me after one night. So, I worked hard to get you to stay."

A little girl gasped, making Darion pause to smile.

"I promise to keep making you want to stay," he said. "Forever. I love you, Tina Marie Schwartz. Will you marry me?"

The photographer was waiting, his camera raised to his face. The park seemed suspended, everyone close by, holding their souvenirs, their children, the hands of the person they loved.

Time stood completely still. I looked down at Darion, his riot of black hair, those earnest eyes. I guess this is what a normal life looked like. I had never pictured it before. But the canvas was right here, waiting to be painted. It didn't matter what scene went behind it. Wealth. Poverty. Sickness. Health. What mattered is that you captured the feelings you had.

And right now I knew exactly what I felt, so I said it. "I love you, Dr. Darion Marks. Yes. Yes, I will marry you."

The light flashed from the camera. People cheered and clapped and resumed their motion, their happy day. Darion stood up and slipped the ring on my finger. I would look at it later. Right now I wanted him to kiss me, here where everyone could see.

And he did, thoroughly and long. I sensed a crowd growing around us, then little arms wrapped around my leg. I looked down. Manuelito.

"Little Man!" I said.

We were surrounded. Gavin. Corabelle. Jenny. Frankie. Everybody, even Nurse Angela. Gerald and Cynthia. They tossed flower petals at us, hugging and laughing. And I knew the scene I had just pictured had to be expanded. We didn't need just one person in our lives, but many. To be sheltered didn't simply mean you got married. But that you weaved a safety net of family and friends. We all needed people in our corner. As many as possible.

I took Darion's hands. He looked both relieved and happy. I laughed, realizing he thought I might say no.

I kissed his cheek and whispered, "I need another promise," as our group headed to the base of the castle.

"What's that?" he asked.

"That we never give up on duct-tape panties and meetings in Surgical Suite B."

He picked me up and spun me around one more time. "Now that's the sort of promise I can definitely keep."

THE END

~*'♥'*~

Also by Deanna Roy

Don't miss the other books in the Forever Series

Stella & Dane: Stella is ready to blow out of her honky tonk town when a hot stranger rolls in on a Harley, leading to a dangerous romance that upsets the locals and sparks a tragedy that will change everyone's lives. (Romance)

Baby Dust. Abandoned by friends and haunted by what they've lost, five women forge friendships to survive the death of their babies. (Women's Fiction)

About Deanna Roy

Deanna is a passionate advocate for women who have lost babies. She founded the web site www.pregnancyloss.info in 1998 after the loss of her first baby and continues to run both online and in-person support groups for women who have endured this impossible loss. Find her on Facebook, Twitter, Instagram, Google+, and Goodreads.

Learn more about the author at
www.deannaroy.com

Your review on Amazon is appreciated—it makes a huge difference to authors when readers provide their reactions to a work.

Acknowledgements

Many experts, nurses, EMTs, and hospital personnel were instrumental in helping me understand the world of Dr. Darion. I could not have done this book without them: **Khristie Beaird, Lynn Kennedy, Missy Givens-Norris, Karen Greenberg, and Jon Korfmacher**.

My beta readers helped me make sure I kept a good balance between the series stories and Tina and Darion: **Missy, Jammie, Lindsey, Amy, Maria, and Lisa.** Thank you!

Big thanks to author friends **Mimi Strong** and **Julia Kent** for all the things you know you do! You get it!

I am grateful to all the mothers who placed their children's stories on Caring Bridge. You put up the most succinct details of blood tests and treatments. This was so helpful, and I cried many days and nights over the pain and trials your families suffered.

And to all you fans out there – you enable me to live the life I love ~ *thank you.*

Dedications to Loved Ones Affected by Cancer

- Pat Prouty ~ Extraordinary mom, aunt, and classy feisty lady. ♥
- Shirley McDonald ~ Very much loved and missed by all. ♥
- Barry Peden ~ A classmate and father taken far too soon. ♥
- Linda Sue Bade Witt ♥
- Grandad Julian Everson ~ 1910 - 1984 Forever Loved ♥
- Melba K. ~ Miss you so much. ♥
- Carol ~ A Survivor And The Best Stepmum Ever ♥
- Bobby Aycock ~ Finally at peace 1/1/06 forever loved always ♥
- Ted Lewzey ~ Full of life even in death. ♥
- Linda Nemecek ~ Kicked cancers butt! ♥
- Helen Stump ~ Deeply missed ♥
- Tracy Gordon ~ Deeply missed ♥
- Claudia Isenhour ~ Mom, we miss you every single day! We were lucky to have you in our lives. Love You. ♥
- Lacy Spears ~ Love you always Pawpaw Lacy ♥
- Amber T. My daughter ~ 19 year cancer survivor ♥
- Arianna Kellborn ~ Cancer free for 5 years! ♥
- Marine Sgt. Joshua Lee Franks ~ Our brother, you are not forgotten. ♥
- Patti Varner ~ Three time leukemia survivor ♥
- Monica H. ~ Keep up the positive attitude!!!! ♥

- Nanny Hollis ~ Forever in my Heart, memories I will cherish.
- Aunt Annie ~ Mom & Dad S
- My Mom, Jean. ~ She fought cancer for 12 years.
- Loretta Jean Dinninger ~ 10/2/1926 - 08/16/2002
- My dad, Chris. ~ Loving daddy.
- William Forrest Street ~ Beloved father 10/19/56 - 09/08/13
- James Roy
- Mom (Tami) ~ <3 Greg, Lindsey, Jacob, & Lena
- Lillam Padin ~ The warrior in you inspires every day the fighter in me. I love you Mami! God bless you always...
- Dad -Leonard Wyborn ~ Miss you always xx Kell & Boys
- Squiggy - Wayne Wyborn ~ You kicked cancer's butt. Kell & Boys
- Mom (Annie) ~ You will always be remembered. Until we meet again. Love You!
- Ida Mae L. J. ~ We still have so much to learn from you. Keep fighting. Love you!
- Sandra J ~ I know the sun is always shining wherever you are. You're always in our hearts. Miss you so much mom.
- Margaret Pantano ~ To my mom, forever loved, never forgotten.
- Ray T. ~ Love and miss you Daddy
- Khristie D. Beaird ~ Stage IV Brain cancer. Cancer Free 3 1/2 years and going!!
- Raymond Ballard ~ was the greatest brother ever lost to pancreatic cancer
- Katherine Williams (Granny) ~ Cherished, loved, and hero to many
- Robert Williams, Sr. ~ Lost, but not forgotten
- Willie Moody ~ Those you left will always miss you greatly!
- Gina Marie Laycock ~ Forever Loved
- John Phillip Field ~ Loved and sadly missed lost the battle 22.1.1998

- Christine Lovely ~ To one of the most beautiful people to have ever graced this planet. Your memory will forever live on. ♥
- Josh Primeau ~ I'm so proud of my son. Petscan clear. It's Over. Thank you God ♥
- Odete Maia Chelinho Caetano ~ You won mother! Love you! ♥
- James Andrews Sr. ~ Miss you daddy. Forever in my heart ♥
- Bertie Welck ~ Kicked Cancer's Butt ♥
- Jan Bancroft ♥
- Vicki Zeikus ~ I've been cancer free for 22 years! ♥
- Dreama Poore ~ I PERSONALLY KICKED CANCER'S BUTT - 4/12 years ago (2009) ♥
- Patricia Elliott ~ 11/28/03 Gone but not forgotten ♥
- Gladys Luna ~ Loving mother and grandmother ♥
- Joe ~ My dad died on 19 Aug 2005 of lung cancer, I would give my arms up to have him back ♥
- Lucille C ~ fought and won!! ♥
- Grandma P. ~ Our bond was short lived but our memories will last forever. Miss & love you forever and always. ♥
- Sonia Delaney ~ Forever riding waves and bikes in Heaven ♥
- Danielle (Ah-Ah) ~ Survivor/Mommy 9/24/02 Love you! ♥
- Sarah Tullai ~ My aunt who beat breast cancer and just finished treatment for another cancer. I love you. ♥
- Catherine "Meemaw" Morrill ~ My inspiration, my guiding light, my hero ♥
- Charles O. Dennis ~ Mesothelioma may have taken you from the earth but you live on in our hearts. Love you Daddy! ♥
- Richard Held ~ Giving cancer its toughest fight until August 2009 ♥
- Walter- Big Papa ~ Strong papa ♥
- Larry Watson ~ Dad, I miss you. ♥
- Vena Ward ~ 2 Time Survivor, MawMaw, Inspiration 2 All ♥
- Barbara K ♥

♥ Susan Marr ♥

♥ Hayden Browne ♥

♥ Susan R. ~ Kidney Cancer Survivor ♥

♥ Wanda E. Garcia ~ 9/15/2009 lost to cancer, Miss Dearly ♥

♥ CWV ~ 7/27/2013 You are missed. ♥

♥ Aunt Nancy ~ 7-Jun-99 ♥

♥ Uncle Allen ♥

♥ Grandma O. ~ Wish I could have known you! ♥

♥ George W. ~ You're my hero, buddy! ♥

♥ Alice ~ Kicked the big C with grace! Love u! ♥

♥ Anna Siringo ~ "Believe" ♥

♥ Sara Lynne Hinds Suffridge ~ 12/12/03 I miss your smile mom! ♥

♥ Kristi VH ~ I'm glad that she made it. She was only 10 years old when she got cancer. She's so strong. Love her. ♥

♥ Eleanor Cataffo ~ She didn't make it. I was sad to see her go. She was my grandma and had throat cancer. ♥

♥ Wanda Mayberry-Thick ♥

♥ Sierra McBride ♥

♥ John Mayberry ~ Beloved Granddad and Great-Granddad ♥

♥ Ann Sefcovic ~ LYAYMLILFY ♥

♥ Lottie M ~ My grandma was a very strong woman who died from ovarian cancer at 75. She fought for a long time. I was glad that she was my grandma. ♥

♥ Karen Wickes ~ You're my inspiration! GIBTAT! ♥

♥ Joy O'Donnell ~ Your a Survivor! ♥

♥ William Leslie Fox ♥

♥ Anthony Sefcovic ~ Miss You Poppy! ♥

♥ John W. McKay SR. ~ Beloved Father and Grandfather, sadly missed by all. ♥

♥ Grammy Dea ~ I love and miss you so much. <3 ♥

- Sherie Ann Holgate ~ We love and miss you!! ♥
- Maria DeBartolo ~ I miss you mom everyday. ♥
- Dorothy ~ Love & miss you my other mother ♥
- John (Fritz) Staib ~ Dad, you died too soon. I can't believe you've been gone since 3/1/81. Love Doll ♥
- Denise ~ My sister and BFF, miss you ♥
- Barb WZ ~ Miss you my fav cousin. ♥
- Uncle Jake ~ Miss your smiling face. ♥
- John W. McKay SR. ~ Beloved Father and Grandfather, sadly missed by all. ♥
- Uncle Don B ~ Miss you and your faith in us all. ♥
- Mom ~ You are strong and you are woman, live strong. ♥
- JC Quintana-Trujillo 1/19/85-6/11/09 Colon Cancer. Your family and friends miss you J! ♥
- My Dad Sonny Price ~ He died aged 46 in 1976 when I was only 6yrs old. And I think of him every day and wonder "what if". ♥
- Ellen G. Chalfant ~ 4/10/1941 - 6/2/2011 All my love forever. ♥
- Papa ~ 1929-2001 Gone But Never Forgotten ♥
- Mom ~ Bravery and Strength 10 Years Cancer Free ♥
- Gaby Gonzalez Galas ~ Dedicado a mi hermana sobreviviente de cancer de mama ♥
- Sherry Sac ~ Gone too soon 1950 - 2012 ♥
- J & C Raymond ~ One Very lucky couple ♥
- My loving mother, Pam ~ Gone but not forgotten. 3/22/14 Love you Kari ♥
- Linda H. ~ SURVIVOR (x2) Mother of Kimberly N. and Mark N. ♥
- Lola Ivy ~ Rollerskating in Heaven ♥
- Brenda B. ~ May 2011 - Gone too soon ♥
- Glenda ~ You have always done a lot for me and I will always miss you! <3 ♥

- Brett Savant ~ Always a Warrior, I love you.
- Charlane C ~ 2 X survivor of breast cancer
- Ida Mae Sanders ~ I miss you gran but I'm glad you're home. I feel better knowing you're looking down on me and wishing me luck.
- Laura Nelson ~ Lost battle with lung cancer on December 31, 2011
- Susan Wood ~ Breast Cancer survivor of five years now.
- Aunty Dodie ~ We miss you very much <3
- Deborah M. Arrant ~ Stage 4 Small Cell Lung Cancer. To my hero and my everything you are the epitome of strength and are a true fighter. I love you with all my heart!
- Gayle Marquardt ~ Mom, we miss you every day. Always in our hearts. Love you
- Jane Papas ~ Survivor
- Rhonda Cox ~ Missing you always
- Bridgett Thompson ~ You inspire me!
- Eric Oesterreicher ~ Gone but never forgotten. 2/24/11
- Wanda Oesterreicher ~ Strong Survivor and an Inspiration
- Net ~ Cancer took your life, but not our memories sis
- Harveleh ~ with love
- Cathy D. LeBourdais ~ 1953-2004 Mom, you will always be missed
- George Silvestri ~ I love you papa and miss you.
- Erlinda Yenchai ~ Caring Nurse. Loving Mom. 11-25-2011
- Donald McNeely ~ Beloved Husband & Father, We miss and love you so much!
- Sheila Gensler ~ an angel here and above...forever missed
- Rex Gladden ~ My beloved husband, who lost his life too young.
- Lynnette Edwards ~ Gone but not forgotten, love you mom, always 01/04/02
- Grandma Helen ~ She survived 11 years from a stroke. She lived a month after we found out she had cancer.

- Brandy Ratcliff ~ Once a Warrior, Always an Angel ♥
- Jonathan ~ This is my nephew he made it through leukemia when there was several times when we didn't think he make it. ♥
- Vivian I Mendoza ~ I still love you mom ♥
- Kim Siefkas ~ The loveliest mother in the world ♥
- Grandma Rosie ~ I still feel you near, even after all these years. ♥
- Grandpa Joe ~ You would have loved our lil Ro Bug :) ♥
- Aunt Rosalind ~ with all my love, you are missed. ♥
- Robert Brian Whitney(my superman) ~ love and miss you everyday daddy ♥
- Shirley Fick ~ I will always miss you ♥
- Dede ~ You were the best stepmom ever! ♥
- Kelly Hillis ~ The love that you brought will never be forgotten, you strength gives me hope, I will never forget you ♥
- Nola Pearl ~ Lost, but forever loved. ♥
- Herb Fink ~ 12/29/2013 ♥
- Edna W. Patterson ~ My mom who died too young to breast cancer. ♥
- Sierra Jean ~ My daughter taken too soon by Neuroblastoma 2/27/99-3/19/99 ♥

CPSIA information can be obtained at www.ICGtesting.com
Printed in the USA
LVOW07s0533180714

394663LV00001B/6/P